THE
UNDERTAKER'S
DAUGHTER

BOOKS BY SARA BLAEDEL

THE LOUISE RICK SERIES

The Missing Persons Trilogy

The Forgotten Girls

The Killing Forest

The Lost Woman

The Camilla Trilogy

The Night Women

The Running Girl

The Stolen Angel

THE UNDERTAKER SERIES

The Undertaker's Daughter

THE
UNDERTAKER'S
DAUGHTER

SARA BLAEDEL

TRANSLATED BY
MARK KLINE

GRAND CENTRAL
PUBLISHING

New York   Boston

Copyright © 2018 by Sara Blaedel
Translated by Mark Kline, translation © 2018 by Sara Blaedel
Hachette Book Group supports the right to free expression and the value of copyright. The purpose of copyright is to encourage writers and artists to produce the creative works that enrich our culture.

The scanning, uploading, and distribution of this book without permission is a theft of the author's intellectual property. If you would like permission to use material from the book (other than for review purposes), please contact permissions@hbgusa.com. Thank you for your support of the author's rights.

Grand Central Publishing
Hachette Book Group
1290 Avenue of the Americas
New York, NY 10104
Hachettebookgroup.com

Grand Central Publishing is a division of Hachette Book Group, Inc.
The Grand Central Publishing name and logo is a trademark of Hachette Book Group, Inc.

The Hachette Speakers Bureau provides a wide range of authors for speaking events. To find out more, go to www.hachettespeakersbureau.com or call (866) 376-6591.

The publisher is not responsible for websites (or their content) that are not owned by the publisher.

Library of Congress Cataloging-in-Publication Data

Names: Blaedel, Sara, author. | Kline, Mark, translator.
Title: The undertaker's daughter / Sara Blaedel; translated by Mark Kline.
Other titles: Bedemandens datter.
Description: First edition. | New York: Grand Central Publishing, 2018.
Identifiers: LCCN 2017023764| ISBN 9781455541119 (hardcover) | ISBN 9781478940289 (audio download) | ISBN 9781455541096 (ebook)
Subjects: LCSH: Fathers and daughters—Fiction. | Widows—Fiction. | Murder—Investigation—Wisconsin—Racine—Fiction.
Classification: LCC PT8177.12.L33 B4313 2018 | DDC 839.813/8—dc23
LC record available at https://lccn.loc.gov/2017023764

Printed in the United States of America

LSC-H

First edition: February 2018
10 9 8 7 6 5 4 3 2 1

FEB 0 6 2018

To Victoria

THE
UNDERTAKER'S
DAUGHTER

1

"What do you mean you shouldn't have told me? You should have told me thirty-three years ago."

"What difference would it have made anyway?" Ilka's mother demanded. "You were seven years old. You wouldn't have understood about a liar and a cheat running away with all his winnings; running out on his responsibilities, on his wife and little daughter. He hit the jackpot, Ilka, and then he hit the road. And left me—no, he left *us* with a funeral home too deep in the red to get rid of. And an enormous amount of debt. That he betrayed me is one thing, but abandoning his child?"

Ilka stood at the window, her back to the comfy living room, which was overflowing with books and baskets of yarn. She looked out over the trees in the park across the way. For a moment, the treetops seemed like dizzying black storm waves.

Her mother sat in the glossy Børge Mogensen easy chair in the corner, though now she was worked up from her rant, and her knitting needles clattered twice as fast. Ilka turned to her. "Okay," she said, trying not to sound shrill. "Maybe you're right. Maybe I wouldn't have understood about all that. But you didn't think I was too young to understand that my father was a coward, the way he suddenly left us, and that he didn't love us anymore. That he was an incredible asshole you'd never take back if he ever showed up on our doorstep, begging for forgiveness. As I recall, you had no trouble talking about that, over and over and over."

"Stop it." Her mother had been a grade school teacher for twenty-six years, and now she sounded like one. "But does it make any difference? Think of all the letters you've written him over the years. How often have you reached out to him, asked to see him? Or at least have some form of contact." She sat up and laid her knitting on the small table beside the chair. "He never answered you; he never tried to see you. How long did you save your confirmation money so you could fly over and visit him?"

Ilka knew better than her mother how many letters she had written over the years. What her mother wasn't aware of was that she had kept writing to him, even as an adult. Not as often, but at least a Christmas card and a note on his birthday. Every single year. Which had felt like sending letters into outer space. Yet she'd never stopped.

"You should have told me about the money," Ilka said, unwilling to let it go, even though her mother had a point. Would it really have made a difference? "Why are you telling me now? After all these years. And right when I'm about to leave."

Her mother had called just before eight. Ilka had still been in bed, reading the morning paper on her iPad. "Come over, right now," she'd said. There was something they had to talk about.

Now her mother leaned forward and folded her hands in her lap, her face showing the betrayal and desperation she'd endured. She'd kept her wounds under wraps for half her life, but it was obvious they had never fully healed. "It scares me, you going over there. Your father was a gambler. He bet more money than he had, and the racetrack was a part of our lives for the entire time he lived here. For better and worse. I knew about his habit when we fell in love, but then it got out of control. And almost ruined us several times. In the end, it did ruin us."

"And then he won almost a million kroner and just disappeared." Ilka lifted an eyebrow.

"Well, we do know he went to America." Her mother nodded. "Presumably, he continued gambling over there. And we never heard from him again. That is, until now, of course."

Ilka shook her head. "Right, now that he's dead."

"What I'm trying to say is that we don't know what he's left behind. He could be up to his neck in debt. You're a school photographer, not a millionaire. If you go over there, they might hold you responsible for his debts. And who knows? Maybe they wouldn't allow you to come home. Your father had a dark side he couldn't control. I'll rip his dead body limb from limb if he pulls you down with him, all these years after turning his back on us."

With that, her mother stood and walked down the long hall into the kitchen. Ilka heard muffled voices, and then Hanne appeared in the doorway. "Would you like us to

3

drive you to the airport?" Hanne leaned against the door-frame as Ilka's mother reappeared with a tray of bakery rolls, which she set down on the coffee table.

"No, that's okay," Ilka said.

"How long do you plan on staying?" Hanne asked, moving to the sofa. Ilka's mother curled up in the corner of the sofa, covered herself with a blanket, and put her stockinged feet up on Hanne's lap.

When her mother began living with Hanne fourteen years ago, the last trace of her bitterness finally seemed to evaporate. Now, though, Ilka realized it had only gone into hibernation.

For the first four years after Ilka's father left, her mother had been stuck with Paul Jensen's Funeral Home and its two employees, who cheated her whenever they could get away with it. Throughout Ilka's childhood, her mother had complained constantly about the burden he had dumped on her. Ilka hadn't known until now that her father had also left a sizable gambling debt behind. Apparently, her mother had wanted to spare her, at least to some degree. And, of course, her mother was right. Her father *was* a coward and a selfish jerk. Yet Ilka had never completely accepted his abandonment of her. He had left behind a short letter saying he would come back for them as soon as everything was taken care of, and that an opportunity had come up. In Chicago.

Several years later, after complete silence on his part, he wanted a divorce. And that was the last they'd heard from him. When Ilka was a teenager, she found his address—or at least, an address where he had once lived. She'd kept it all these years in a small red treasure chest in her room.

"Surely it won't take more than a few days," Ilka said.

"I'm planning to be back by the weekend. I'm booked up at work, but I found someone to fill in for me the first two days. It would be a great help if you two could keep trying to get hold of Niels from North Sealand Photography. He's in Stockholm, but he's supposed to be back tomorrow. I'm hoping he can cover for me the rest of the week. All the shoots are in and around Copenhagen."

"What exactly are you hoping to accomplish over there?" Hanne asked.

"Well, they say I'm in his will and that I have to be there in person to prove I'm Paul Jensen's daughter."

"I just don't understand why this can't be done by e-mail or fax," her mother said. "You can send them your birth certificate and your passport, or whatever it is they need."

"It seems that copies aren't good enough. If I don't go over there, I'd have to go to an American tax office in Europe, and I think the nearest one is in London. But this way, they'll let me go through his personal things and take what I want. Artie Sorvino from Jensen Funeral Home in Racine has offered to cover my travel expenses if I go now, so they can get started with closing his estate."

Ilka stood in the middle of the living room, too anxious and restless to sit down.

"Racine?" Hanne asked. "Where's that?" She picked up her steaming cup and blew on it.

"A bit north of Chicago. In Wisconsin. I'll be picked up at the airport, and it doesn't look like it'll take long to drive there. Racine is supposedly the city in the United States with the largest community of Danish descendants. A lot of Danes immigrated to the region, so it makes sense that's where he settled."

"He has a hell of a lot of nerve." Her mother's lips barely moved. "He doesn't write so much as a birthday card to you all these years, and now suddenly you have to fly over there and clean up another one of his messes."

"Karin," Hanne said, her voice gentle. "Of course Ilka should go over and sort through her father's things. If you get the opportunity for closure on such an important part of your life's story, you should grab it."

Her mother shook her head. Without looking at Ilka, she said, "I have a bad feeling about this. Isn't it odd that he stayed in the undertaker business even though he managed to ruin his first shot at it?"

Ilka walked out into the hall and let the two women bicker about the unfairness of it all. How Paul's daughter had tried to reach out to her father all her life, and it was only now that he was gone that he was finally reaching out to her.

2

The first thing Ilka noticed was his Hawaiian shirt and longish brown hair, which was combed back and held in place by sunglasses that would look at home on a surfer. He stood out among the other drivers at Arrivals in O'Hare International Airport who were holding name cards and facing the scattered clumps of exhausted people pulling suitcases out of Customs.

Written on his card was "Ilka Nichols Jensen." Somehow, she managed to walk all the way up to him and stop before he realized she'd found him.

They looked each other over for a moment. He was in his early forties, maybe, she thought. So, her father, who had turned seventy-two in early January, had a younger partner.

She couldn't read his face, but it might have surprised him that the undertaker's daughter was a beanpole: six feet tall without a hint of a feminine form. He scanned her up and down, gaze settling on her hair, which had never been an attention-getter. Straight, flat, and mousy.

He smiled warmly and held out his hand. "Nice to meet you. Welcome to Chicago."

It's going to be a hell of a long trip, Ilka thought, before shaking his hand and saying hello. "Thank you. Nice to meet you, too."

He offered to carry her suitcase. It was small, a carry-on, but she gladly handed it over to him. Then he offered her a bottle of water. The car was close by, he said, only a short walk.

Although she was used to being taller than most people, she always felt a bit shy when male strangers had to look up to make eye contact. She was nearly a head taller than Artie Sorvino, but he seemed almost impressed as he grinned up at her while they walked.

Her body ached; she hadn't slept much during the long flight. Since she'd left her apartment in Copenhagen, her nerves had been tingling with excitement. And worry, too. Things had almost gone wrong right off the bat at the Copenhagen airport, because she hadn't taken into account the long line at Passport Control. There had still been two people in front of her when she'd been called to her waiting flight. Then the arrival in the US, a hell that the chatty man next to her on the plane had prepared her for. He had missed God knew how many connecting flights at O'Hare because the immigration line had taken several hours to go through. It turned out to be not quite as bad as all that. She had been guided to a machine that requested her fingerprints, passport, and picture. All this information was scanned and saved. Then Ilka had been sent on to the next line, where a surly passport official wanted to know what her business was in the country. She began to sweat but then pulled herself together and explained that she was simply visiting family, which in a way was true. He stamped her passport, and moments later she was standing beside the man wearing the colorful, festive shirt.

"Is this your first trip to the US?" Artie asked now, as they approached the enormous parking lot.

She smiled. "No, I've traveled here a few times. To Miami and New York."

Why had she said that? She'd never been in this part of the world before, but what the hell. It didn't matter. Unless he kept up the conversation. And Miami. Where had that come from?

"Really?" Artie told her he had lived in Key West for many years. Then his father got sick, and Artie, the only other surviving member of the family, moved back to Racine to take care of him. "I hope you made it down to the Keys while you were in Florida."

Ilka shook her head and explained that she unfortunately hadn't had time.

"I had a gallery down there," Artie said. He'd gone to the California School of the Arts in San Francisco and had made his living as an artist.

Ilka listened politely and nodded. In the parking lot, she caught sight of a gigantic black Cadillac with closed white curtains in back, which stood first in the row of parked cars. He'd driven there in the hearse.

"Hope you don't mind." He nodded at the hearse as he

opened the rear door and placed her suitcase on the casket table used for rolling coffins in and out of the vehicle.

"No, it's fine." She walked around to the front passenger door. Fine, as long as she wasn't the one being rolled into the back. She felt slightly dizzy, as if she were still up in the air, but was buoyed by the nervous excitement of traveling and the anticipation of what awaited her.

The thought that her father was at the end of her journey bothered her, yet it was something she'd fantasized about nearly her entire life. But would she be able to piece together the life he'd lived without her? And was she even interested in knowing about it? What if she didn't like what she learned?

She shook her head for a moment. These thoughts had been swirling in her head since Artie's first phone call. Her mother thought she shouldn't get involved. At all. But Ilka disagreed. If her father had left anything behind, she wanted to see it. She wanted to uncover whatever she could find, to see if any of it made sense.

"How did he die?" she asked as Artie maneuvered the long hearse out of the parking lot and in between two orange signs warning about roadwork and a detour.

"Just a sec," he muttered, and he swore at the sign before deciding to skirt the roadwork and get back to the road heading north.

For a while they drove in silence; then he explained that one morning her father had simply not woken up. "He was supposed to drive a corpse to Iowa, one of our neighboring states, but he didn't show up. He just died in his sleep. Totally peacefully. He might not even have known it was over."

Ilka watched the Chicago suburbs drifting by along the long, straight bypass, the rows of anonymous stores and cheap restaurants. It seemed so overwhelming, so strange, so different. Most buildings were painted in shades of beige and brown, and enormous billboards stood everywhere, screaming messages about everything from missing children to ultracheap fast food and vanilla coffee for less than a dollar at Dunkin' Donuts.

She turned to Artie. "Was he sick?" The bump on Artie's nose—had it been broken?—made it appear too big for the rest of his face: high cheekbones, slightly squinty eyes, beard stubble definitely due to a relaxed attitude toward shaving, rather than wanting to be in style.

"Not that I know of, no. But there could have been things Paul didn't tell me about, for sure."

His tone told her it wouldn't have been the first secret Paul had kept from him.

"The doctor said his heart just stopped," he continued. "Nothing dramatic happened."

"Did he have a family?" She looked out the side window. The old hearse rode well. Heavy, huge, swaying lightly. A tall pickup drove up beside them; a man with a full beard looked down and nodded at her. She looked away quickly. She didn't care for any sympathetic looks, though he, of course, couldn't know the curtained-off back of the hearse was empty.

"He was married, you know," Artie said. Immediately Ilka sensed he didn't like being the one to fill her in on her father's private affairs. She nodded to herself; of course he didn't. What did she expect?

"And he had two daughters. That was it, apart from

11

Mary Ann's family, but I don't know them. How much do you know about them?"

He knew very well that Ilka hadn't had any contact with her father since he'd left Denmark. Or at least she assumed he knew. "Why has the family not signed what should be signed, so you can finish with his…estate?" She set the empty water bottle on the floor.

"They did sign their part of it. But that's not enough, because you're in the will, too. First the IRS—that's our tax agency—must determine if he owes the government, and you must give them permission to investigate. If you don't sign, they'll freeze all the assets in the estate until everything is cleared up."

Ilka's shoulders slumped at the word "assets." One thing that had kept her awake during the flight was her mother's concern about her being stuck with a debt she could never pay. Maybe she would be detained; maybe she would even be thrown in jail.

"What are his daughters like?" she asked after they had driven for a while in silence.

For a few moments, he kept his eyes on the road; then he glanced at her and shrugged. "They're nice enough, but I don't really know them. It's been a long time since I've seen them. Truth is, I don't think either of them was thrilled about your father's business."

After another silence, Ilka said, "You should have called me when he died. I wish I had been at his funeral."

Was that really true? Did she truly wish that? The last funeral she'd been to was her husband's. He had collapsed from heart failure three years ago, at the age of fifty-two. She didn't like death, didn't like loss. But she'd already lost her father many years ago, so what difference would it have made watching him being lowered into the ground?

"At that time, I didn't know about you," Artie said. "Your name first came up when your father's lawyer mentioned you."

"Where is he buried?"

He stared straight ahead. Again, it was obvious he didn't enjoy talking about her father's private life. Finally, he said, "Mary Ann decided to keep the urn with his ashes at home. A private ceremony was held in the living room when the crematorium delivered the urn, and now it's on the shelf above the fireplace."

After a pause, he said, "You speak English well. Funny accent."

Ilka explained distractedly that she had traveled in Australia for a year after high school.

The billboards along the freeway here advertised hotels, motels, and drive-ins for the most part. She wondered how there could be enough people to keep all these businesses going, given the countless offers from the clusters of signs on both sides of the road. "What about his new family? Surely they knew he had a daughter in Denmark?" She turned back to him.

"Nope!" He shook his head as he flipped the turn signal.

"He never told them he left his wife and seven-year-old daughter?" She wasn't all that surprised.

Artie didn't answer. *Okay*, Ilka thought. *That takes care of that*.

"I wonder what they think about me coming here."

He shrugged. "I don't really know, but they're not going

to lose anything. His wife has an inheritance from her wealthy parents, so she's taken care of. The same goes for the daughters. And none of them had ever shown any interest in the funeral home."

And what about their father? Ilka thought. *Were they uninterested in him, too?* But that was none of her business. She didn't know them, knew nothing about their relationships with one another. And for that matter, she knew nothing about her father. Maybe his new family had asked about his life in Denmark, and maybe he'd given them a line of bullshit. But what the hell, he was thirty-nine when he left. Anyone could figure out he'd had a life before packing his weekend bag and emigrating.

Both sides of the freeway were green now. The landscape was starting to remind her of late summer in Denmark, with its green fields, patches of forest, flat land, large barns with the characteristic bowed roofs, and livestock. With a few exceptions, she felt like she could have been driving down the E45, the road between Copenhagen and Ålborg.

"Do you mind if I turn on the radio?" Artie asked.

She shook her head; it was a relief to have the awkward silence between them broken. And yet, before his hand reached the radio, she blurted out, "What was he like?"

He dropped his hand and smiled at her. "Your father was a decent guy, a really decent guy. In a lot of ways," he added, disarmingly, "he was someone you could count on, and in other ways he was very much his own man. I always enjoyed working with him, but he was also my friend. People liked him; he was interested in their lives. That's also why he was so good at talking to those who had just lost someone. He was empathetic. It feels empty, him not being around any longer."

Ilka had to concentrate to follow along. Despite her year in Australia, it was difficult when people spoke English rapidly. "Was he also a good father?"

Artie turned thoughtfully and looked out his side window. "I really can't say. I didn't know him when the girls were small." He kept glancing at the four lanes to their left. "But if you're asking me if your father was a family man, my answer is, yes and no. He was very much in touch with his family, but he probably put more of himself into Jensen Funeral Home."

"How long did you know him?"

She watched him calculate. "I moved back in 1998. We ran into each other at a local saloon, this place called Oh Dennis!, and we started talking. The victim of a traffic accident had just come in to the funeral home. The family wanted to put the young woman in an open coffin, but nobody would have wanted to see her face. So I offered to help. It's the kind of stuff I'm good at. Creating, shaping. Your father did the embalming, but I reconstructed her face. Her mother supplied us with a photo, and I did a sculpture. And I managed to make the woman look like herself, even though there wasn't much to work with. Later your father offered me a job, and I grabbed the chance. There's not much work for an artist in Racine, so reconstructions of the deceased was as good as anything."

He turned off the freeway. "Later I got a degree, because you have to have a license to work in the undertaker business."

They reached Racine Street and waited to make a left turn. They had driven the last several miles in silence. The streets were deserted, the shops closed. It was getting dark, and Ilka realized she was at the point where exhaustion and jet lag trumped the hunger gnawing inside her. They drove by an empty square and a nearly deserted saloon. Oh Dennis!, the place where Artie had met her father. She spotted the lake at the end of the broad streets to the right, and that was it. The town was dead. Abandoned, closed. She was surprised there were no people or life.

"We've booked a room for you at the Harbourwalk Hotel. Tomorrow we can sit down and go through your father's papers. Then you can start looking through his things."

Ilka nodded. All she wanted right now was a warm bath and a bed.

"Sorry, we have no reservations for Miss Jensen. And none for the Jensen Funeral Home, either. We don't have a single room available."

The receptionist drawled apology after apology. It sounded to Ilka as if she had too much saliva in her mouth.

Ilka sat in a plush armchair in the lobby as Artie asked if the room was reserved in his name. "Or try Sister Eileen O'Connor," he suggested.

The receptionist apologized again as her long fingernails danced over the computer keyboard. The sound was unnaturally loud, a bit like Ilka's mother's knitting needles tapping against each other.

Ilka shut down. She could sit there and sleep; it made absolutely no difference to her. Back in Denmark, it was five in the morning, and she hadn't slept in twenty-two hours.

"I'm sorry," Artie said. "You're more than welcome to stay at my place. I can sleep on the sofa. Or we can fix up a place for you to sleep at the office, and we'll find another hotel in the morning."

Ilka sat up in the armchair. "What's that sound?"

Artie looked bewildered. "What do you mean?"

"It's like a phone ringing in the next room."

He listened for a moment before shrugging. "I can't hear anything."

The sound came every ten seconds. It was as if something were hidden behind the reception desk or farther down the hotel foyer. Ilka shook her head and looked at him. "You don't need to sleep on the sofa. I can sleep somewhere at the office."

She needed to be alone, and the thought of a strange man's bedroom didn't appeal to her.

"That's fine." He grabbed her small suitcase. "It's only five minutes away, and I know we can find some food for you, too."

The black hearse was parked just outside the main entrance of the hotel, but that clearly wasn't bothering anyone. Though the hotel was apparently fully booked, Ilka hadn't seen a single person since they'd arrived.

Night had fallen, and her eyelids closed as soon as she settled into the car. She jumped when Artie opened the door and poked her with his finger. She hadn't even realized they had arrived. They were parked in a large, empty lot. The white building was an enormous box with several attic windows reflecting the moonlight back into the thick darkness. Tall trees with enormous crowns hovered over Ilka when she got out of the car.

17

They reached the door, beside which was a sign: JENSEN FUNERAL HOME. WELCOME. Pillars stood all the way across the broad porch, with well-tended flower beds in front of it, but the darkness covered everything else.

Artie led her inside the high-ceilinged hallway and turned the light on. He pointed to a stairway at the other end. Ilka's feet sank deep in the carpet; it smelled dusty, with a hint of plastic and instant coffee.

"Would you like something to drink? Are you hungry? I can make a sandwich."

"No, thank you." She just wanted him to leave.

He led her up the stairs, and when they reached a small landing, he pointed at a door. "Your father had a room in there, and I think we can find some sheets. We have a cot we can fold out and make up for you."

Ilka held her hand up. "If there is a bed in my father's room, I can just sleep in it." She nodded when he asked if she was sure. "What time do you want to meet tomorrow?"

"How about eight thirty? We can have breakfast together."

She had no idea what time it was, but as long as she got some sleep, she guessed she'd be fine. She nodded.

Ilka stayed outside on the landing while Artie opened the door to her father's room and turned on the light. She watched him walk over to a dresser and pull out the bottom drawer. He grabbed some sheets and a towel and tossed them on the bed; then he waved her in.

The room's walls were slanted. An old white bureau stood at the end of the room, and under the window, which must have been one of those she'd noticed from the parking lot, was a desk with drawers on both sides. The bed was just inside the room and to the left. There was also a small coffee table and, at the end of the bed, a narrow built-in closet.

A dark jacket and a tie lay draped over the back of the desk chair. The desk was covered with piles of paper; a briefcase leaned against the closet. But there was nothing but sheets on the bed.

"I'll find a comforter and a pillow," Artie said, accidentally grazing her as he walked by.

Ilka stepped into the room. A room lived in, yet abandoned. A feeling suddenly stirred inside her, and she froze. He was here. The smell. A heavy yet pleasant odor she recognized from somewhere deep inside. She'd had no idea this memory existed. She closed her eyes and let her mind drift back to when she was very young, the feeling of being held. Tobacco. Sundays in the car, driving out to Bellevue. Feeling secure, knowing someone close was taking care of her. Lifting her up on a lap. Making her laugh. The sound of hooves pounding the ground, horses at a racetrack. Her father's concentration as he chain-smoked, captivated by the race. His laughter.

She sat down on the bed, not hearing what Artie said when he laid the comforter and pillow beside her, then walked out and closed the door.

Her father had been tall; at least that's how she remembered him. She could see to the end of the world when she sat on his shoulders. They did fun things together. He took her to an amusement park and bought her ice cream while he tried out the slot machines, to see if they were any good. Her mother didn't always know when they went there. He also took her out to a centuries-old amusement park in the forest north of Copenhagen. They stopped at Peter Liep's, and she drank soda while he drank beer. They sat outside and watched the riders pass by, smelling horseshit and sweat when the thirsty riders dismounted and draped the reins over the hitching post. He had loved horses. On the other hand, she couldn't remember the times—the many times, according to her mother—when he didn't come home early enough to stick his head in her room and say good night. Not having enough money for food because he had gambled his wages away at the track was something else she didn't recall—but her mother did.

Ilka opened her eyes. Her exhaustion was gone, but she still felt dizzy. She walked over to the desk and reached for a photo in a wide mahogany frame. A trotter, its mane flying out to both sides at the finishing line. In another photo, a trotter covered by a red victory blanket stood beside a sulky driver holding a trophy high above his head, smiling for the camera. There were several more horse photos, and a ticket to Lunden hung from a window hasp. She grabbed it. Paul Jensen. Charlottenlund Derby 1982. The year he left them.

Ilka didn't realize at the time that he had left. All she knew was that one morning he wasn't there, and her mother was crying but wouldn't tell her why. When she arrived home from school that afternoon, her mother was still crying. And as she remembered it, her mother didn't stop crying for a long time.

She had been with her father at that derby in 1982. She picked up a photo leaning against the windowsill, then sat down on the bed. "Ilka and Peter Kjærsgaard" was written on the back of the photo. Ilka had been five years old when her father took her to the derby for the first time. Back then, her mother had gone along. She vaguely remembered going to the track and meeting the famous jockey, but suddenly the odors and sounds were crystal clear. She closed her eyes.

"You can give them one if you want," the man had said as he handed her a bucket filled with carrots, many more than her mother had in bags back in their kitchen. The bucket was heavy, but Ilka wanted to show them how big she was, so she hooked the handle with her arm and walked over to one of the stalls.

She smiled proudly at a red-shirted sulky driver passing by as he was fastening his helmet. The track was crowded, but during the races, few people were allowed in the barn. They were, though. She and her father.

She pulled her hand back, frightened, when the horse in the stall whinnied and pulled against the chain. It snorted and pounded its hoof on the floor. The horse was so tall. Carefully she held the carrot out in the palm of her hand, as her father had taught her to do. The horse snatched the sweet treat, gently tickling her.

Her father stood with a group of men at the end of the row of stalls. They laughed loudly, slapping one another's shoulders. A few of them drank beer from bottles. Ilka sat down on a bale of hay. Her father had promised her a horse when she was a bit older. One of the grooms came over and asked if she would like a ride behind the barn; he was going to walk one of the horses to warm it up. She wanted to, if her father would let her. He did.

"Look at me, Daddy!" Ilka cried. "Look at me." The horse had stopped, clearly preferring to eat grass rather than walk. She kicked gently to get it going, but her legs were too short to do any good.

Her father pulled himself away from the other men and stood at the barn entrance. He waved, and Ilka sat up proudly. The groom asked if he should let go of the reins so she could ride by herself, and though she didn't really love the idea, she nodded. But when he dropped the reins and she turned around to show her father how brave she was, he was back inside with the others.

Ilka stood up and put the photo back. She could almost smell the tar used by the racetrack farrier on horse hooves. She used to sit behind a pane of glass with her mother and follow the races, while her father stood over at the finish line. But then her mother stopped going along.

She picked up another photo from the windowsill. She was standing on a bale of hay, toasting with a sulky driver. Fragments of memories flooded back as she studied herself in the photo. Her father speaking excitedly with the driver, his expression as the horses were hitched to the sulkies. And the way he said, "We-e-e-ell, shall we…?" right before a race. Then he would hold his hand out, and they would walk down to the track.

She wondered why she could remember these things, when she had forgotten most of what had happened back then.

There was also a photo of two small girls on the desk. She knew these were her younger half sisters, who were smiling broadly at the photographer. Suddenly, deep inside her chest, she felt a sharp twinge—but why? After setting the photo back down, she realized it wasn't from never having met her half sisters. No. It was pure jealousy. They had grown up with her father, while she had been abandoned.

Ilka threw herself down on the bed and pulled the comforter over her, without even bothering to put the sheets on. She lay curled up, staring into space.

3

At some point, Ilka must have fallen asleep, because she gave a start when someone knocked on the door. She recognized Artie's voice.

"Morning in there. Are you awake?"

She sat up, confused. She had been up once in the night to look for a bathroom. The building seemed strangely hushed, as if it were packed in cotton. She'd opened a few doors and finally found a bathroom with shiny tiles and a low bathtub. The toilet had a soft cover on its seat, like the one in her grandmother's flat in Bagsværd. On her way back, she had grabbed her father's jacket, carried it to the bed, and buried her nose in it. Now it lay halfway on the floor.

"Give me half an hour," she said. She hugged the jacket, savoring the odor that had brought her childhood memories to the surface from the moment she'd walked into the room.

Now that it was light outside, the room seemed bigger.

Last night she hadn't noticed the storage boxes lining the wall behind both sides of the desk. Clean shirts in clear plastic sacks hung from the hook behind the door.

"Okay, but have a look at these IRS forms," he said, sliding a folder under the door. "And sign on the last page when you've read them. We'll take off whenever you're ready."

Ilka didn't answer. She pulled her knees up to her chest and lay curled up. Without moving. Being shut up inside a room with her father's belongings was enough to make her feel she'd reunited with a part of herself. The big black hole inside her, the one that had appeared every time she sent a letter despite knowing she'd get no answer, was slowly filling up with something she'd failed to find herself.

She had lived about a sixth of her life with her father. *When do we become truly conscious of the people around us?* she wondered. She had just turned forty, and he had deserted them when she was seven. This room here was filled with everything he had left behind, all her memories of him. All the odors and sensations that had made her miss him.

Artie knocked on the door again. She had no idea how long she'd been lying on the bed.

"Ready?" he called out.

"No," she yelled back. She couldn't. She needed to just stay and take in everything here, so it wouldn't disappear again.

"Have you read it?"

"I signed it!"

"Would you rather stay here? Do you want me to go alone?"

"Yes, please."

Silence. She couldn't tell if he was still outside.

"Okay," he finally said. "I'll come back after breakfast." He sounded annoyed. "I'll leave the phone here with you."

Ilka listened to him walk down the stairs. After she'd walked over to the door and signed her name, she hadn't moved a muscle. She hadn't opened any drawers or closets.

She'd brought along a bag of chips, but they were all gone. And she didn't feel like going downstairs for something to drink. Instead, she gave way to exhaustion. The stream of thoughts, the fragments of memories in her head, had slowly settled into a tempo she could follow.

Her father had written her into his will. He had declared her to be his biological daughter. But evidently, he'd never mentioned her to his new family, or to the people closest to him in his new life. Of course, he hadn't been obligated to mention her, she thought. But if her name hadn't come up in his will, they could have liquidated his business without anyone knowing about an adult daughter in Denmark.

The telephone outside the door rang, but she ignored it. What had this Artie guy imagined she should do if the telephone rang? Did he think she would answer it? And say what?

At first, she'd wondered why her father had named her in his will. But after having spent the last twelve hours enveloped in memories of him, she had realized that no matter what had happened in his life, a part of him had still been her father.

She cried, then felt herself dozing off.

Someone knocked on the door. "Not today," she yelled, before Artie could even speak a word. She turned her back to the room, her face to the wall. She closed her eyes until the footsteps disappeared down the stairs.

The telephone rang again, but she didn't react.

Slowly it had all come back. After her father had disappeared, her mother had two jobs: the funeral home business and her teaching. It wasn't long after summer vacation, and school had just begun. Ilka thought he had left in September. A month before she turned eight. Her mother taught Danish and arts and crafts to students in several grades. When she wasn't at school, she was at the funeral home on Brønshøj Square. Also on weekends, picking up flowers and ordering coffins. Working in the office, keeping the books when she wasn't filling out forms.

Ilka had gone along with her to various embassies whenever a mortuary passport was needed to bring a corpse home from outside the country, or when a person died in Denmark and was to be buried elsewhere. It had been fascinating, though frightening. But she had never fully understood how hard her mother worked. Finally, when Ilka was twelve, her mother managed to sell the business and get back her life.

After her father left, they were unable to afford the single-story house Ilka had been born in. They moved into a small apartment on Frederikssundsvej in Copenhagen. Her mother had never been shy about blaming her father for their economic woes, but she'd always said they would be okay. After she sold the funeral home, their situation had improved; Ilka saw it mostly from the color in her mother's cheeks, a more relaxed expression on her face. Also, she was more likely to let Ilka invite friends home for dinner. When she started eighth grade, they moved to Østerbro, a better district in the city, but she stayed in her school in Brønshøj and took the bus.

"You *were* an asshole," she muttered, her face still to the wall. "What you did was just completely inexcusable."

The telephone outside the door finally gave up. She heard soft steps out on the stairs. She sighed. They had paid her airfare; there were limits to what she could get away with. But today was out of the question. And that telephone was their business.

Someone knocked again at the door. This time it sounded different. They knocked again. "Hello." A female voice. The woman called her name and knocked one more time, gently but insistently.

Ilka rose from the bed. She shook her hair and slipped it behind her ears and smoothed her T-shirt. She walked over and opened the door. She couldn't hide her startled expression at the sight of a woman dressed in gray, her hair covered by a veil of the same color. Her broad, demure skirt reached below the knees. Her eyes seemed far too big for her small face and delicate features.

"Who are you?"

"My name is Sister Eileen O'Connor, and you have a meeting in ten minutes."

The woman was already about to turn and walk back down the steps, when Ilka finally got hold of herself. "I have a meeting?"

"Yes, the business is yours now." Ilka heard patience as well as suppressed annoyance in the nun's voice. "Artie has left for the day and has informed me that you have taken over."

"*My* business?" Ilka ran her hand through her hair. A

bad habit of hers, when she didn't know what to do with her hands.

"You did read the papers Artie left for you? It's my understanding that you signed them, so you're surely aware of what you have inherited."

"I signed to say I'm his daughter," Ilka said. More than anything, she just wanted to close the door and make everything go away.

"If you had read what was written," the sister said, a bit sharply, "you would know that your father has left the business to you. And by your signature, you have acknowledged your identity and therefore your inheritance."

Ilka was speechless. While she gawked, the sister added, "The Norton family lost their grandmother last night. It wasn't unexpected, but several of them are taking it hard. I've made coffee for four." She stared at Ilka's T-shirt and bare legs. "And it's our custom to receive relatives in attire that is a bit more respectful."

A tiny smile played on her narrow lips, so fleeting that Ilka was in doubt as to whether it had actually appeared. "I can't talk to a family that just lost someone," she protested. "I don't know what to say. I've never—I'm sorry, you have to talk to them."

Sister Eileen stood for a moment before speaking. "Unfortunately, I can't. I don't have the authority to perform such duties. I do the office work, open mail, and laminate the photos of the deceased onto death notices for relatives to use as bookmarks. But you will do fine. Your father was always good at such conversations. All you have to do is allow the family to talk. Listen and find out what's important to them; that's the most vital thing for people who come to us.

29

And these people have a contract for a prepaid ceremony. The contract explains everything they have paid for. Mrs. Norton has been making funeral payments her whole life, so everything should be smooth sailing."

The nun walked soundlessly down the stairs. Ilka stood in the doorway, staring at where she had vanished. Had she seriously inherited a funeral home? In the US? How had her life taken such an unexpected turn? What the hell had her father been thinking?

She pulled herself together. She had seven minutes before the Nortons arrived. "Respectful" attire, the sister had said. Did she even have something like that in her suitcase? She hadn't opened it yet.

But she couldn't do this. They couldn't make her talk to total strangers who had just lost a relative. Then she remembered she hadn't known the undertaker who helped her when Erik died either. But he had been a salvation to her. A person who had taken care of everything in a professional manner and arranged things precisely as she believed her husband would have wanted. The funeral home, the flowers—yellow tulips. The hymns. It was also the undertaker who had said she would regret it if she didn't hire an organist to play during the funeral. Because even though it might seem odd, the mere sound of it helped relieve the somber atmosphere. She had chosen the cheapest coffin, as the undertaker had suggested, seeing that Erik had wanted to be cremated. Many minor decisions had been made for her; that had been an enormous relief. And the funeral had gone exactly the way she'd wanted. Plus, the undertaker had helped reserve a room at the restaurant where they gathered after the ceremony. But those types of details were apparently already taken care of here. It seemed all she had to do was meet with them. She walked over to her suitcase.

Ilka dumped everything out onto the bed and pulled a light blouse and dark pants out of the pile. Along with her toiletry bag and underwear. Halfway down the stairs, she remembered she needed shoes. She went back up again. All she had was sneakers.

The family was three adult children—a daughter and two sons—and a grandchild. The two men seemed essentially composed, while the woman and the boy were crying. The woman's face was stiff and pale, as if every ounce of blood had drained out of her. Her young son stared down at his hands, looking withdrawn and gloomy.

"Our mother paid for everything in advance," one son said when Ilka walked in. They sat in the arrangement room's comfortable armchairs, around a heavy mahogany table. Dusty paintings in elegant gilded frames hung from the dark green walls. Ilka guessed the paintings were inspired by Lake Michigan. She had no idea what to do with the grieving family, nor what was expected of her.

The son farthest from the door asked, "How does the condolences and tributes page on your website work? Is it like anyone can go in and write on it, or can it only be seen if you have the password? We want everybody to be able to put up a picture of our mother and write about their good times with her."

Ilka nodded to him and walked over to shake his hand. "We will make the page so it's exactly how you want it." Then she repeated their names: Steve—the one farthest from the door—Joe, Helen, and the grandson, Pete. At least she thought that was right, though she wasn't sure because he had mumbled his name.

"And we talked it over and decided we want charms," Helen said. "We'd all like one. But I can't see in the papers whether they're paid for or not, because if not we need to know how much they cost."

Ilka had no idea what charms were, but she'd noticed the green form that had been laid on the table for her, and a folder entitled "Norton," written by hand. The thought struck her that the handwriting must be her father's.

"Service Details" was written on the front of the form. Ilka sat down and reached for the notebook on the table. It had a big red heart on the cover, along with "Helping Hands for Healing Hearts."

She surmised the notebook was probably meant for the relatives. Quickly, she slid it over the table to them; then she opened a drawer and found a sheet of paper. "I'm very sorry," she said. It was difficult for her not to look at the grandson, who appeared crushed. "About your loss. As I understand, everything is already decided. But I wasn't here when things were planned. Maybe we can go through everything together and figure out exactly how you want it done."

What in the world is going on? she thought as she sat there blabbering away at this grieving family, as if she'd been doing it all her life!

"Our mother liked Mr. Jensen a lot," Steve said. "He took charge of the funeral arrangements when our father died, and we'd like things done the same way."

Ilka nodded.

"But not the coffin," Joe said. "We want one that's more upscale, more feminine."

"Is it possible to see the charms?" Helen asked, still tearful. "And we also need to print a death notice, right?"

"Can you arrange it so her dogs can sit up by the coffin during the services?" Steve asked. He looked at Ilka as if this were the most important of all the issues. "That won't be a problem, will it?"

"No, not a problem," she answered quickly, as the questions rained down on her.

"How many people can fit in there? And can we all sit together?"

"The room can hold a lot of people," she said, feeling now as if she'd been fed to the lions. "We can squeeze the chairs together; we can get a lot of people in there. And of course you can sit together."

Ilka had absolutely no idea what room they were talking about. But there had been about twenty people attending her husband's services, and they hadn't even filled a corner of the chapel in Bispebjerg.

"How many do you think are coming?" she asked, just to be on the safe side.

"Probably somewhere between a hundred and a hundred and fifty," Joe guessed. "That's how many showed up at Dad's services. But it could be more this time, so it's good to be prepared. She was very active after her retirement. And the choir would like to sing."

Ilka nodded mechanically and forced a smile. She had heard that it's impossible to vomit while you're smiling, something about reflexes. Not that she was about to vomit; there was nothing inside her to come out. But her insides contracted as if something in there was getting out of control. "How did Mrs. Norton die?" She leaned back in her chair.

She felt their eyes on her, and for a moment everyone was quiet. The adults looked at her as if the question weren't her business. And maybe it was irrelevant for the planning, she thought. But after Erik died, in a way it had been a big relief to talk about him, how she had come home and found him on the kitchen floor. Putting it into words made it all seem more real, like it actually had happened. And it had helped her through the days after his death, which otherwise were foggy.

Helen sat up and looked over at her son, who was still staring at his hands. "Pete's the one who found her. We bought groceries for his grandma three times a week and drove them over to her after school. And there she was, out in the yard. Just lying there."

Now Ilka regretted having asked.

From underneath the hair hanging over his forehead, with his head bowed, the boy scowled at his mother. "Grandma was out cutting flowers to put in vases, and she fell," he muttered.

"There was a lot of blood," his mother said, nodding.

"But the guy who picked her up promised we wouldn't be able to see it when she's in her coffin," Steve said. He looked at Ilka, as if he wanted this confirmed.

Quickly she answered, "No, you won't. She'll look fine. Did she like flowers?"

Helen smiled and nodded. "She lived and breathed for her garden. She loved her flower beds."

"Then maybe it's a good idea to use flowers from her garden to decorate the coffin," Ilka suggested.

Steve sat up. "Decorate the coffin? It's going to be open."

"But it's a good idea," Helen said. "We'll decorate the chapel with flowers from the garden. We can go over and pick them together. It's a beautiful way to say good-bye to the garden she loved, too."

"But if we use hers, will we get the money back we already paid for flowers?" Joe asked.

Ilka nodded. "Yes, of course." Surely it wasn't a question of all that much money.

"Oh God!" Helen said. "I almost forgot to give you this." Out of her bag she pulled a large folder that said "Family Record Guide" and handed it over to Ilka. "It's already filled out."

In many ways, it reminded Ilka of the diaries she'd kept in school. First a page with personal information. The full name of the deceased, the parents' names. Whether she was married, divorced, single, or a widow. Education and job positions. Then a page with familial relations, and on the opposite page there was room to write about the deceased's life and memories. There were sections for writing about a first home, about becoming a parent, about becoming a grandparent. And then a section that caught Ilka's attention, because it had to be of some use. Favorites: colors, flowers, season, songs, poems, books. And on and on it went. Family traditions. Funny memories, role models, hobbies, special talents. Mrs. Norton had filled it all out very thoroughly.

Ilka closed the folder and asked how they would describe their mother and grandmother.

"She was very sociable," Joe said. "Also after Dad died. She was involved in all sorts of things; she was very active in the seniors' club in West Racine."

"And family meant a lot to her," Helen said. She'd stopped crying without Ilka noticing. "She was always the one who made sure we all got together, at least twice a year."

Ilka let them speak, as long as they stayed away from talking about charms and choosing coffins. She had no idea how to wind up the conversation, but she kept listening as they nearly all talked at once, to make sure that everything about the deceased came out. Even gloomy Pete added that his grandmother made the world's best pecan pie.

"And she had the best Southern recipe for macaroni and cheese," he added. The others laughed.

Ilka thought again about Erik. After his funeral, their apartment had felt empty and abandoned. A silence hung that had nothing to do with being alone. It took a few weeks for her to realize the silence was in herself. There was no one to talk to, so everything was spoken inside her head. And at the same time, she felt as if she were in a bubble no sound could penetrate. That had been one of the most difficult things to get used to. Slowly things got better, and at last—she couldn't say precisely when—the silence connected with her loss disappeared.

Meanwhile, she'd had the business to run. What a circus. They'd started working together almost from the time they'd first met. He was the photographer, though occasionally she went out with him to help set up the equipment and direct the students. Otherwise, she was mostly responsible for the office work. But she had done a job or two by herself when they were especially busy; she'd seen how he worked. There was nothing mysterious about it. Classes were lined up with the tallest students in back, and the most attractive were placed in the middle so the focus would be on them. The individual portraits were mostly about adjusting the height of the seat and taking enough pictures to ensure that one of them was good enough. But when Erik suddenly wasn't there, with a full schedule of jobs still booked, she had taken over. Without giving it much thought. She did know the school secretaries, and they knew her, so that eased the transition.

"Do we really have to buy a coffin, when Mom is just going to be burned?" Steve said, interrupting her thoughts. "Can't we just borrow one? She won't be lying in there very long."

Shit. Ilka had blanked out for a moment. Where the hell was Artie? Did they have coffins they loaned out? She had to say something. "It would have to be one that's been used."

"We're not putting Mom in a coffin where other dead people have been!" Helen was indignant, while a hint of a smile appeared on her son's face.

Ilka jumped in. "Unfortunately, we can only loan out used coffins." She hoped that would put a lid on this idea.

"We can't do that. Can we?" Helen said to her two brothers. "On the other hand, if we borrow a coffin, we might be able to afford charms instead."

Ilka didn't have the foggiest idea if her suggestion was even possible. But if this really was her business, she could decide, now, couldn't she?

"We *would* save forty-five hundred dollars," Joe said.

Forty-five hundred dollars for a coffin! This could turn out to be disastrous if it ended with them losing money from her ignorant promise.

"Oh, at least. Dad's coffin cost seven thousand dollars."

What is this? Ilka thought. *Are coffins here decorated in gold leaf?*

"But Grandma already paid for her funeral," the grandson said. "You can't save on something she's already paid for.

You're not going to get her money back, right?" Finally, he looked up.

"We'll figure this out," Ilka said.

The boy looked over at his mother and began crying.

"Oh, honey!" Helen said.

"You're all talking about this like it isn't even Grandma; like it's someone else who's dead," he said, angry now.

He turned to Ilka. "Like it's all about money, and just getting it over with." He jumped up so fast he knocked his chair over; then he ran out the door.

His mother sent her brothers an apologetic look; they both shook their heads. She turned to Ilka and asked if it were possible for them to return tomorrow. "By then we'll have this business about the coffin sorted out. We also have to order a life board. I brought along some photos of Mom."

Standing now, Ilka told them it was of course fine to come back tomorrow. She knew one thing for certain: Artie was going to meet with them, whether he liked it or not. She grabbed the photos Helen was holding out.

"They're from when she was born, when she graduated from school, when she married Dad, and from their anniversary the year before he died."

"Super," Ilka said. She had no idea what these photos would be used for.

The three siblings stood up and headed for the door. "When would you like to meet?" Ilka asked. They agreed on noon.

Joe stopped and looked up at her. "But can the memorial service be held on Friday?"

"We can talk about that later," Ilka replied at once. She

needed time to find out what to do with 150 people and a place for the dogs close to the coffin.

After they left, Ilka walked back to the desk and sank down in the chair. She hadn't even offered them coffee, she realized.

She buried her face in her hands and sat for a moment. She had inherited a funeral home in Racine. And if she were to believe the nun in the reception area laminating death notices, she had accepted the inheritance.

She heard a knock on the doorframe. Sister Eileen stuck her head in the room. Ilka nodded, and the nun walked over and laid a slip of paper on the table. On it was an address.

"We have a pickup."

Ilka stared at the paper. How was this possible? It wasn't just charms, life boards, and a forty-five-hundred-dollar coffin. Now they wanted her to pick up a body, too. She exhaled and stood up.

4

Ilka walked out into the high-ceilinged hall and glanced around. The two glass showcases against the wall looked like they came from a jewelry store. One of them held small, elaborately carved wooden boxes and something that resembled the mantel clock over the fireplace at her grandmother's place in Bagsværd. She walked out to the reception area to find Sister Eileen and talk her way out of the pickup.

"No one else can drive," Sister Eileen said without looking up. She was sorting through the day's mail, slitting envelopes open and laying them on a pile without looking inside. "But maybe you don't have a driver's license?"

"I have one, yes," Ilka said, before realizing she should have said no.

"Good. The keys are in the car. Here's the morgue's address. You need to make sure you bring along gloves and masks. It sounds like he's been mangled badly." She pointed

40

at a door at the end of the hall. "You have to walk by the preparation room to get to the garage. Gloves, masks, and body bags are on the top shelf. And take a look at the coffins in storage; see if there are any unvarnished coffins. Apparently, the deceased was a homeless person; it's possible that no one will cover the expenses. But you'll have to take that up with Artie."

Ilka had stopped listening. She had to call Artie and talk him into coming. She lifted her phone out of her pocket and noted a backlog of messages from her mother; the phone had been on mute.

"Niels will do jobs tomorrow and Friday, but can't next week. You have four jobs Monday when you get home."

"The code to get into the garage is six-seven-eight-nine," the nun said, adding that Ilka would need help to pick up the deceased. "It takes two."

"I'll figure it out," Ilka said, looking for Artie's phone number in her address book.

"By the way, someone sent you a bouquet," Sister Eileen said as Ilka walked out. "I put it in Mr. Jensen's office."

Ilka turned in surprise. "Who's it from?"

"There's a card." The nun looked up suddenly now, as if she'd finally noticed Ilka. "You look like your father. You have the same nose. And chin." She smiled. "Please let me know if there's anything I can do for you."

Something in the sister's voice gave Ilka the impression she had been close to her father: her familiar tone. Ilka was puzzled for a moment; then she smiled and thanked the nun.

She returned to the room to change into a pair of jeans and a long-sleeved T-shirt. The wrapped bouquet stood on the small coffee table beside the bed. Written on the card: "We look forward to closing the deal with you." It was signed by Golden Slumbers Funeral Home.

She stared at the card for a moment before sticking it back in the flamboyant purple and white flowers. She went upstairs and grabbed her fleece jacket from the pile of clothes on the bed. She would have to ask Artie what the hell this was all about.

It was one thing to put her to the test. See what she was made of. Have a little laugh at her expense. Fine. And if they were going to get involved with another business in town, honestly, she was more than fine with that. She might even avoid having to figure out how to dismantle her father's business. But she was getting annoyed at how it was happening drip by drip. Why couldn't they just sit down and talk about things? Hatch a plan and divvy up what needed to be done. She punched in the code to the garage. Then it hit her: She was the one who had yelled no, every time Artie had knocked on the door trying to talk with her. She was also the one who had signed the IRS document without reading it.

"Just get this over with," she muttered to herself. She froze when she stepped into the garage.

The space was as large as what she'd seen of the funeral home's first floor. Right inside stood an open coffin. Glossy black, with large gilded handles. It looked to her like something for a head of state, or at least someone who didn't want their final journey to go unnoticed. The coffin had a white satin lining, with a pillow featuring embroidered initials, and it was open in a way that gave Ilka the impression that a person had just sat up, climbed out, and walked off. A coffin that looked a bit less pretentious stood up against a wall, but what she couldn't tear her eyes from was the refrigerator at the far end of the garage. Not exactly like what she'd seen in large restaurant kitchens and institutions, but something along those lines. Unburnished steel, about six feet wide and not as tall as a normal refrigerator, with three drawers. A few rugs and a box had been tossed on top. The whole garage seemed a bit messy.

Ilka knew she shouldn't do it, but her feet were already on the way. When she opened the top drawer, the cold reached out and zapped her. But the tray was empty. She needed to open the next drawer only a crack to see the bluish foot on the steel tray inside. She shivered, closed the drawer, and looked out the window, checking the view—the same as from the room where she'd slept. In other words, her lodgings were above the funeral home's morgue.

She was being silly; she understood that. And yet she was caught in a mood that made her stare momentarily at the drawers of rust-free steel. The boy's grandmother lay inside. The smell— It was true, the air smelled like death. And cold. And like something that had been disinfected. Mostly it smelled cold to Ilka, even though she couldn't put her finger on what that meant.

Thoughts roiled in her head, but she knew she was only stalling. She had an address and a body waiting for her, and she needed to figure out how to go about picking it up. She'd called Artie a few times, but he hadn't answered. At last she pulled herself together and walked over to the hearse, which was parked just inside.

A wheeled stretcher, like the ones used in ambulances, stood against the opposite wall. Under the stretcher were blankets lined with thick plastic and straps to fasten down a corpse. There was also a low cart, something that looked like a forklift. She didn't need anyone to explain it was for transporting coffins.

Ilka was unsure whether she was supposed to take along an unvarnished wooden coffin, or if she should just see if there were any left. To start with, she needed to find where the coffins were stored. She pressed the button to open the door to the funeral home's spacious backyard.

An addition to the house stood next to the parking lot. An overhang under which a vehicle could be backed connected the garage and the addition. FLOWERS was written on the door beside the garage. Ilka walked by a large Dumpster with a biohazard sticker, and over by the next door she noticed a small sign: STORAGE.

Ilka walked in. The room seemed cramped. She turned the light on; she was right, the room was filled from floor to ceiling. In the back, two coffins had been stood up, one a light metallic blue, the other in imitation oak. She recognized the American coffins from films, yet these seemed to her even bigger and more pretentious. She also spotted one that was simple and unfinished—surely the one the nun had been talking about. It looked like a coffin from an old Western, rough wood, no carving or decoration whatsoever.

She ran into Sister Eileen on her way back to the garage.

"You haven't left yet?" the nun asked. It sounded like an accusation.

"I need to talk to Artie before I leave." She looked for plastic gloves and masks on the shelves. She'd called him several times now, but he hadn't answered. She tried again, but no luck. "Unless," she added, "you can come along and help me."

Immediately the sister shook her head. "I can't, and calling him will do you no good. He's gone fishing; he always leaves his phone—"

"I've decided I'm going to help until we figure out what to do with the business." She spoke sharply—*too* sharply, she thought. "And if I have to bring in a corpse, I will drive the hearse. But I'm not going alone."

The nun handed her a note. "Pick him up on the way. Drive as far as you can down the last road. The last stretch before the lake is a bit steep."

Ilka looked at the note and shook her head. Sister Eileen had planned on having her pick Artie up the entire time; she'd been testing her. Ilka was about to say something, but she realized it wasn't the right time for a show of authority. In fact, right now she had little authority to show. How had it suddenly become her job to pick up a dead person? She hadn't even eaten since her flight, apart from the chips she'd wolfed down during the night.

She took the note. "I'll find him. Do I need documents or something to pick up the deceased?"

Suddenly memories from before her father had abandoned them popped up, of him saying, "I have a pickup." She had misunderstood and asked if he'd forgotten something, but then he explained it was called a pickup when he had to go someplace—a nursing home, for example—to put a dead person in a coffin and drive them to the funeral home. He also explained to her that you didn't call a dead person a corpse. You always called the dead person "the deceased." It was all about respect for the person. She had even gone along on pickups, but she'd never been allowed to go inside. She'd sat out in the hearse and waited until he came out with the coffin and rolled it into the back. And by then, the lid of the coffin had been screwed down.

"You won't need any documentation when Artie is with you. They know him." The sharpness in Sister Eileen's voice had disappeared. "This is a very simple pickup; you can handle it easily. But remember to take a stretcher to wheel the deceased on. And bring along some extra plastic. It sounds like it might be a mess."

Ilka nodded and smiled, reminding herself that it would soon be over.

5

Ilka settled in behind the wheel of the hearse and adjusted the mirrors; she quickly checked out the instrument panel. She wasn't used to an automatic, so the car jerked when she braked at first. Tense now, she looked in the side mirror; this boat seemed twice as long as the station wagon she drove back home. The engine growled as she slowly backed out of the garage. She realized that a sensor would warn her if she was about to back into something. It actually did feel as if she were navigating a large boat instead of driving a car. The axles creaked noisily.

Was the rear door completely shut? She'd tried to fit the stretcher to the tracks, but it hadn't seemed to sit exactly right, or maybe the wheels underneath hadn't been pushed up well enough. Finally, she had shoved it in and slammed the door shut as best she could. Hopefully it was heavy enough that it wouldn't spring open while she was driving.

She turned around in the parking lot behind the funeral home, then punched in the address on the GPS. It wouldn't take more than ten minutes to drive to where she hoped Artie was still fishing, she saw. It was just outside town.

She drove down the broad residential street. It was deserted, but she noticed a school across the way from the funeral home. A group of kids were laughing as they hung over a fence and tossed their school bags down on the ground.

The houses in the area all looked the same. Front porches and lawns open to the street, hedges to the sides. The Stars and Stripes swayed over several of the porch railings, and every house had the classic American mailbox in front. Ilka followed the directions given by the GPS, turning from one street to the next. She passed a supermarket with its doors open, though there seemed to be no one inside, no cars parked outside. She'd just turned onto the main street when her phone rang.

"He can't take care of your jobs on Friday after all," her mother said, after asking how things were going. "Can you make it home by then?"

Ilka assured her that everything was going fine. She sensed that her mother held back from asking more. "I don't think I can be back that soon. But I'll probably leave on Friday. Otherwise this weekend. Call West District School Photography. They usually have trainees; maybe we can borrow one. If we can't, call back." The GPS said to turn and drive over a small canal that looked like it ran far into the city. She seemed to be in an old industrial area, long since abandoned, though ships still lined the wharf.

And though stores were open, the downtown streets

were also empty. The town simply seemed deserted. As if it once had been alive but now was gasping for breath, about to give up the ghost. Ilka reminded herself it was early September. Maybe there had been tourists all summer; the atmosphere might have been different earlier. But when she drove up a hill and shortly after found herself leaving town, she doubted there had been much life here. Ever.

Everything around her was green. Horses grazed in large pastures on the left, and on the right, toward Lake Michigan, she glimpsed houses built on the cliff facing the lake. She slowed and tried to look down, but her view was blocked by high fences and hedges.

Quite the place—nice! she thought. She drove by a white-washed lighthouse. For a moment, she was tempted to drive down there, but the GPS said she would reach her destination in two minutes. She drove on until it told her to turn right.

The road was winding and quite steep. Ilka drove so slowly that a person could easily have walked beside her. The vehicle swayed and floated its way down to a fence with an open gate; she wasn't at all sure she could make it through. Slowly she coaxed the big Cadillac forward, and only one side mirror scraped as she slipped between the gateposts. She stopped at a cliff, where a small path led to the water. She slammed the door hard, hoping Artie would hear and not be too surprised when she appeared.

She started down the path, and within short order, a breathtakingly magnificent sight spread out before her. Had she not known better, she would have thought Lake Michigan was an ocean; the calm waters looked boundless. So beautiful and peaceful. It smelled of freshwater, and despite the mirror surface on the lake, a light breeze was blowing.

"Two men drowned down there last week."

The voice from behind almost scared her to death. Artie. She tried to hide her embarrassment.

Two fishing rods were clamped under his arm, and he was carrying a lidded white plastic bucket. He didn't seem at all surprised to see her; maybe Sister Eileen had had better luck getting through to him. He waved his bucket and said there would be fish on the grill if she wanted to stay and eat.

Ilka shook her head and handed him the keys to the hearse. She didn't at all care to listen to him talk about food. She was so hungry she could almost eat the fish in the bucket raw. "We have to work. A dead man at the morgue is waiting to be picked up. I brought along gloves, masks, and extra plastic, because they say he's in bad shape."

Artie broke out into a broad smile at the sight of the hearse parked with its front grille just above the cliff. He shook his head at her, his grin still smeared all over his face. "You think we can get it back up?"

She didn't bat an eye. "Of course. If it can get down, it can get back up. Okay?"

He opened the rear door and stood for a moment looking at the stretcher. Then he placed the bucket with the fish beside it.

"You're bringing the fish?" She couldn't believe it, but Artie didn't answer.

"Let's go." He got in behind the wheel and backed the hearse up slowly.

They reached the gate without speaking. "Yes, thank you very much, the meeting with the Nortons went well," Ilka said. Artie backed the hearse between the posts. "They would like to hold a funeral service on Friday. Can they? You don't need to answer right now, because you'll be talking to them tomorrow."

He stared straight into the side mirror. "You talked to them?"

"They showed up, and you weren't there. Someone had to do it."

Obviously, he was thoroughly amused by the situation he'd put her in. "Friday is out. Maybe Saturday. How'd it go otherwise?"

"It went fine." She explained that the family wanted to do the flowers themselves. "The deceased loved her garden, and they all believed it would be a beautiful thing if the flowers came from there."

"Joanne won't be happy about that," Artie said without looking at her.

"Joanne?"

"The flower shop that usually delivers for the big funeral services. I'm assuming the family wants everything as magnificent and successful as when Mr. Norton passed away."

"I don't know anything about that. But anyway, they want to do the flowers. The deceased is to be cremated, and they want to buy some charms. What are they?"

Artie looked over at her. "A charm is a piece of jewelry that can hold some of the ashes of a deceased. They can hang from a bracelet or a necklace. Don't you have them in Denmark? They're really popular over here."

Back in town now, he drove down the main street in the opposite direction from where they'd arrived the evening before.

"They expect between one hundred and one hundred

fifty people," Ilka continued. "And they want to borrow a coffin for the funeral service."

"Borrow a coffin?" He almost lost his grip on the wheel. Ilka ignored him.

"And I promised that everyone can log on the memorial page we're setting up for them. I don't know how it works with passwords, but they want everyone to have access."

Artie ignored her right back. "We don't loan out coffins. They'll have to buy one."

"She will only be inside one for a few hours. There's no reason to pay forty-five hundred dollars when she'll be burned up anyway."

She felt his eyes on her. Then he shook his head, but not in respect, not like the way he had when he saw she'd driven the hearse down to the cliff. "The coffin's already paid for. We don't make refunds on anything prepaid that the deceased requested."

"After the funeral service we can move Mrs. Norton over to one of the cheap wooden coffins. They can pay for that."

He shook his head again; she knew what he was going to say wouldn't be nice, and she cut him off. "Before my father moved over here, he owned a funeral home in Denmark that he left to my mother. One of the ways her employees cheated her was, after a funeral they took off the coffin lids and reused them. They bought coffins without lids and sold them for full price."

Ilka remembered how it had driven her mother crazy, but there was nothing she could do about it. Without the two undertakers, she couldn't run the business, and without running the business, she couldn't sell it.

"Sometimes they even took the body out of the coffin

after the services and put it in a box they made out of this, whatever it's called, cheap wood stuff, and then they drove it to the place where people are burned."

This was one of the many stories her mother had told in the years after selling the funeral home.

"We loan out coffins," she declared. Artie had handed the reins of the conversation over to her. She owned the business; she made the decisions. "About money, we'll figure something out. Like I said, they want to buy some charms, so we have to take care of that. We agreed that you will talk about that with them tomorrow."

His expression was closed up now, the smile that cast nets of wrinkles from the corners of his eyes long gone. "Okay. Now's the time for you to learn what's going on with your dad's business. It was all in the letter I gave you, but I guess you haven't read it."

A message beeped in, and she grabbed her phone. She didn't want to hear what Artie Sorvino had to say.

She nodded. "I know that I've inherited the business."

"This came out after he died," he began, again without looking at her. "At the same time we found out about you." He paused for a moment, as if weighing his words.

"I don't know anything about the business's books. Never have; that was your dad's department. I guess I might as well tell you straight out that he owes a hell of a lot of money. And when you say we can just lend them a coffin, so they can save money, I say, sure! That's a hell of a good idea! Let's just make the debt bigger. Listen, we can't afford to lose the income from selling coffins. And we can't afford higher prices from the crematorium because we change things around so they can't send the coffins to a scrap-metal dealer to earn a little bit extra. The books are in bad shape; the business is about to be turned over to the creditors. I've managed to buy a little time with the IRS; I told them I had to bring you over from Denmark. It wasn't easy to delay them, but now we have until Friday afternoon before they come in and shut us down. And that means," he added, his tone hinting that there was more to come, "it's too late to save anything. After Friday, you will not have access to your father's private belongings. It's all going to be seized until the government makes sure it has enough assets to cover what it's owed. Then a long process is going to start; it's something neither one of us wants to go through. And it's probably not going to end before we have one foot in the grave. So right now, every single hour that goes by without us fighting to save your father's business is a complete waste of time."

"But you went fishing and forced that meeting on me, instead of staying and telling me how things were," she muttered.

He nodded. "I had to find a way to get you out of that room. We don't have time for you to lie in there and whine. We've got until Friday to put our rescue plan into action. You need to understand that this isn't only going to hurt you. It's our skins, too, if your dad's business closes down this way. But I didn't think you'd go through with the meeting. And I really didn't think you'd put your signature on something without reading it, either."

He might as well have slapped her, several times.

"What about my father's new family? You say they live in a big house in West Racine. It must be worth something too."

The crow's-feet spreading out from the corners of his

eyes returned for a moment. Single strands of his long hair, which was combed back over his head, drooped down alongside his face. "What Paul and Mary Ann had together is her own property. You won't get anything there. Whether it was her who saw it could end up bad, or your dad who wanted to protect her and the girls, I don't know. But the debt is in his business, so if the IRS needs to seize assets any other place, to cover the losses in the funeral home, the first place they'll go to is your property."

She heard her mother's voice in the back of her head: *If you go over there, you risk being liable for something you can't get out of. And they might even arrest you.*

Artie glanced at her. "Do you own anything?"

She shook her head. "I don't have anything valuable, and no, I don't own anything."

"Probably the first thing the tax authorities will do is investigate your financial situation in Denmark. But we do have an offer that can save everything your dad built up."

"But there must be money coming in, too," she said, ignoring her knifelike pangs of hunger. "Because it looks like you're busy enough. And with those prices! It's not exactly cheap to die here."

They were outside the city again, driving down a long, straight stretch of highway with nothing but an occasional house and a few large barns. "I can't say what he spent his money on, but he milked the business dry; no doubt about that." Artie spoke with a seriousness that made it absolutely clear to Ilka: Her situation right now was desperate.

She took a deep breath. *Story of my life*, she thought. She tried, really tried to get a grip on her life, and yet it always ended up with other people or circumstances controlling her.

"Tell me about this offer. It wouldn't be coming from a place called Golden Slumbers Funeral Home, would it?"

Artie looked surprised. He nodded. "Yeah, the Oldham family runs the biggest undertaker business in the entire region. They have their own crematorium and can hold funeral services for over a thousand people. They can put up as many as sixty people when relatives show up from out of town. And they want to take over your dad's business. To stop the IRS from freezing the assets, we must pay sixty thousand dollars before banks close on Friday. And that's just a sort of deposit. We don't have the money, but the Oldhams are willing to pay it if we sign a statement that we're in the process of transferring the business to them."

"It sounds like you've already talked with them."

"Your dad started the negotiations before he died." It seemed like Artie understood just how lousy the situation felt to Ilka, being dragged into the middle of a deal already taking place.

"What do they want?" Ilka tried to ignore her hunger and jet lag, to keep her head clear, because she had a bad feeling about this.

"They'll take over the order book and all the debt in the business. That means you won't be involved financially in the settlement with the IRS or with any of the other creditors. You would still be able to take any of your dad's personal belongings you want."

"What does it mean—they'll take over the order book?"

They drove into a parking lot behind a long gray building. Artie nodded to a security guard and showed his ID, and they parked near a gateway leading to a ramp. "It means they'll take over all the funerals paid for in advance. A lot of people begin making payments for their funerals when they're young, so their relatives don't have to borrow money to bury them. Like you said, it's very expensive to die in this country."

"So the Golden Slumbers people take over the funerals already paid for? And my father already spent that money?"

"No. That money can't be touched; it's in a special account."

"But what do they get by taking over the business?"

"They also get a list of people who have signed up for a funeral but haven't paid yet. Because of the expense, some people take out funeral insurance and pay on it their entire lives, and the insurance covers the funerals when they die."

Ilka nodded. "Okay, so that's what they're going after."

"If you'd bothered to read what I gave you, you'd know your dad's will says that Sister Eileen and I have the preemptive rights, the right to buy, if you decide to sell the business."

"Okay," she said, without understanding what would be left to buy.

While they were sitting in the parking lot, another hearse had driven up to the gateway. Two people had gone into the morgue, but they must have returned without Ilka noticing them, because the hearse drove off.

"I'd like to buy the house, if we manage to get out of this situation. But that won't happen unless we avoid everything being frozen and then getting dragged into bankruptcy."

"The house isn't part of the deal with the Oldhams?"

Artie shook his head. "All they want is the actual business. I'll buy the house from you, so at least you get something out of coming all this way."

Ilka was certain the deal with the Oldhams was to their advantage, but she didn't care, as long as she avoided being held inside the US with an enormous debt. "Let's get this deal going."

He nodded and asked if she was ready to go inside.

6

Artie handed Ilka a mask and a pair of white latex gloves, then walked behind the hearse and opened the rear door to pull out the stretcher. He shoved the bucket of fish to the side.

"Have you ever been in a morgue before?"

Ilka shook her head. She had been to the Forensic Institute in Copenhagen to see her husband one last time after his autopsy, and it had been horrible. She wasn't sure why, whether it had been because no one had been careful enough to conceal the Y-incision in his body, or if it was more because he'd been lying there grayish and cold, and it all had happened too fast for her to realize he was truly gone. The autopsy had been unavoidable, because his death had come out of the blue. No illness, no sign that the end was in sight. Suddenly he was just lying there.

"Okay then, I'll see if there's someone inside who can help lift, but I might need some help out here."

She nodded and followed him down the long hallway with frosted glass panes in the doors.

"Wait here," Artie said. A double door opened automatically and closed behind him as he walked around a corner.

Ilka leaned against the wall. She was dizzy and weak from hunger. She should call her lawyer and get her opinion on this deal with Golden Slumbers. The time difference between Racine and Denmark, however, was seven hours; she would have left work long ago. Ilka tried anyway, and to her surprise she got an answer.

"Hello!" her lawyer repeated. She had worked for Erik long before Ilka had met him, and after his death, Ilka had kept her. The phone connection was breaking up on every third word because of the thick morgue walls, so Ilka walked back outside. The piercing voice of the lawyer came through again, loud and clear.

"No, I don't know if there's a mortgage on the house," Ilka said after she explained her situation.

"Do not sign anything before I've read it," the lawyer warned her. "Send it over right away."

"I've already signed something."

The wind was warm, but Ilka was freezing, and she gave a start when she heard a long, mournful scream behind her. The morgue door was open; a woman was being helped down the ramp by two uniformed police officers. She wore a light summer jacket and walked bent over with both hands clutched to her chest, as if she were afraid her heart was about to fall out. The sounds she made were those of an animal. Between her screams rising and falling in waves, she sobbed desperately, sobs that cut into the place where Ilka had stowed away her own sorrow.

"What in the world is going on? Are you there?" the lawyer asked, but before Ilka could answer, Artie walked out the door, pushing the stretcher. He was still wearing the mask and gloves, but now he also had on a disposable lab coat with rust-red stains from dried blood.

"I have to run," Ilka said. She hung up and hurried down the ramp.

"Someone beat him to death," Artie said after they had rolled the stretcher to the hearse. "He might as well have been hit by a train."

Ilka nodded at the police car. She was still shaken by the anguished screaming, though the woman had stopped and now was sobbing deeply. "Is that a relative?" she asked after the police car drove off.

Artie shook his head and nodded toward the morgue. "She's the mother of a little girl in there who drowned earlier today on a class trip. They just got hold of her; she works at the pharmacy in Racine, but today is her day off. She was in Chicago visiting her mother. The lake is a big part of people's lives here, but it's dangerous. It looks peaceful enough, but it's cold and it's deep, and it's windy once you get away from land. It takes a seaworthy boat to sail out there."

Ilka watched the police car drive off. "Is he from town too?" She glanced at the stretcher, which Artie was sliding into the hearse.

He shrugged. "Looks like he's been living on the street; he only had a few clothes in a bag. The police are trying to locate his relatives. A security guard found him behind one of the empty factories at the edge of town, lying in the grass.

The police report says he died at the crime scene; maybe he'd been sleeping there and someone attacked him."

He shrugged again and closed the back door. "Usually the funeral homes in town take turns handling the homeless. Sometimes we get a small fee from the state, but it hardly covers the cremation, not to mention the cost of a coffin."

"So it's not something you're crazy about doing," she said.

He shook his head. "When you become an undertaker you take this oath, that everyone has the right to a dignified departure from this world. And that includes the people who can't pay. But you're right; we don't fight over these jobs. Like I said, we take turns."

They pulled out of the parking space. Ilka's phone rang. "No one can do your jobs," her mother said. She sounded tired and irritable. "I've tried everyone, but now I would really like to go to bed."

"Shit! Would you please try again tomorrow? I'm sitting in a hearse; we've just picked up a homeless person in a morgue. I'm tired and I'm hungry and really, I don't know what to do—"

"Don't worry," her mother said, her own warm voice on the edge of breaking from anxiety. "We'll find a solution."

"Thanks, Mom," Ilka said, quickly adding, "Say hi to Hanne."

Ilka hung up before her mother could say anything more. She sank in her seat and sighed deeply.

Artie glanced over at her. "Problems?"

Ilka shrugged and stared out the window, letting him know she didn't want to involve him in something he wouldn't understand anyway.

※

"Is it okay with you if we stop to get something to eat?" Artie asked when they reached the town square. He parked the hearse across from Oh Dennis!, the saloon where Artie had met her father, Ilka remembered.

"Yes, it's very okay." As she stepped out of the car, she glimpsed the body behind the curtains in back, packed under a blanket and strapped in place. Before shutting her door, she said, "Shouldn't we deliver him first?"

"It'll only take a minute," he said. "They have the best chicken wings in town, and the ribs are good too. What would you like?"

"Chicken wings and ribs; that's fine. Anything."

Loud music was playing when they walked in, and sports channels blazed out from two televisions on both sides of the bar, just under the ceiling. Artie obviously knew the young woman behind the counter, who was juggling several enormous glasses. The diner smelled greasy and a bit sour, the floor felt sticky, but Ilka couldn't care less. All she wanted was something to eat. Two older men sat across from each other in a corner, their eyes glued to the two televisions. One of them had hair combed forward from the back of his head.

She heard Artie order at the counter, and she shook her head when he turned to her and asked if she wanted a beer. She went to look for the bathrooms. On her way to the door at the back of the diner, she stopped and put a few coins in one of the slot machines hanging on the wall. One-armed bandits, her father had called them. Nothing happened, and she put a few more quarters in. Ten quarters tumbled out. The machine's reels clicked every time they came to a stop.

Artie and the woman were talking and laughing together. A couple came in and sat down by the window.

Ilka won five more quarters and fed them back into the machine; then she went into the bathroom. Their food was ready when she came out. Artie had drunk his beer and packed the food into two large paper sacks. Ilka nodded at the waitress and followed him to the car. The odor from the paper sacks seemed out of place in the hearse.

"There's also curly fries and sliders," he said. He handed her the bags, which felt heavy enough to feed an army. "I'll probably be working late this evening."

He explained he was repairing a face that had been caved in on one side. "He lived in senior housing, and he fell against the edge of a table and hit his temple. It keeps collapsing. The family is coming tomorrow, before I drive him over to the church, so I've got to get going on the makeup and then dress him. They just sent me the clothes. His grown-up daughter wanted to choose them, and she just got in from Minneapolis this afternoon."

Artie backed the hearse under the carport next to the house; then he punched the code to the door. Ilka grabbed the sacks of food, and after getting out she remembered the bucket of fish in back. She didn't want to look in there.

Artie pulled the stretcher out of the hearse. He'd obviously had much practice locking the wheels down and pushing it into the passageway. Ilka followed. The pungent odor of formaldehyde rammed into her. The first time she'd held her breath and rushed through so fast that she had barely registered it; now it seemed to cling to her skin, the inside of her nose, her eyes. She eyed the sacks and retreated a few steps to keep them away from the odor while she waited for Artie.

A cat meowed, then sauntered over and rubbed against her leg. It had white markings on its chest and down over its stomach; otherwise it was coal black. A second later it was on its way into one of the sacks. Ilka lifted it up and set it down off to the side. She was ready to eat straight from the sacks herself if Artie didn't hurry up. She heard him open the refrigerator in the garage and glimpsed him setting the fish bucket in the bottom. After locking the garage behind him, he walked into the preparation room and turned on the powerful fan; a glaring light streamed down from the ceiling.

"This'll only take a sec," he said.

Ilka noticed a long steel table over by the wall, where in place of the countertop was a grating over a drain in the floor. In the middle of the room, another table stood under a large, broad operating room lamp.

He walked back and stood in the hallway, as if he didn't notice the stink. "What do you want to drink? Beer, water, iced tea?"

"Water is fine." She followed him into the office and started emptying the sacks. Two small mountains of meat soon lay on the table. Ilka suppressed any thoughts of death and formaldehyde and dove into the food.

"Why in the world do you want this house?" she asked after wolfing down five enormous chicken wings and noting that even though the doors to the hallway were closed, a whiff of death and formaldehyde still hung around. *Who would want a house that had been a funeral home?* she wondered. She looked around.

Shelves of urns lined the walls, and a poster demonstrated how a large machine could thaw the ground if a coffin had to be lowered in the winter.

He laid his spareribs down and wiped his hands on a napkin; then he looked at her. "When your dad was alive, he did the talking with the relatives. I did it occasionally, after he was gone. But for the most part it was his job. I took care of the deceased. We did the pickups together."

She started eating again while he spoke. "And when we get out of this mess, hopefully, I'm going to start working for the Oldhams. But as a freelancer, so I can help the other undertakers around here, too. That way I'll only be doing the embalming, reconstructions, preparation, makeup. I'll make sure the deceased look the way they'd want to be remembered."

Ilka nodded. She wasn't all that surprised to hear he already had a deal in place. But if he wanted to take over the house and had arranged things to his advantage, that was fine with her too. "And Sister Eileen, what about her? Is she also an employee? And what does she actually do?" Her mouth was half-full of coleslaw.

Artie smiled briefly. "She's from a parish west of here. A lot of nuns work voluntarily in different places, in daycare centers, schools, nursing homes, funeral homes. Some nuns are supported by the parish; other places pay for their services. That's the way it is here. Your dad always took good care of Sister Eileen. She lends a hand; she gives our clients a sense of peace. It's her calling to help wherever she can, wherever she sees it's needed. She wants to work where it's cooler than down south. The heat bothers her."

Ilka was getting full now, and it was hard to ignore the stink of death in her nose. They could have it all, lock, stock, and barrel, as far as she was concerned. Really.

"I just don't want to get dragged out of bed in the middle of the night anymore, when someone dies. And I don't want to scrape people up off the highway, either. You know what? Crushed bones feel like jelly when you lift them over into a coffin. And I won't have to pick up anyone dead so long that their skin slips off like overcooked chicken. I just want to do the creative work; it's what I'm best at."

Ilka nodded. She was finished eating now, and an image of the chickens she cooked for soup was not something she wanted stuck in her head. She always covered chicken bones on her plate with a napkin; it was instinct. "So you want to keep the house as your workshop." That made sense.

"I can take on customers from the entire area. When a funeral director gets severe accident victim cases they can't do anything with, they can send them to me. Just like we pay the Oldhams for using their crematorium."

Artie stood and began picking things up. There was still food left in the sacks. When he walked into the preparation room, she went to look for the cat. It was right outside, and it made plenty of noise when Ilka opened the door. She squatted down and gave it some chicken; then she stroked its back. She turned around and jumped at the sight of Sister Eileen in front of her.

"I made the reservation at the hotel. I'm very sorry about the misunderstanding, but now it's taken care of. Your room is ready, and you can use your father's car." She held out a set of keys. "You won't have to pay for your stay at the hotel, of course."

Who will? Ilka wondered. Artie walked out pushing a stretcher holding the old man who had fallen. Music from the room streamed out: "California Girls." The Beach Boys.

He hummed along as he slipped his arms into a long white lab coat and covered his loud shirt. She couldn't care less if they turned her father's funeral home into a beauty salon for the dead. She just wanted out. Now that she'd eaten, her exhaustion returned.

"But I don't mind staying here," she said. "In fact I'd rather sleep in my father's room. I go to bed early anyway." She walked over to Artie's door to say she was on her way up. She'd stopped holding her hand over her mouth, but the embalming fluids still seemed to line her throat, all the way down.

He promised to gather up all the papers dealing with her inheritance and the upcoming sale, so she could mail them back to her lawyer. Then he walked inside and closed the door.

"I've already moved your belongings," Sister Eileen said, behind her now. "Everything's ready, and your father's car is outside, parked in the large space." She pointed down at the asphalt behind the trees.

"You've already been up and packed my things?" Ilka asked.

"Yes, everything's at the hotel, but I didn't unpack for you. I thought you'd rather do it yourself."

Ilka could see the pile of clothes on the bed, the empty potato chip bag. What else had been lying there? "I'd rather stay here." She tried to smile. "I also have to go through my father's things and decide what to take home with me."

"We can do that together. Do you know where the hotel is?"

Ilka's head began to spin. She needed to lie down, be alone.

"When you pull out, just drive straight ahead and then to the right," Sister Eileen explained, but before she could continue, Ilka raised her hand.

"I'm staying here. I'll pick my things up at the hotel, and please make sure I'm not locked out when I return."

The nun stood for a moment, looking like a child who had just been bawled out, but then she nodded. "Of course. You're quite welcome to stay. I just thought it wouldn't be nice for you sleeping upstairs while Artie works. We've all gotten used to that, also to the smell. But you are more than welcome if it doesn't bother you."

7

"No," Ilka told the receptionist. "I won't be needing the room. I'm just here to pick my things up."

"But we can't cancel a reservation when the room has already been occupied," he argued. He was so big that Ilka couldn't see the chair he was sitting in. His arms filled the sleeves of his blazer, and when he moved them, she smelled stale sweat and something else she couldn't put a finger on.

"Yesterday you didn't have a room, even though we'd reserved one, so doesn't this even things up?" Ilka didn't care if it cost her a night's fee, or rather, if it cost Artie and Sister Eileen.

There was a small coffee bar across from the reception desk. Unmanned. Ilka could stand a cup of coffee, and she looked around for someone to serve her while the receptionist conferred with a coworker. Several minutes passed, and she couldn't hear anything from the back room, only the insistent whining sound she'd heard the day before, like a telephone ringing somewhere.

At last she gave up and walked through the hotel lobby. The nun had given her the room card along with the car keys. When Ilka walked past a wide ice machine, the humming drowned out the monotone whining sound for a moment. The room smelled of cigarettes when she walked in; she was glad to know the embalming fluids hadn't ruined her sense of smell. Sweat and smoke apparently trumped the scents in a morgue.

Her suitcase lay on the bed beside her neatly folded coat.

The reception desk was still empty when she returned. She laid the room card on the desk, walked outside, and threw her suitcase into her father's silver-gray Chevrolet. She got in behind the wheel and sat for a moment with her eyes closed. Again, she felt as if he were with her, though not because she recognized anything in the car. It was more a presence.

Inside the pocket on the door was a package of gum, an empty water bottle, a Post-it with an address, and a receipt from a parking machine. Ilka leaned over and opened the glove compartment. A pile of papers lay under the car manual, and she glanced at them. A questionnaire from a car wash—how was the service? A reminder from the dentist; a chimney sweep was coming. Things that come in the mail, but nothing about him. She stuffed the papers back in, but then she had second thoughts.

She brought out the reminder from the dentist and punched into the GPS the address it had been sent to. It would take ten minutes to reach the destination, she was told.

Ilka headed toward the harbor. A large, open area behind the hotel looked like a construction site that had been deserted for years, from the way the weeds and small trees had taken over. The windows of enormous warehouses closer to the city were boarded up, but a new park had been built in the southern part of the harbor area. It would have looked nice had there been people around. Someone here must have been ambitious, had wanted to accomplish something, she thought, but likely had failed. For a moment, the sense of emptiness and abandonment overwhelmed her. She looked at the GPS. Who knew what she'd find at that little black-and-white marker?

The residential street looked like the ones she'd driven around on earlier. But behind the house where her father had lived with his new family, the ground sloped down to a river with large trees leaning out over the banks. It wasn't hard to see that this was one of the town's better neighborhoods. Ilka approached the house slowly. She took in everything around her, tried to imagine how it had been for him to come home to the life being lived here. It was far from Brønshøj Square, in every way.

She parked in front of the large, square, white wooden house with a porch extending all the way across the front. It took her a moment to notice someone on the porch, a woman in a wheelchair moving toward the front door. The small, frail woman's light hair was pinned up on her head. Her father's wife; Ilka was sure of it. The front door opened, and a blond woman appeared carrying a tray. The two women spoke; then the younger woman looked over toward the car. She took the tray back into the house. The woman in the wheelchair stayed outside, but she didn't look Ilka's way.

Suddenly Ilka realized she was clenching the wheel. The engine was still running, and the car jerked when she stepped on the gas and drove away. Obviously, they had recognized the Chevy.

She reached the end of the street before noticing it was blocked, leaving her no choice but to turn around and drive back. This time she drove past the house without slowing. Out of the corner of her eye, she saw the other woman in the doorway, this time without the tray.

8

Ilka blinked as the bright sun shone directly in her eyes. Mentally, she felt dead tired, and she was thirsty. Annoyed by the sunlight, she turned her head to the side. After her little excursion to her father's house, she had tiptoed up to his room and closed and locked the door. She'd sat on the bed for a while before pulling out the drawers in his desk one by one, first carefully, then with greater impatience. She wanted answers. She felt his presence strongly, all the time, not only there in the room but when driving his car. At his enormous box of a house, with the charming front porch and the lawn that looked as if it had been trimmed with nail scissors, she hadn't sensed him at all.

She curled up. Later she realized she had fallen asleep with her clothes on. Her pants pinched her waist. She raised herself onto her elbows and noticed that the pile of letters she'd found in her father's desk drawer the evening before was about to fall behind the bed.

Some of the letters she'd found were hers, the ones she'd sent him over the years, bound by a wide rubber band and stuffed in the top drawer. The envelopes had been cut open, the letters unfolded. And read. She could see that from the dog-eared corners and creases. She felt a lump in her throat when she found them, and when she read the last one, the one in which she had written about Erik's death, she began sobbing. The letter was stained; it had been read more than once; that much was certain. But it wasn't that pile she had knocked over in her sleep. Another, smaller pack of letters had been stored in the desk, letters he had written to her. Her name was on the envelopes, but they had never been stamped and sent.

There were birthday cards and Christmas cards, and a photo of a little pony had been enclosed in the first letter. A date had been written in the right-hand upper corner April 1983, six months after he'd left Denmark.

"See who's here waiting for you, you'll be the finest little horse and rider." The photo had been taken in front of a large racetrack, and her father posed beside the pony. There wasn't a word in the letter about him leaving for good. It was only a happy note from a father to his little daughter.

Almost eight months passed before he had written again. On December 2, 1983, he was looking forward to showing her how Americans decorated for Christmas. "They don't hold back," he wrote. "Wait until you see the elf arrangement in one of the fancy department stores in Chicago, and they also put caramel in the hot chocolate. I'm looking forward to seeing you again, Trotter, the pony is doing fine."

Trotter. She'd forgotten that name. His little trotting horse. Images began popping up. Lost memories, pulled up from out of the deep. Summer evenings at Havnsie Lake, where they ate fried eel, her father's favorite food, at the inn. One of his friends from the racetrack had owned a summer-house down there, and occasionally they had borrowed it. They had eaten outside in the small yard. She'd been given extra scalloped potatoes, which she mashed.

She could almost physically recall what it had been like, walking down to the harbor to look at all the boats. The smell of tarred bulwarks, the sound of the water lapping against the railing. She'd held her father's hand while carrying an ice cream cone, her mother smiling from under her broad summer hat.

After the first few years, the letters became less frequent.

"My big girl," one of them said. "I think about you. And I think about how your mother is doing. Nothing went like I expected it to, we know that now. I have so often thought about the direction your life has taken. Do you have children? Have you found a good husband?"

There were fourteen letters in the pile. The last one had been written four years ago. Of course, that wasn't many over a thirty-three-year period, yet she was shaken. Why had he never sent them?

She heard a faint knock on the door. Sister Eileen called out.

"Just a moment," Ilka called. Quickly she gathered up her father's letters and put them back in the drawer; then she walked over and opened the door.

The gray-clad nun stood holding a breakfast tray. Tea, toast, jam, and a glass of juice. "I am so very sorry about the inconvenience you had yesterday, having to fetch your things at the hotel. I hadn't understood that you preferred to stay here."

Ilka stepped aside. "It wasn't a problem. Please don't worry." The sister walked in and set the tray down.

Ilka needed a shower, and she still had to unpack her suitcase properly. Even though it wouldn't affect her appearance much, given how little she'd brought along to wear.

"I only thought that you might have felt uncomfortable sleeping in your father's bed." Sister Eileen glanced over at the bed.

"I'm okay with that; it's no problem for me being here."

The nun wouldn't leave it alone. "Some people would probably not like it. We don't know exactly how long he lay there before he was found."

Now Ilka looked over at the bed. "You mean this is where he died?" For some reason, she had assumed it had happened at his home.

"Yes, this is where he departed this life."

Ilka stood for a moment, not knowing what to say, and Sister Eileen misinterpreted her silence. "Of course I changed the bedclothes immediately."

"Wasn't my father living with his family?" Ilka asked, ignoring this bed business. She told the sister about driving by his house and seeing the two women on the porch, one in a wheelchair, the other younger.

"Your father and Mary Ann were involved in a serious traffic accident eighteen years ago. She was injured worse than he was, she never walked again, but he was also affected by it." She stepped over to the window. "He was driving the car."

Ilka had unconsciously moved away from the bed. Yet she didn't feel uncomfortable knowing he had died there. It was more as if she were standing in a very private space, very intense, which her father filled even more now.

"It was probably Leslie you saw on the porch; she's their oldest daughter. She stayed home to take care of her mother, even though Amber also has been living there since your father died. But make no mistake, he lived there, even though he often spent the night here. I believe he did so mostly out of consideration to his wife and daughter, so they wouldn't be woken when he was dragged out of bed."

Ilka nodded. That made sense. She set down the glass of orange juice she'd been drinking. "It's very sweet of you, but you don't have to take care of my breakfast. I don't want anyone to be bothered because I'd rather stay here. It's no problem for me to use the kitchen."

"It's no bother whatsoever," the nun said. "I'm happy to help. The business is yours now, so if there's anything I can do, please let me know."

She stood with her hands clasped in front of her.

Ilka nodded. True, the business was hers now, as if for one happy moment she could have forgotten.

She poured herself a cup of tea and walked over to the window. A woman was sitting on a bench by the parking lot, staring up at the room, or so it seemed. Hadn't she been sitting there yesterday, too, when Ilka came home? Ilka leaned forward and studied her. "Do you know that woman on the bench down there?"

Sister Eileen shrugged. "Don't worry about her," she said, without even glancing outside. "Two men are waiting for you downstairs."

Ilka looked at her in surprise. "Who?"

"Policemen. They would like to talk to you." The nun grabbed the empty juice glass and headed for the door.

Ilka set her teacup down and checked the clothes she'd slept in. "Police! How long have they been waiting?"

"They arrived when I was about to come up with the tea. Go ahead and eat your breakfast; it won't hurt them to wait. They could have called and let us know they were coming."

Ilka promised to be ready in ten minutes. An idea suddenly came to her. "I'd like to give away all my father's clothes to your parish, if you think they could use them. I could also take them there."

Sister Eileen looked a bit confused for a second. "That's very thoughtful of you." She added that she could have them sent; Ilka wouldn't have to bother. "If you'll just sort them, so we can put them in plastic sacks. Thank you so much. I'm certain people will be very pleased."

After the sister closed the door, Ilka gobbled down the two pieces of toast and found her toiletry bag. Ten minutes later, she stepped into the arrangement room where she'd sat with the Norton family the day before. "Can I help you?" She looked at the two police officers.

All sorts of thoughts had rushed through her head while she'd taken a lightning-quick shower and put on clean clothes. She still hadn't sent the papers to her lawyer, so if the visit had anything to do with legal matters, she was very much on her own. Which she was anyway, no matter what the reason for their visit, she thought, as she studied the two uniformed men who had stood when she came in.

One of them was an older man with a thick, full beard;

the other looked to be in his early thirties. He had strong features and broad shoulders. Ilka noticed the brown cardboard box on the floor beside them.

"Morning, ma'am!" the older officer said. He stuck his hand out and introduced himself as Officer Stan Thomas. He was trying—and failing—to hide how astonished he was by Ilka's appearance. No doubt he wasn't expecting a tall beanpole of a woman with wet hair, wearing jeans and sneakers.

Ilka held the hand of the younger policeman longer than necessary, mostly to see how he reacted. It didn't seem to bother him; on the contrary, he smiled. "Officer Jack Doonan."

"Sorry if we're interrupting anything," the other officer said.

Ilka was still looking at the younger man's prominent chin and the line leading up to his cheekbone. His face was like something out of the comics, where masculine men looked as if they had been carved from granite. *He's on the list,* she decided, even though he wasn't exactly her type. The list of possible decent screws in Racine, which had only one name: his.

"You're not interrupting anything." She wrenched her eyes away. They weren't here just to chat. Should she offer them something? Should she be a bit more aloof before she found out what was up? Would it be better to ask them to come back when Artie was around? He had messaged her once last night; he wasn't coming in until the meeting with the Norton family. He'd worked until two in the morning and wanted to sleep in.

She cleared her throat when they sat down. "I'm sorry, would you repeat that?"

The officer nodded seriously. "We think we know who he is." He leaned forward, as if he thought she might not understand English so well. "Is it Denmark, where you come from?"

Ilka nodded. "You think you know who *who* is?" She was confused, and now she was the one who leaned forward.

"At least we have a very strong suspicion of who he could be."

"He," she said, impatient now. "Who do you mean?"

"The man you picked up at the morgue yesterday."

"Okay!" Her shoulders slumped. "And now you need to see him again?"

The younger officer shook his head, and he pointed down at the box to say something, but his partner beat him to it. "I would like to have a look at him, in fact." He nodded. "We believe it's a guy from here in town. He disappeared twelve years ago, but I knew him back when he was a boy. And I know his mother. His dental records are arriving later today, but we're still waiting to hear from his former doctor. So, our identification isn't confirmed yet, which is why we haven't contacted his relatives."

"You're very welcome to go out and look at him," Ilka said, well knowing she would have to pull out all three of the refrigerator drawers, because she didn't know where Artie had put him.

"There was a bag close to where he was assaulted, and our techs found his fingerprints on it," said Officer Doonan, the younger of the two. "We brought along his belongings."

Ilka nodded hesitantly and remembered what Artie had said about the expense of taking in deceased homeless. Maybe that problem was solved? "I'll make sure his belongings are taken care of." She tried to remember the code for the garage. "Why did he disappear?"

The officers followed her past the preparation room. They kept discreetly in the background when she punched the code in to unlock the door. The black coffin was gone. In its place was the plainer one that had been standing up against the wall, trimmed and ready to go. Suddenly Ilka realized there must be another room where the deceased were placed after being embalmed and laid into a coffin. She thought about the door between the preparation room and the door out to the garage.

"Mike Gilbert was a seventeen-year-old boy back then, or maybe he'd just turned eighteen," Officer Thomas said. "The way I remember it, he and Ashley had been going together a few months when it happened."

"Ashley?" Ilka held the door for them.

"A girl from here in town. She was a year ahead of him in school, a real head-turner. And Mike wasn't anything special." The way he said this made Ilka think he'd turned his head for a look at her a few times himself.

"The afternoon it happened, they'd planned to meet after school down at the lake, at the south end of town. It was freezing. I couldn't understand what they were doing down there."

They reached the refrigerator.

"Later we found out they met there when they wanted to be sure they were alone. Mike had a little sister, so it was their hideout, guess you could say. There's a little fishing cabin up on the cliff by the lake; they had blankets and a few sleeping bags stowed away there. Afterward Mike admitted they'd smoked pot and had sex; then he'd left a few hours later for work. She was found on the shore, at the bottom of the cliff. But he claims she was still alive when he left her, still in the cabin."

"Did you think he pushed her?"

Officer Thomas shook his head. "First we thought she'd slipped on the ice. Some places around here it's hard to see in the winter where Lake Michigan ends and the beach begins. Unfortunately, there are way too many serious accidents on the lake, and not only in winter. But the dirt on her clothes indicated she fell from above, even though there's heavy underbrush along the cliff up by the cabin. You don't just step off into empty space there. And the next day, like we said, Mike came into the station and admitted he and Ashley had been at the cabin. He insisted she was alive when he left, and her phone was in her pants pocket; we could see she'd sent a message to her father at four thirty. That gave Mike an alibi, because he showed up at work at four, and his boss and others at the shop confirmed he'd been there all the time. He was our main suspect, though, but we never managed to charge him. And then suddenly one day he was gone. We haven't seen him since, and that sort of supported what we all thought we knew. That he'd done it. But what happened, and how he managed to slip out of town, I don't know. He just disappeared, and that's one way to admit you're guilty."

Now the younger officer asked, "But you didn't have any leads when he disappeared?"

Officer Thomas shook his head. "Not even one. He left his phone in his room, but we put a wiretap on his mother's phone just in case he called home anyway. No luck. He didn't make any cash withdrawals, and his mother says he couldn't have had more than ten or fifteen dollars on him when he left. We started thinking he was dead too. In a lot of ways, it resembles a case from 1988, where a young man from Milwaukee disappeared the same way. Though he wasn't suspected of murder. He was going to visit a friend but never showed up. The police thought he'd run into a serial killer who later was sentenced for killing several young men in Wisconsin."

"But now you believe Mike Gilbert came back?" Ilka pulled out the top drawer—old Mrs. Norton. Gilbert was in the middle drawer, and Ilka stepped back to give the two officers room.

Officer Thomas's face changed expression when he pulled the steel tray out to view the battered corpse. Artie hadn't worked on the deceased, since there was no money for embalming or reconstructing the battered face, and the body was still covered with blood and dirt from where he was found.

The policeman stepped back. "If we hadn't identified him from fingerprints, it would've been nearly impossible."

The young man had a full beard and head of hair; splotches of dried blood clung to his head. His face was puffed up badly, and both eyes were swollen shut. It was indeed difficult to recognize a face so badly beaten as this one.

Why am I staring down at this? Ilka thought. The officer shook his head and pushed the tray back in again. She hadn't intended to look. And it did her no good to see someone in such bad shape. Thirty years old, and beaten to death.

Shit! she said to herself. Not so much because the dead young man lying below her bedroom had probably murdered a girl, but while alive he had possibly been on the run most of his adult life, and now he lay in her funeral home, a shattered wreck that no one wanted anything to do with. Even if she had to pay Artie herself, she decided that at the very least he would be washed off before being interred. She followed the two officers back.

"I'll give the box of his things to Artie Sorvino," she said.

"Thanks," Officer Thomas said. "And, of course, you'll hear from us when we get a definite identification; his family will have to cover the expenses. Though I just heard his sister is sick; they think it's cancer, so if the family doesn't have good health insurance, don't expect to get much out of them."

Ilka nodded, but she already knew she didn't have the heart to squeeze money out of a mother who had lost her son many years ago, a son who'd finally returned, only to be killed.

Artie walked in the door and stopped when he saw the two officers. He glanced over at Ilka.

"I let them look at the man we picked up from the morgue," she said. "They think they know who he is."

"Yeah?" Artie said. Ilka thought he looked relieved that the policemen weren't there regarding the funeral home's demise.

"We have a good idea," Officer Thomas said, "but it hasn't been officially confirmed."

"Mike Gilbert," the younger officer said, as if the entire town should know who that was.

"Really? I didn't see that coming." He pulled the refrigerator drawer out and studied the body for a moment before closing it again. "It can't be his face you recognized."

9

"Do you know anything about what happened to him?" Ilka asked when the policemen left. She followed Artie out into the kitchen.

"I know his mother." He grabbed a few plates out of a cupboard. "She never got over it. I didn't know him or the girl, either, but they were the talk of the town."

Ilka shook her head when he asked if she had eaten. He handed her some silverware, and she asked if he was ready to talk to the Norton family.

"I already talked to them. I stopped by on the way; they were all at the mother's house. The funeral service will be on Saturday. They're keeping the coffin, as was agreed with the deceased, and they're also going to buy four charms and a silver chain; I've billed them for that. But we kept the agreement on the flowers from the mother's garden."

Ilka nodded. She thought about a waiter she once knew.

He'd taken pride in his ability to convince guests who ordered meatballs to drink an expensive burgundy. It was all in the way you sell, he'd said. And she'd had to agree. Though it said more about him than about the customers at his restaurant.

After Artie finished bragging about his sale, he said the Golden Slumbers Funeral Home had invited them over, so Ilka would have the chance to meet the new owners before starting in on the transfer of ownership. "We can grab a bite to eat before we go; I started the grill." He nodded toward the back before walking into the garage for the white bucket of fish. "They need to be eaten today."

Ilka nodded. Not because she was particularly wild about eating the fish he'd put in the back of the hearse, but she could see in Artie's look that he was testing her again.

Why in hell is there a grill in a funeral home? she asked herself, though she kept her face blank.

"What would you like to drink?" Artie walked over to the refrigerator. "I'm having a beer."

His words were innocent enough, but something in his tone and, again, the look in his eye annoyed her. "I don't drink alcohol."

"Not at all? Never a beer, never a glass of wine?" He eyed her. "You have a drinking problem?"

She tilted her head and gazed at him. Whenever she turned down an offer of alcohol, the obligatory question followed: Why? She weighed which version would be best to throw at him. "I don't have a problem with alcohol. It's just I don't like it."

She read his eyes; he seemed to accept her explanation and presumably categorized her as a bore. "So you don't smoke, either?" he asked later, when he returned with the grilled fish.

Ilka shook her head and found a root beer in the back of the refrigerator.

She held her plate out, and he gave her two delicious-looking pieces of fish, which he offered to fillet. She squeezed lemon juice over them. "There's bread in the kitchen too," he said.

"Do you ever miss your gallery and your life in Florida?" she asked.

He slid some fish onto his own plate. "I do, yes." He spooned up some coleslaw and dumped it over his fish; then he passed it over to her. "I miss the life, sitting in the sun and watching people on Duval Street while I work. It's a little hard to do that here."

Ilka asked if he ever painted or sculpted anymore.

"I do wood carving. You'll see that if you ever stop by my place."

"But don't you miss people coming into your gallery and getting excited about what you've created?" She remembered how proud Erik had been when people praised his photographic portraits at the few exhibitions he'd held.

He chewed without looking at her. "It's more that I miss talking to people, like when they stopped by to see Artie the Artist."

She almost laughed but stopped herself when she saw he was serious.

"I miss all the variety, the diversity, the tolerance. You probably won't be here long enough to see how people in this town all think the same way. How little anyone stands out, how much gets left unsaid, because no one thinks it's worth making someone mad. I miss the crazy guy with the big hat who got drunk and sang on the way home from Sloppy Joe's bar. I miss the tourists kissing on the beach at sundown. Keith telling crazy stories he made up about Hemingway. Bald-faced lies. All the pleasuremongers and street artists. And the women. You meet the best women in Key West. And then of course I miss the climate," he added. "It's cold as a well-digger's ass up here, most of the time. And everybody talks about the weather, *all* the time."

"We do that in Denmark, too. In many ways, we're lucky to live where the weather is always changing. At least it gives people something to talk about."

He smiled and took the last bite of his fish. Ilka looked him over for a moment. It was easy to imagine Artie the Artist on a porch, wearing his Hawaiian shirt, listening to the Beach Boys. In fact, it was harder to picture this gaudy undertaker behind a closed door with the big fan roaring.

"And I miss the food," he added.

"Why didn't you go back?" She drank the rest of her root beer, which tasted like bubblegum in a bottle.

Artie checked his watch before standing and picking up their plates. He nodded toward the preparation room. "If I weren't here, who would make sure they look decent?"

"There must be others who could. Surely you don't need an art education to learn how to embalm."

"Anyone can do the embalming, but not many people can re-create a face and bring it back to life."

Ilka didn't ask, but then she didn't need to. It wasn't hard to see that the appreciation of a deceased's relatives was much deeper and more meaningful than remarks from happy tourists strolling by Artie the Artist on the main street of Key West.

He carried the plates into the small kitchen and returned. "Ready to go?"

She nodded; then she asked if Sister Eileen ever ate with him.

"Once in a while. Mostly she eats lunch by herself at her place."

His black pickup was parked just outside the door. Artie pointed to the end of the addition that held the coffin storage room. "She has a little apartment; she likes to go over there on breaks. I don't know how it is in Denmark, but here, she's not on salary. She's a volunteer, and she receives donations for the work she does. She gives most of the money to the church. Occasionally your dad put on small charity auctions; the profit was donated to her parish. She liked your dad a lot, and he understood how important it was to her to be useful. But nuns aren't allowed to take salaried jobs. I haven't said anything to her yet, but if I take over, she can stay with me."

Ilka got into the passenger side of the pickup.

"Even though there probably won't be much to do at first. All this business with laminating and bookmarks and folders, I won't need that. But she'll still talk to people and greet them, and a lot of them like how the church is represented here, sort of."

They drove past several small bars and restaurants she hadn't noticed before. On the sidewalk in front of a big Harley-Davidson dealership, enormous bikes were lined up in an impressive row. But it still seemed like no one was home in Racine. Artie hung a right on the coast road, and after a few hundred yards he turned in. They drove past an impressive building and farther on to a large parking lot that spread out on both sides of the road; Ilka thought it was the city hall until she noticed the sign with cursive script—GOLDEN SLUMBERS FUNERAL HOME. Behind the parking lot, Lake Michigan was completely calm, and the American flag on the enormous flagpole barely moved. The flagpole was fenced in on a small plot of grass in the middle of the parking lot.

Artie led her to a back door with EMPLOYEES ONLY written on it. A tall body-builder type in his early thirties stood outside nearby, smoking a cigarette. His face had delicate features, and he nodded when they approached and told them to go on in. Ilka couldn't help looking closely. His dark eyes were so deep set that his forehead cast a shadow over his irises. Otherwise he was handsome enough.

"What are we actually going to talk about in here?" she whispered. She looked around. "I haven't heard from my lawyer yet. I don't dare sign anything that has to do with the deal, not before she contacts me."

They walked down a long, high-ceilinged passageway with big windows on both sides that reminded Ilka of the party tents rented out in Denmark, except the passageway was wood. A red deep-pile runner lay on the floor, and small decorative gold rosettes lined the walls. Three short steps at the end led up to the building itself. Red rugs also covered the floors inside, and behind a massive mahogany desk sat a nun who looked like Sister Eileen's twin. She stood and smiled when they approached; then she asked them to follow her. She wore the same type of shoes as Sister Eileen, beige and soft, almost indistinguishable from her tightly woven skin-toned nylons.

"We're just here to say hello; they want to meet you," Artie said. She felt his hand on her back, as if he were leading her on a dance floor.

"They're waiting for you. Please go on in!"

Ilka hadn't thought much about what to expect, but she froze when she walked into the enormous high-paneled room with heavy draperies and an oval conference table, high-gloss finish, made from the same massive mahogany as the desk outside.

At one end of the table sat a plump but elegant elderly woman wearing a dark blue suit, her hair piled on top of her head. A man sat at the other end. Ilka guessed he was in his early sixties. His hair was neatly cut and almost white, and he wore a vest under a dark blue suit with a muted tie. A small, neatly folded handkerchief stuck up out of his suit pocket. A thin woman a few years younger than Ilka sat between the two. Carlotta was arrogant and snobbish; Artie had told her before they walked in. That sounded accurate to Ilka, the way the woman watched her as she walked around the table shaking hands. Beside her sat her older brother, David, a stocky man with acne scars. He stared down at a stack of papers. The third brother, Jesse, was still outside smoking. All three of Phyllis's children had deep-set eyes that gave their faces an oddly anonymous look.

Artie had explained that Phyllis Oldham inherited the funeral home from her husband, Douglas. He had run the business with his brother, Howard, the English-gentleman type at the end of the table.

Mrs. Oldham stood up and warmly welcomed Paul Jensen's Danish daughter to Racine. Her large ice-blue eyes sparkled. The children must have gotten their eyes from their father, Ilka thought, which a glance at their uncle confirmed.

"Have you been to the museum? There's a great deal about the Danish immigrants who came to Racine in the late 1800s. Two-thirds of the townspeople at the time were once from Denmark, did you know that? You'll meet many of their descendants out in West Racine." She added that some of them still spoke Danish.

"Coffee will be served in a moment," Howard said, "and we also have kringles. After all, you Danes did bring the kringle to our town." *You Danes*—it was almost as if Ilka personally had introduced the pastry to Racine.

"We have three Danish bakers famous for their kringles. Thanks to them, Racine is known as Kringle Town." He laughed. "President Obama even visited one of our bakers in 2010 to try out a kringle before a meeting."

The sister knocked on the door and came in with a large white cardboard box containing an oval kringle with icing. "A black currant kringle." She set it on the table and then handed out cups to everyone.

Ilka bit into what they proudly called the "famous Danish kringle." Unlike the kringles in Copenhagen bakeries, it was as heavy as a rum ball. There was nothing light, airy, and sugary about the clump of dough with thick icing, so sweet that her teeth screamed. Everyone else seemed happy with it, though; Artie had already gobbled his up before coffee was poured.

"We were very fond of Paul," Mrs. Oldham said after everyone had been served. "He was a good and loyal colleague, though we of course were competitors. But we always chose to think of ourselves as colleagues; that's a much better way to do business in a small town like Racine. We were all very sad when we heard he passed away."

The door behind them opened, and Jesse, the son who had been standing outside smoking, walked in. He sat down beside his mother and helped himself to a piece of the kringle.

None of the children had spoken; it was easy to decode the hierarchy at Golden Slumbers.

"We were also very sorry to hear about the difficulties your father fell into before his death," Mrs. Oldham continued. "And as we told Artie, we would like to help you out of this unfortunate situation."

Ilka said nothing, though it annoyed her that the family matriarch made it sound as if they only wanted to bail an old friend out of trouble. To top it off, an old *dead* friend. As if they were forking over sixty thousand dollars only as a personal favor.

"Fortunately we're also able to act quickly. Tomorrow is the IRS deadline, isn't that right?"

Artie nodded.

"What exactly happens with this type of business deal?" Ilka asked. "As I understand, it's not the physical assets of my father's business you're buying, only…the business part."

Phyllis and Howard Oldham both nodded. "Business activities, yes."

"And now you'll be dealing with the tax authorities?" she added.

They nodded again. The three siblings sitting in silence like stone statues were getting on Ilka's nerves. Apparently, they were following the conversation; each sat with a pen and sheet of paper, onto which they occasionally scribbled something.

"We are completely okay with that," Howard said. "The first thing to take care of is the sixty thousand dollars to be paid tomorrow. After that, the final amount will be settled, presumably within the next…maybe six months."

"But you can take over all the business activities immediately?" Ilka asked. She was thinking of the man they had just picked up at the morgue. It would certainly be nice to avoid the expenses connected with him, especially now that it looked like his family wouldn't be able to pay for his burial.

Howard nodded. "Of course that's contingent on you signing the sales agreement; that has to be done by noon tomorrow at the latest to avoid having the IRS freeze all the assets. But if everything goes smoothly, we'll be ready to take over by this weekend. We'll be able to handle the current clients you have and all those who might come in."

He pointed at the sons. "Jesse handles the pickups in our business; his older brother and I do the embalming; while Phyllis and Carlotta handle all contact with the relatives, all sales and marketing and printed material."

"But we'd like to show you around," Mrs. Oldham said. "You haven't even seen what we have to offer." She pointed at her eldest son and asked him to take Miss Nichols around. "Have a look across the street, too."

He looked terrified; his mother might as well have grabbed a belt and whipped him. He uttered a weak excuse about having to go downstairs, something about a coffin that needed to be sent to the crematorium before three.

Mrs. Oldham's eyes lingered on him for a moment. Then

she straightened up, smiled at Ilka, and told her she would be very pleased to take over. She immediately stood and strode toward the door. "Follow me; I'll show you our business."

Ilka was already impressed when they reached the second floor, where a large display room was practically decorated with coffins. As if it were a safari hunter's trophy room, they had hung the ends of coffins in perfectly spaced rows on all the walls. Coffins of all colors, coffins with carvings and without any decoration. Varnished and unvarnished. It was like stepping into a luxury catalog; nothing was ordinary. Urns of gold and glazed clay, large centerpieces to be decorated with photos and placed on coffins. There was even an example of how it would look if an enlarged photo of the deceased covered the entire coffin lid. Overwhelming, and way too much. Nothing could be further from the more Spartan Danish mentality concerning funeral and burial ceremonies.

After Erik died, Ilka didn't get out of her pajamas for three days. The funeral director had come to their house and showed her a folder. Photos of various coffins that looked absolutely nothing like what hung from the walls here. Ilka had also chosen the chapel from pictures he brought out. Also, the decoration for the coffin, though she changed her mind later. Erik's coffin had been covered with yellow tulips, a flower he had loved.

They walked back downstairs. Phyllis Oldham was agile and a fast talker. Ilka noticed the same stink of formaldehyde as in their funeral home, not only in the hallway but all over the first floor. Heavy paintings in gaudy frames hung from the walls. It was all overwhelming, yet it also projected authority, proof that the Oldham family was successful and had been for many years. One wall was devoted to pictures of the family over four generations; *it probably goes even further back*, Ilka thought. She followed Mrs. Oldham across the street to an even larger building.

"These rooms are for larger funeral arrangements we can't handle across the street." She nodded at the building they'd just left. "We also have live music here. We've had gospel choirs as well as string orchestras."

They walked into a large, high-ceilinged hall with seats and a stage at the end, like a theater. It was beautiful. And it could hold almost one thousand people, Mrs. Oldham said. "We rent this out for weddings when there are no funeral arrangements. The acoustics in here are so good that we've also put on a few concerts open to the public."

Ilka smiled. She wondered how her father had made any sort of a living, having to compete with Golden Slumbers.

Mrs. Oldham smiled back at Ilka. "There will always be a need for funeral homes." She turned off the lights in the large crystal chandelier, and they headed back to the office across the street. "It's a bit like hairdressers and lawyers."

She walked faster now, though it seemed wrong somehow, moving so fast through a funeral home. Ilka could barely keep up.

"As I said, David takes care of preparation. We have an elevator, so the deceased comes directly up to Reception from the parking lot. We have two large cold rooms in there, and out back the florist has her own room. When they come to decorate, they can just walk in. They can also decorate out here when necessary. And we have our own crematorium; it's on the outskirts of town."

Earlier, Ilka had thought that the crematorium might be

at the rear of the building, that they burned the deceased in the middle of town, which made her uneasy. But Artie had explained there were small apartments in back that they rented to relatives arriving from out of town.

"All of our marketing material is upstairs," Mrs. Oldham said. "We send representatives to all the senior citizen fairs, and we visit nursing homes to speak with the elderly. Carlotta has begun arranging home parties; they've been an enormous success. It's like Tupperware parties, where female friends and families get together and hear about all our offers. Jewelry for ashes has become incredibly popular."

Ilka gawked, though she said nothing.

"We have to protect our interests. Paul would have said the same. Now that people can order coffins on the Internet, we have to emphasize service and extras."

"Time to go," Artie said when they returned to the arrangement room, where Ilka had laid her jacket. The kringle box was empty, and it appeared he'd had the pleasure of the snobbish daughter's company the entire time Ilka had been gone.

"You're welcome to walk through the garage," Mrs. Oldham suggested after they said their good-byes and thanked her for the pastry.

Artie nodded, but instead he led her out the way they had come. "She just wants you to see their two new hearses and the escort cars to lead them." He held the door for her.

10

Ilka had just sat down in her father's office chair to take a look at his will and the legal papers on the transfer of activities when her phone beeped: an e-mail from her lawyer in Denmark. The attorney was furious that right off the bat, Ilka had signed papers confirming she was Paul Jensen's daughter. Now Ilka was stuck with the consequences. This wasn't good. On the other hand, it was unavoidable, because, quite likely, their relationship would have been confirmed anyway. And presumably Ilka had a way out of the hopeless situation she'd put herself in.

"Just don't count on any financial windfall. You'll be lucky to get out of this without losing anything. If you enter into a transfer agreement with Golden Slumbers Funeral Home, it looks like they can take over your debt. Both to the IRS and the other creditors. But it's important to pay the sixty thousand dollars tomorrow, to prevent the governmental wheels from starting to turn. Otherwise you risk them making a claim on your assets in Denmark."

Ilka was about to write back that she had just visited the Oldhams, that everything was ready to be signed, when Sister Eileen appeared in the doorway and asked her to come.

"Can it wait a moment?" Ilka glanced at her father's will with a mixture of fear, excitement, and anxiety; she had decided to put off looking at it until last.

The nun shook her head. "No, unfortunately. You should come right now. There's someone you need to talk to."

"Can't Artie handle it?"

Sister Eileen shook her head again and began walking back to the reception area. Ilka followed her. She noticed the woman from a distance, sitting on one of the high-backed chairs along the wall. Her hair was in a loose ponytail, and she wore an oversized cardigan, a white blouse, and a pair of dark pants. It was her shoes, however, that revealed she'd left home in a hurry. Red Crocs with splotches of paint and blades of grass clinging to them.

Ilka looked in puzzlement at Sister Eileen, who said, "The police sent her here."

The woman walked over to them. "I want to see him." She took both of Ilka's hands in her own and looked pleadingly at her. "I have to see him."

Her face was pale, her lips pressed together to keep from sobbing, but tears appeared anyway when she began talking and slowly shaking her head. "It can't be true," she murmured.

"Go get Artie," Ilka said, sending Sister Eileen off with a gentle but firm shove.

"Let's go in here, into the arrangement room, shall we?"

she said to the woman—Mike Gilbert's mother, Ilka was sure. They had just sat down when Artie walked in, but she stood and walked to him.

"Oh, Shelby!" He put his arm around her.

"You never met Mike, but I've got to know if it's my son they found," she said. Artie murmured something soothing; Ilka couldn't hear what. Obviously, they knew each other well. "The police say they're sure. Fingerprints and dental records match."

She looked exhausted, but she settled down as Artie spoke to her. Her head and shoulders sank, and suddenly her clothes looked much too big, as if she had shrunk. Tears dripped onto the floor, and Artie held her. Ilka left the room, but she heard him say the woman couldn't see her son.

"What do you mean?" she sobbed. "You don't have the right to stop me."

Artie spoke calmly. "I can't show him to you the way he is now. That wouldn't be good for anyone, least of all you. Give me a little time, and I'll get him ready. Come in tomorrow afternoon; then you can see him."

She pulled herself together and nodded. For a moment, she stared straight ahead; then she lifted her shoulders. Artie offered her a chair.

Ilka went out into the tiny kitchen, found some cups, and filled a carafe. She dumped some small wrapped chocolates into a bowl, then brought it all in and set it on the table and went back for a few bottles of water. She wasn't used to serving in this sort of situation, but she used what they had. Quickly she moved everything around on the table to make it look appealing, but it wasn't her strong suit; she realized that. Finally, she gave up and left everything alone.

Shelby Gilbert sat down. Pale, stone-faced, weeping. And so small and alone in her sorrow, Ilka thought.

"Do you have a photo of Mike?" Artie asked. He pulled a chair over and sat beside her.

Shelby didn't react, so he repeated his question and added, "I'll do everything I possibly can to make your son look like himself. But I need to see how he looked before he disappeared."

"But I can't afford it," she sobbed, gasping for breath. "First I thought I'd have to sell the house, now that Emma is sick, so I could pay for her treatment. Then Mike wrote that he was coming home to help us. But now he's dead, and I can't afford to pay for his funeral."

That surprised Artie. "You've been in contact with him?"

Ilka offered her a cup of coffee in the pause that followed. Shelby nodded, then lifted a Kleenex out of the box and dried her cheeks. "I knew all the time he was out there. And I knew he would get in touch when he was ready. And he did; three years ago, he sent me a post office box address I could write to. We were careful; we only wrote a few letters a year. We were scared the police would come for him if they knew where he was. It's hard when you've been made the scapegoat. But then I wrote to him when his sister got the diagnosis. I just thought he should have the opportunity to say good-bye to her, if it came to that."

She began crying again, and Ilka felt her eyes growing damp as well at the thought of Shelby Gilbert's son lying in there. No one had been given the chance to say good-bye to him.

"We'll find a way," Artie said. "Don't be thinking about the money. But help me with the photo, so I can re-create his face. Unfortunately, there's been a lot of damage."

"Is it that bad? How bad?" Shelby looked straight into Artie's eyes. "What did they do to him?"

Artie ignored her question. "I won't be finished this weekend, but tomorrow I'll let you see him. And next week he'll be ready so you can say your good-byes. Do you want a funeral service?"

Shelby shook her head. "We just want to say good-bye, real quiet. It'll only be Emma and me, and of course I'll let their father know. He can come if he wants."

Artie nodded and suggested that Ilka and Shelby talk some more about the interment. Or the inurnment, if she chose to have him cremated. He motioned for Ilka to follow him outside; then he closed the door behind them. "This is going to be on us, but try to keep the expenses down." He left, and shortly after she heard the fan start and the garage door open.

Keep the expenses down. Great idea, but how? How could she save money in this crazy undertaking business? She shook her head and walked back inside.

A pale Shelby Gilbert sat in the arrangement room, staring off into space. She'd stopped crying, but the corners of her mouth were quivering. Ilka handed her a cup of coffee. She set it down without drinking.

"She was no good," she said, her voice low now. "I warned him, told him she was a devilish girl; you can just tell, the kind of girl she was. She had him wrapped around her little finger, talked him into skipping school. And he admitted to smoking pot; he'd never done anything like that before. But he wouldn't listen; he was in love. And now they're both dead. So young."

Ilka sat down beside her in the chair Artie had pulled out. "But he came back," she said. She asked if he had seen his sister after he had returned.

"No. I didn't know he was back in town. The plan was that he would go to Milwaukee and I would meet him there. He wanted to visit Emma; she's in All Saints Hospital here in Racine, but I was scared that people would recognize him if he showed up here."

Her mouth began quivering again; her voice sounded brittle. "He didn't do it. You know that, right?" she asked, even though she had to be aware that Ilka couldn't know what had happened back then. "He wasn't the one who killed her. They used him as a scapegoat and ran him out of town. The town he was born and raised in. Jesus!"

She hid her face in her hands for a moment; then she straightened up and reached for Ilka's hand. "I can't pay for a big expensive funeral. I can't even pay the bills for my daughter's treatments. Our health insurance has turned us down because she has a brain tumor; they don't cover it when there's too big a risk to operate. But when I get the house sold, I hope there'll be enough money to cover your expenses with Mike."

She looked down at her hands. "I've already taken out a bank loan to cover Emma's first round of chemotherapy, so I'm not sure I can borrow any more. But the house should be easy to sell if I price it low enough."

Her tears began falling again. "I just want to see him one last time, so much," she murmured.

Ilka stroked her hand. "It sounds like you and Artie have already made a deal, and if you don't mind a plain coffin, I know we can work something out." She thought of the unvarnished wooden coffin they had decided to give to the homeless man, who as it turned out wasn't actually homeless.

"We'll need some clothes for him," Ilka said, and she asked if there was anything special Shelby wanted him to wear.

"I don't know if he can fit into anything he left behind. I haven't seen how much he's grown."

Ilka smiled at her. "Go home and have a look. Otherwise we'll find something. It was just if there was something you preferred."

They were standing up now, and Ilka noticed that the coffee had been left untouched again. Maybe she was doing something wrong during these conversations?

11

After her meeting with Shelby Gilbert, Ilka had gone up to her room and stuffed most of her father's clothes in some large grocery bags she'd found in the kitchen. Sister Eileen could send them to her parish. She'd placed a note on the nun's desk in the reception area, informing her that she could have the sacks of clothes in the hall. Later she dropped by the taco shop two blocks from the funeral home and grabbed a bite to eat. Then she shopped at the supermarket and picked up water, crackers, and a bag of chips. And some bread she could toast the next morning. She surveyed the refrigerator; the bread Artie had mentioned was more cardboard than bread. On the way to the checkout, Ilka had dropped two cream sodas in her cart.

Now everything was lined up on the desk, and she was reading the will from the very beginning.

"I bequeath everything I own except my funeral home business to my wife, Mary Ann Jensen, and my two daughters, Leslie Ann Jensen and Amber Ann Jensen. That includes the money deposited in my private accounts and the contents of the bank box in Mid-America Bank, 21075 Swenson Dr., Suite 100, Milwaukee, Wisconsin. Everything is to be divided equally among the three, as my wife is wealthy. In addition, the house is in her name, and she has purchased most of the contents of the house. I bequeath Jensen Funeral Home to my daughter from my first marriage, Ilka Nichols Jensen. The business is to be transferred directly to her, and she is to be the sole owner of the business. If, however, she wishes to sell the funeral home business, Artie Sorvino and Sister Eileen O'Connor are to have first right of refusal before it is put on the market, at a price set by a person knowledgeable of the funeral home business."

Ilka was interrupted by her phone. Most likely not her mother, she thought; it was the middle of the night back home in Denmark, and hopefully she was sound asleep.

"Can you do a pickup?" Artie asked. Music was playing in the background.

"Not just now. I'm about to eat," she muttered. "And I'm reading through my father's papers." Also, she had an offer on Tinder. Some guy a few blocks away had invited her to meet him at a bar. "You'll have to take it yourself."

"You can be here in fifteen minutes; I'll be ready," he said, ignoring her objections. "Bring along plastic and the light stretcher. It's up on the second floor."

He hung up. A moment later, he'd messaged her his address.

It's a quick pickup. You'll be back in an hour.

She sighed and gathered the papers, laid them on the desk, and grabbed her fleece jacket from the bed.

She recognized the lighthouse as she drove the twisting road north along Lake Michigan, but the GPS told her to continue past it before turning right. The road down wasn't quite as steep as when she had picked up Artie and his fish. Houses lined both sides of the small side street. Nothing big; more like summerhouses, with short driveways. At the end of the street, she reached a turnaround and a small path that led to the last house, which faced the lake. The surface of the water looked like quicksilver, an artificial gray metallic sheen.

Ilka was about to shut the engine off when a young, light-haired woman came prancing out of the house; her hair was a mess, and her jacket sat crooked, as if it were a bathrobe. She waved at Ilka energetically, a sign that she was satisfied now, that it was okay with her for Artie to go to work.

Who the hell does he think he is? Ilka slammed the door of the hearse extra hard. He ordered her around to give himself time to finish screwing. Before she reached the path, Artie came walking toward her. He looked like he was about to invite her in for a tour, and she promptly turned on her heel and strode back to the car. "We'd better get going."

"It's probably best that you drive," he said, and headed for the passenger side.

She was about to protest, but then she dropped it. It would be asking too much of him to be on standby 24/7 for pickups. On the other hand, she felt it was tactless of him to get drunk and screw someone while she was going through her father's will.

"I was in the middle of an important telephone call," she said, after they were inside the hearse. "You maybe don't know this, but I have a business to run in Denmark and I can't just drop everything because you want a night off."

He ignored her complaint. "Isn't it nighttime in Denmark? There's seven hours' time difference, if I remember right."

"We have early meetings. I thought you put off the pickup until tomorrow."

He nodded. "This is a new one. An older man. He's been dead quite a while, maybe a week, maybe longer. He lived alone with his dog. The police think the dog tried to wake him up; it nearly licked his cheek off. The people in the apartment below found him. The dog's dead too; we'll take it along, now that the police are finished."

The hearse swayed and the shocks creaked when Ilka sped up on the steep gravel road. She liked the personality of the hearse, a bit grouchy but with a strong will. The lake looked like an enormous gray river in the broad side mirror, a river that disappeared when she cautiously turned onto the highway.

"We're taking a dog along?" she said, suspicious now. "Can't the people living below bury it?"

"The dog was all he had. It's part of the deal." Artie leaned his head against the window while she drove. "We'll put it in a coffin before we go to the crematorium; they won't even know it's there. It's only right that the two of them leave this world together."

She turned to him "Are you drunk, or what?"

He shook his head. "I'm fine, I just need to…"

She shook her head too; then she turned on the radio and twisted the worn, leather-covered button. She found a station playing an old Paul Simon song.

The police car pulled out just as they arrived. A light on the top floor was still on, and from the side window she saw a couple walk out on the front steps as she turned into the driveway. Artie had told her to back into the parking space so they wouldn't have to carry the deceased so far. Meanwhile he'd dozed off, and she elbowed him after she had parked in front of the main building. "We're here." She stared at him in annoyance.

Darkness shielded them, allowing them to work without interference from neighbors and passersby. Ilka was fine with that; she wasn't sure what she'd see up on the second floor, and she didn't know how she would react. There was that business about the cheek, too.

The couple standing in the doorway shook their hands. "We've been gone all week; that's why we didn't notice Ed hadn't been down with his dog," the woman explained apologetically as they walked up the steps. Her husband opened the door to the small hallway and told them Ed was in the living room.

The police had been thoughtful enough to leave several windows open, but the stink was nauseating anyway. Ilka discreetly pulled the hood on her jacket around and covered her mouth and nose.

"We've always looked out for each other; we'd never have let him lie here like this," the woman continued. "You hear so much about lonely people dying alone. But we got along really well. And we kept an eye on each other."

Her voice was wispy and anguished, as if she expected someone would blame her for not discovering the man living above them had been dead so long.

"But you're the ones who found him," Ilka said. "You haven't done anything wrong. Lots of people don't have good neighbors who look out for each other. Of course you should be able to travel. No one could know this would happen."

Ilka had no idea where all these words were coming from. Just as she didn't know if she was trying to comfort them or if she was stalling to avoid going into the living room.

She felt a cold wind blowing from in there, and she remembered to breathe in through her mouth, as Artie had recommended. He'd already brought the stretcher in, and now he handed her a pair of gloves.

"What about a mask?" she whispered before entering the room.

He shook his head and explained that masks were necessary only when there was a threat of infection. And when dealing with the homeless, because you could never know what they might have.

"This guy here is okay. It's not a pretty sight, but there's no danger of catching something."

Ilka pulled on her gloves and followed him. She noticed the bulky furniture and heavy picture frames, big pillows on the sofa, wide armchairs. Everything was nice, attractive. Ed McKenna was on the floor by the open bedroom door, lying on his side with his arms folded. His dog lay curled up beside him.

Ilka froze. Seeing them lying there felt like a punch to the gut. Loneliness and solidarity. Together they had left the world behind. She felt Artie's eyes on her, aware that he was giving her a minute. The sight must also have hit him hard.

She nodded and joined him as he squatted down to turn McKenna over. Standing over the body, Ilka realized her anxiety had disappeared. Sure, it stank in there, and he was bloated, his skin was gray, but she'd thought it would be worse.

They carried the stretcher over and pulled the wheels up so it lay on the floor beside him. "You take hold of his legs; I'll grab his shoulders," Artie said. He was on his knees, ready to go.

Ilka leaned down and gripped the back of his knees.

"Get a good hold on him; he'll be middle-heavy when we lift him," Artie said. He counted to three. "Kneel down and lift with your legs. Tighten your stomach muscles; careful with your back."

Ilka concentrated on lifting and moving him slowly, not looking at him until he was on the stretcher. The skin on the left side of his face was missing. The exposed muscle was dark, but in one spot his cheekbone was visible.

"Might be insects," Artie said as they strapped the body down. "We'll come back for the dog."

Ilka nodded. She felt so sad it had taken so long to discover Ed McKenna was dead. That no one had missed him. Except his dog. They carried him slowly down the steps, Artie in front, Ilka leaning over a bit to level out the stretcher. The couple had returned to their apartment, but now they came out. "What about everything up there?" the man asked.

Artie shrugged and said they would have to contact the police, to hear if he had any relatives.

"He does; Ed has a daughter," the woman said from behind her husband.

"But you haven't contacted her?"

The couple looked at each other before shaking their heads. "Matter of fact, we haven't. We should have, of course we should, but coming home and finding him like this, it shocked us. We called the police at once."

"We don't have her number, either," the man added. "She lives somewhere over in upstate New York, but I don't know where."

"Most likely the police have found her; she's probably on her way. Or she'll show up in the morning." Artie was reassuring them; Ilka was very surprised he'd shaken off the drinking and sex and was acting as if he'd just been sitting around, waiting to be called to take care of Ed McKenna. "We'll also speak with his family. They may want him buried closer to them."

He pushed the stretcher into the car and told Ilka to get in, that he would get the dog.

She nodded. Though it hadn't been as bad as she had feared, she was relieved to not have to go back up there. She watched him come down with the dog, which he'd packed in a sheet. He slammed the rear door.

"Okay, we'll drive back and get him and the dog taken care of, and then I'd appreciate you driving me home. You mind if I roll down the window and smoke a cigarette?"

She shook her head and held her fingers out toward him in a V.

He looked questioningly at her; then he tapped an extra

cigarette out of the pack. They smoked in silence as Ilka drove back to the funeral home. After she tossed the butt out the window, she held her hand out, asking for another.

She couldn't stop thinking about McKenna and the dog. The loneliness. She chain-smoked three of Artie's cigarettes before reaching the funeral home.

12

Ilka dropped Artie off and finally arrived home just before midnight.

She left the engine running as she got out and punched in the code to open the garage door. The cat appeared and snaked around her legs as she walked back. Gently she pushed the cat away, got in behind the wheel, and maneuvered the big, klutzy vehicle into the garage. The cat was right there when she shut off the engine and stepped out.

"Okay, okay," she muttered as she closed the garage door and yawned. She called the cat to follow her through the garage and into the passageway. Then she went into the kitchen for the rest of the grilled fish.

She made small talk to herself as she walked; she knew she would fall asleep if she didn't keep moving. Mumbling helped her cope with the deep stillness of the funeral home. And the darkness.

She laid the fish on a small plate and opened the door to the carport just outside. "Dinnertime, kitty," she called. The cat hopped up on its hind legs before she could set the plate down. "You're a hungry little thing, aren't you?"

She shook her head at herself and let the cat do what cats do. She walked upstairs. The sacks full of her father's clothes and shoes were gone; Sister Eileen must have taken them. Ilka liked the idea of his clothes having a new life somewhere else, worn by people unaware that the dark suits had been a funeral home director's uniform.

The burritos on the desk were still unopened, but she was too tired to care about food.

Ilka had also been too exhausted to pull the curtains before collapsing on the bed. It was still dark outside when she woke up. She lay there listening, disoriented and unsure of what had woken her. A thud from something falling. Or was it a door slammed shut? She concentrated as she lay staring up into the dark, trying to isolate the sound, but now everything was silent. She'd just closed her eyes when she heard it again. And again. Had she forgotten to close the door after feeding the cat?

Still half-asleep, she swung her legs out of bed, stuck her feet in her shoes, and wrapped a sweater around her shoulders.

She glanced at the clock: three thirty. She'd slept some, but not much. Out by the stairway, she fumbled for the light switch, then started down. Somewhere she heard an engine, or perhaps a transformer. The ceiling light hummed.

Halfway down, she stopped. She heard the noise again, and now she was sure a door had been slammed. Her footsteps were muffled by the thick dark blue carpet as she made her way through the office and past the kitchen. She took a deep breath and opened the door to the passageway.

The silence and darkness outside pressed in on her. The door leading to the carport was closed; she hadn't forgotten that one. Ilka walked over to the door to the cold room. Locked. She opened it slowly and turned on the light. The man and his dog still lay on the stretcher. She shivered. The two coffins were in the same place as the last time she'd been there. Maybe she'd heard the ventilation system? It rattled slightly, the only noise in the room.

She shook her head at herself; then she walked over to the garage and punched in the code. It was dark in there, too. When she finally found the light switch, the fluorescents sputtered a few moments before showering the entire garage in white.

Nothing. Refrigerator shut and garage door down. Everything exactly the way it had been when she had parked the hearse.

Don't be so stupid! she told herself. She was letting her imagination run wild over the slightest noise—ridiculous! As if she believed that the dead could rise and walk around. And she'd never heard of anyone breaking into a funeral home. What was there to steal? Formaldehyde and coffins. *Get hold of yourself!*

She switched the lights off and shut the door, checked the garage doorknob an extra time to make sure it was locked, then walked back upstairs. *Relax*, she told herself. In two or three days, she'd be on her way back to Copenhagen.

She had no idea whether ten minutes or an hour had gone by when she was awakened again. The noise was back, and this time she was certain. She lay a few minutes before resolutely throwing off the comforter, pulling on a pair of pants, and slipping her shoes on. She was determined to shove out this final shred of the fear of darkness inside her. At no time had she been bothered by sleeping over a morgue. The dead would be the last to come up here and haunt her. But rattling noises in dark, strange places had never been her cup of tea. Usually she could control her fear, but she was too exhausted to stop her imagination from running away with her. She tried to calm herself while sneaking downstairs. What she really needed was a decent meal, a good screwing, and a good night's sleep. Then she'd feel strong enough to handle these ghosts. She realized she'd stood up her Tinder date. She'd completely forgotten about him.

Down on the first floor, Ilka switched the passageway light on. She was determined to check every door. If she didn't get at least a few more hours' sleep, she would be too spaced-out to think clearly when signing the transfer agreement over at the Oldhams.

Door to the carport—locked. Preparation room—locked. Cold room—locked. Garage—locked. She punched in the code, turned on the light, and was on her way to the big garage door when she spotted him. In shock now, she saw the open middle drawer of the refrigerator, the empty steel tray pulled out. Mike Gilbert lay on the floor, twisted and battered. Dark splotches of blood on his face stood out as grotesque shadows. He lay on his back, his arms spread like someone being arrested and patted down, his legs splayed out crookedly.

Ilka's heart hammered as she stood frozen in the middle of the garage, staring at the dead man. Silence; that's all there was now, a deep silence. Except for the low hum from the ventilation fan. She had no idea what to do, and Artie wouldn't be coming in for several hours. Instinctively she backed up until she hit the wall. Her legs prickled; her arms felt weak. What in hell was going on?

A thought struck her: There might be someone there. Without budging an inch, she surveyed the entire garage; then she knelt down to look under the two trolleys. No one there. She was alone, she was sure. Almost sure, anyway. She struggled to think clearly; mostly she wanted to run up to her room and lock the door and wait for Artie. Her phone was in the room. Why hadn't she brought it along? *Idiot*, she muttered to herself. Then she realized she couldn't just leave the deceased lying there on the floor. It was undignified; it looked all wrong.

Slowly she approached him, but then she turned to get the stretcher over by the wall. She maneuvered it around the coffins, pushing it in front of her like a shield. Sweat ran down her back as she wrestled to put up the wheels. The noise she made was unnaturally loud. Should she call Artie? The police? Get Sister Eileen?

Her fingers had forgotten how to work together; she couldn't find the mechanism to release the wheels so she could lower the stretcher to the floor. Finally, though, she succeeded. Simply doing something helped her fight off panic. Without thinking, she leaned over to take hold of Mike Gilbert's torso.

She slipped her arms under his shoulders to get the best possible hold on him, but suddenly she pulled them back, an instinctive reaction. What was she doing? Could this be considered a crime scene? And it felt as if she'd grabbed a pile of wet sand. Scared now, she looked down at the man, but then she took hold again, squatted down, and slipped her arms underneath his body. She tried to lift him, but it was hopeless. Only now, sitting with her arms around the dead body, did she realize she might have been mistaken the first time she was down here.

But she had checked everywhere. Ilka was sure he hadn't been lying on the floor. She fought down her uncertainty. It must have happened after she'd gone back to bed.

She considered again whether to leave the body there until Artie came, let him decide what to do. Her palms were sweaty, the back of her T-shirt wet. Her eyes darted around the garage, into the nooks and crannies.

She gave it one more shot, but it was impossible to lift him by herself. Instead of going back to bed, though, she opened the garage door and walked over to the addition. It was much too quiet outside, in contrast to all the noise in her head. It felt all wrong. And then there was the mauled body on the floor a few yards away.

The darkness made it difficult to make out what was written on the doors, but the one down at the end seemed to be the main entrance. She pushed the doorbell hard, let go, pushed it again. And again, and again, until a light came on in a room facing the parking lot.

She retreated a few steps and waited until Sister Eileen came to the door in a nightgown.

"I'm sorry," Ilka began. Suddenly she realized she was standing there in a sleep shirt, her hair tangled up. "Something's happened in the garage. I need your help."

The nun frowned and shook her head. She pulled the door shut behind her, as if she was afraid Ilka might push past her and make an even bigger nuisance of herself.

"Someone has been in there. Someone pulled Mike Gilbert out of the refrigerator and left him on the floor."

"Wasn't the door locked?" the sister asked, as if that changed something about the fact that he was lying on the floor.

Ilka shrugged. "He's lying over there; you have to come help me. I can't pick him up by myself." She was tired, but this had to be done. Now.

Sister Eileen nodded and went back inside. A moment later she came out wearing her practical office shoes, with a long cardigan wrapped around her.

They walked back to the garage without speaking. The garage door was still open; the light inside fanned out into the yard.

"I don't like being woken up in the night," the nun finally said when they reached the garage.

"I don't either," Ilka replied shortly. She made a gesture, signaling that she wanted Sister Eileen to grab his legs, while she would take his arms. "If we can lift him up on the stretcher, we'll find a way to get him over on the steel tray."

They counted to three and lifted. This time Ilka ignored the feel of the dead body.

After carrying him to the refrigerator, the nun asked, "Is he wet?" She pointed to the large wet blotch covering his battered chest. Ilka leaned over and felt his hair, which was wet and sticky. It gleamed in the glaring ceiling light. She pulled her hand away.

Gasoline, was her first thought. She straightened up and looked around. If someone had planned to cremate Mike Gilbert directly on the garage floor, the entire funeral home would probably have burned down. But she should have been able to smell gas right off when she'd leaned over and lifted. She crouched down again and sniffed; then she sat for a moment and gathered herself before standing up and drying her hands on her T-shirt. "Urine. Somebody pissed all over him."

Ilka studied the broken face for a moment, the entire right side caved in. Not that she was an expert on these things, but it looked like his cheekbone was crushed. There was a hollow under his eye, as if a bone was missing or had been pulverized just under the skin.

She looked away and closed her eyes. Hoped that Artie would show up early so he could make Mike Gilbert look presentable before his mother saw him. Otherwise there was a rough day ahead for Shelby. Ilka took a deep breath and nodded at Sister Eileen to help lift him onto the steel tray; then they pushed him back into the refrigerator.

After shutting the door, the nun shook her head in irritation and left without a word of good-bye.

"Okay, well, good night, then," Ilka said to the closed door.

13

It was a terrible night's sleep. Adrenaline surged through Ilka's body, and several times during the night she had convinced herself she was hearing sounds in the garage. Half-asleep, she heard the dead coming to life and walking around the building, pulling each other out of the refrigerator, drinking coffee in the kitchen. She hadn't dared go down, and anyway, she knew it was all in her head. In the moments she was wide awake, she'd pulled the comforter tightly to her and thought about how strange it was, being stuck in the middle of the daily life her father had led for so many years, so far away from her. All those years she had needed him in her own life.

It wasn't because she was any closer to understanding him after these few days in Racine. But his physical presence felt strong to her. She was surrounded by her father, his odor and belongings and the people he'd been with every day.

Still, though, she hadn't learned more about him, nor did she have the faintest idea how abandoning them had left its mark on him.

He had asked for a divorce less than two years after he left. At that time her mother was still struggling to turn the funeral home into a profitable business that could be sold without too big a loss. Ilka hadn't been aware of her reaction to his request—Ilka hadn't even known about the divorce before it was final. One evening her mother came into her room while she was doing homework.

"Your father and I are divorced," was all she said. Ilka still remembered the first thing she thought: *He must have come home.* Which meant she could see him. But her mother explained that he was still in the US, that their lawyers handled everything.

She'd rested her hand on Ilka's shoulder. "It means he's decided to stay over there. Without us."

As she lay in bed and gazed around the small room, Ilka couldn't understand why her father had traded owning a Brønshøj funeral home in the red with owning a Racine funeral home in the red. Racine, a town with less life on a weekday than Brønshøj Square on a Sunday morning.

And yet she knew he must have had a reason. But had he just been looking for adventure? Or did he run away from something? She knew everything had been going downhill for him—her mother had told her that much—yet Ilka had always looked at it as him leaving the two of them. It was telling, though, that he'd started up a new funeral home. And he'd fled suddenly, without making any arrangements. Maybe his reason for leaving did have to do with the business he'd taken over from his own father. But then there were the horses, of course. Her mother thought he'd accumulated a debt he'd never be able to pay, so he took off.

She'd loved it when he took her out to the horses. Except for that one time they'd never told her mother about.

It had been a sunny day. She'd been standing behind the living room door while he spoke on the phone, too low for her to hear. But when he noticed her, he told her to go out to the car and wait for him. Ilka looked down at the red toes of her shoes, uneasy and a bit scared. Her father usually didn't sound like that.

She'd been looking forward to spending that day with him, but now she wished her mother was there too. He was acting strangely. As if he didn't want her to be there. She grabbed the car keys on the dresser and picked her sweater up off the floor.

She was hoping they'd go to the racetrack or out to Mogens's. They'd been there before. He had a lot of horses, and last time they were there he'd let her curry one.

"Where are we going?" Luckily he hadn't spoken on the phone very long. He was wearing his brown suede jacket. He lit a cigarette, but he remembered to roll the window down a bit so she wouldn't get carsick. For a few seconds, he sat as if he'd forgotten where they were going; then he flipped his cigarette out the window and into the hedge.

"We're headed out to run and shout." He laughed, and she laughed with him, though there was still something wrong.

They drove a long time before turning down a gravel road with tall old trees on both sides. They had counted the number of yellow cars on the way. She sat up to see if there were any horses, but the corrals were empty.

"Who lives here?" she asked, as they drove in and stopped at a courtyard. She didn't like visiting people she didn't know, and she felt a small knot in her stomach when a dog came running up to the car.

"I'll only be a minute. Just stay out here." He reached into the backseat and grabbed a Donald Duck comic book for her.

Her father wasn't afraid of dogs. Ilka watched him walk over to a barn door; no one had come out to greet him. Maybe no one had heard them coming? She didn't like this. What should she say if someone came while he was gone? Before going inside the barn, he turned and waved at her.

The dog was gone. Ilka sat for a while; then she opened the car door and hopped down onto the courtyard's cobblestones. The air smelled sour, like it did when manure had been spread out on fields—she knew about that from summer vacations when they drove out into the country.

She walked over to the horse barn and opened the door a crack. Riding gear hung all around. She heard voices, and she slowly opened the door and walked inside. The barn smelled of oil, hay, and leather, odors she knew and liked from the racetrack barn. She called out for her father, but the barn was quiet. For a minute, she stood gathering up the courage to walk down the long row of stalls, which were empty. Someone was cleaning them, though; a wheelbarrow full of straw and horseshit was parked there. They must be out back. She called out again, louder this time.

"Daddy!" She froze at the sight of a man she'd never seen before. He was gripping her father, as if he were trying to lift him up, and speaking angrily to him, hissing in his face. She screamed, and the stranger whirled around. But she couldn't move. Not even when her father yelled at her, told her to go back to the car. He walked over and took her hand.

The stranger was still angry. "You'll hear from me!"

It was light outside when Ilka woke up. She must have fallen asleep again. It was a few minutes past eight, and when she walked downstairs, feeling a hundred years old, she heard Artie rummaging around in back. The preparation room had no windows, but the door stood open and the ventilation fan roared like a range hood set on high. She found him in the kitchenette, pouring Red Bull in his coffee. His eyes were tiny, and he'd tied his longish hair in a small bun on top of his head. Something the under-thirty generation would usually do, she'd thought.

He nodded good morning to her and pointed to a plate of doughnuts. "Have one," he said, his voice low; instinctively she understood he preferred a quiet morning. But today he was out of luck.

She grabbed the powdered milk for coffee and started in. "Have you seen the refrigerator?" She followed him out under the carport, where he sat down on the steps with his coffee, doughnut, and cigarette. He shook his head silently and began eating; a small fleck of icing stuck on his mustache. "No," he finally answered, after he'd finished chewing. "But I'll do Mike first. I don't have time to work miracles before Shelby comes, but I can do a cover-up, so she won't see what bad shape he's in."

Ilka sat down beside him. She felt responsible for someone getting into the garage while she was there. And she should have looked for an alarm to turn on. But Artie should have told her; it wasn't all her fault.

127

"Someone has been inside the garage," she said.

Artie listened without interrupting while she explained she had found Mike on the floor last night and had to wake Sister Eileen up to help get him back in the refrigerator. Cigarette smoke curled around his fingers as he ate the rest of his jelly doughnut and sipped his Red Bull coffee without reacting.

"Was he covered with urine when we picked him up at the morgue?" she asked.

Now he looked surprised. "What do you mean?"

"Did he smell like piss?"

He shook his head. "Not that I noticed. Does he now?"

Ilka nodded. "I think someone peed all over him while he was on the floor."

He knocked another cigarette out of the pack and offered one to her, but she waved the pack away. "That sounds bizarre," was all he said.

"You forgot to tell me if there's an alarm," she said, not the least bit bashful to give him some of the blame. But he didn't seem to hear her. He smoked a while without speaking; then he flipped the butt away and stood up.

"There was so much hate simmering in town after what happened. Everybody had an opinion, but most people seemed to think Mike was guilty. And the talk picked up when he left town. There was even a rumor that Ashley was doing it for money; then other people said no, she was doing it for free. The gossip turned vicious, and I know this sounds bad, but it was almost like people enjoyed it. It was like this smear campaign against Mike Gilbert energized the town; people started making up stories and juicing up the ones they'd heard. And now you tell me this. I can't say I'm surprised the hate's flared up again, if someone found out Mike was back."

He opened the door into the garage and walked over to the refrigerator. Ilka followed him. "But Shelby is convinced her son didn't kill the girl."

"Don't you suppose most mothers would feel that way, without conclusive evidence?" He opened the refrigerator to pull the steel tray out. "We'll have to call the police."

He'd already whipped his phone out.

"But his own mother didn't even know he was back."

"Someone must've seen him," Artie said, while waiting for someone to answer.

"Then the same 'someone' must know he's dead. Otherwise they wouldn't have come here."

Artie nodded and turned away after being transferred.

Ilka was sitting out on the steps when the police car turned in and parked. Artie had agreed that someone had soiled Mike Gilbert with urine during the night, but he thought it probably had been poured over him; there was far too much for a single urination.

She hadn't understood what difference it made, but Artie thought pissing on the body could be a spur-of-the-moment act, whereas dousing it with urine meant it was planned. An insult, sick. More emotional.

When she saw the two officers from the day before, she walked over to meet them. Officers Thomas and Doonan nodded to her and asked if there were surveillance cameras in the garage.

She hadn't even thought of that. Artie would have mentioned it if there were, surely, she thought. Then she remembered about the alarm, and she asked them to follow her.

"Do we have surveillance cameras out here?" she asked Artie. Odd, she thought, how natural it was to say "we" after only three days here. A few weeks ago, she hadn't even known the funeral home existed.

"We have some installed, yeah, but it's been a long time since they've been working. Paul had a contract with a security company, but I have the feeling he didn't renew it. So they're just hanging there now."

"What time did you come down here?" Officer Thomas asked Ilka. The two of them had walked outside the garage.

"The first or the second time?"

"When you heard the noise the first time. And you're sure there was nobody here?"

She shook her head. "I don't think so. But I'm not totally sure anymore. I checked the room with the coffins; there was nobody there. Unless someone was hiding in one of the two coffins. I didn't think about that. I didn't check if the preparation room was locked, either, but I know the door was closed."

"It's always locked," Artie said, walking outside.

"The first time I came down, I was thinking mostly about maybe there was an open door banging; I thought that was what woke me up. But it was only the small window I'd left open for the cat. That was at three thirty." She added that the door out to the carport had also been locked.

Artie had pulled Mike out of the refrigerator; his body lay on a stretcher, covered by a sheet.

"Don't touch anything," Officer Thomas said as the two policemen squeezed past the hearse.

They leaned over the body. She heard them mention the stink from the urine. "If there was any doubt before, it's pretty clear now it wasn't a random assault that cost him his life," Officer Doonan said. "Someone knows he came back."

Ilka heard the cat purr before it started rubbing her legs. She squatted down and petted it. Long, soothing strokes, as if she were trying to calm her own nerves.

"We didn't really believe it was random, either," the young officer continued. "Something like this seldom is." He explained that they were looking at the case again, rereading the witness statements. "But we're not so far along yet."

Ilka stood up. The policemen asked Artie again about the surveillance cameras and alarms. And how many garage entrances there were. She herded the cat into the house and was about to lure it out into the kitchen, when Sister Eileen appeared in the doorway and said there was a telephone call for her. "We usually don't allow pets inside the funeral home," she said as Ilka walked into her father's office.

14

A small click made Ilka think the call was from a foreign country, and instinctively she thought of her mother. But then a dark voice introduced himself in a broad American accent. She didn't catch his name, only that he was associated with another funeral home.

The largest funeral home chain in the country, she learned, after listening for a few moments to the words flowing into her ears like melted chocolate, warm and creamy. It took her a while, though, to get what had actually been said.

"Yes," she said, "I'm Paul Jensen's daughter, and I'm the owner of the business."

The stream of words continued, and she grew impatient; she felt she should get back to the policemen in the garage. And they might need her fingerprints. After all, she'd touched the stretcher.

"No, unfortunately," she answered, in an overly polite tone of voice, which she was getting sick and tired of using to keep things civilized. "I already have a plan for the future."

She listened again. "No, I'm not planning to keep it. I'm about to sell to another funeral home in town."

Now there was an unpleasant insistence to his voice, like when a telephone salesperson won't accept you're in the middle of a meal. Erik had come up with a way of ending a call from a telephone company or someone else who had gotten hold of his number. "I'm screwing someone right now," he would say, and usually that worked. But it was way too late now for that trick.

"Fine," she said, breaking him off. "Thank you very much. I understand you are quite interested in buying my father's business. But like I said, the deal is almost done, so unfortunately I'm not interested. But thank you for calling."

She said good-bye and hung up before his next gusher of words erupted.

She held the phone for a moment. She hadn't caught the name of the funeral home chain. Or maybe it was an organization of funeral home businesses? She wasn't sure. But they were big and they were national, the man had emphasized several times.

She went out to join the others in the garage. The cat was gone, the door to the garage was open, and the two policemen were walking around the refrigerator. The stretcher she had used the previous night lay in the middle of the floor, and the big garage door was also open. Ilka noticed the woman on the bench by the parking lot entrance again, looking down at her hands. Ilka couldn't see her face, but her hair was unmistakable.

Ilka studied her for a moment; then she heard Artie's voice. "Could you come inside?" He stepped out from the house; he must have gone in while she was in the office with the door closed. "Phyllis Oldham is here with the papers. They're ready for your signature."

Ilka nodded and followed him. She thought about telling him about the phone call, but then Artie might think she'd begun calling around, putting feelers out. The truth was, she didn't know if she could get an offer from another funeral home better than the one she had.

"Dear!" Mrs. Oldham chirped, when Ilka stepped into the arrangement room. Papers had been spread out in front of an empty chair, and beside them lay a large fountain pen with the Golden Slumbers logo. "Howard and I thought it would be appropriate to celebrate by inviting you out this evening. We have a fine Italian restaurant here in town. What do you say?"

Ilka smiled at the irresistible cheerfulness radiating from the well-tailored suit. Being back in Denmark before Monday had just come a step closer.

"Thank you, that sounds wonderful." She sat down in front of the papers.

"I would suggest we begin with champagne and hors d'oeuvres at our home," the woman said. "And then we'll drive from there."

Ilka grabbed the pen and began scanning the pages in front of her. It was the same as what she'd read before. What her lawyer had approved.

She was about to sign, when Mrs. Oldham said, "It's so

nice we can do business with you. It was more difficult with your father; he couldn't see this is to everyone's advantage."

Ilka looked up.

"Or perhaps he didn't want to see," she continued.

Suddenly Ilka felt cold, all over. She stared at the woman without seeing her. *What is she saying?* Ilka wondered. *He didn't want to sell?*

She noticed Artie looking away deliberately, though he tried to be casual about it. He didn't say a word.

"Please excuse me," Ilka said. She laid the pen down slowly. "Take a cup of coffee. I'm sure we have some out in the kitchen; otherwise, Sister Eileen can quickly make some. This will only take a moment."

She stood and turned to Artie. "Would you please come with me?" She practically spoke through her teeth.

He looked annoyed as he reluctantly stood up and followed her. Out in the hallway, she noticed the police still walking around in the garage, so she pulled him into the office and closed the door. "Can you tell me what the hell she meant by that? He didn't want to sell? You told me this deal was being worked on before he died, but she says he was difficult. Will you explain that?"

Artie was sitting on the desk now. "This is a real good offer they're giving us. Golden Slumbers Funeral Home is the most distinguished funeral home in town, and like you've already seen, they run a big business, do a good job. Their financial situation is excellent, and they're willing to take over right now."

"But he didn't want to sell to them," Ilka said. "This is going a little too fast now. Did my father even really want to sell his business?"

Artie nodded. "We talked about it. Yes! We discussed it several times."

"It sounds to me like the Oldhams tried to talk him into it several times, but he refused."

"If we lose this deal, I can't help you," Artie said, serious now. "I've been down on my knees to get this offer done, and you're not going to get a better deal than what they're bringing to the table."

Oh, really! she was about to say, but then she remembered she didn't know who had called. Before she threw that in his face, she had to find them.

"So what are you planning on doing, huh?" Artie was starting to sound angry. "Are you thinking about sticking around? Keep this sinking ship afloat long enough for us all to drown? Or do you have the money to pay your dad's debt? Because I can guarantee you're not going to sweet-talk the IRS into anything. That money must be paid tomorrow, or else they will show up and throw us out and put big locks on all the doors. Really, I don't think you understand how serious the situation is."

Ilka caught herself holding her breath. She was enraged, close to exploding right in his face; an angry heat spread out on her cheeks and throat. "I'll be back in five minutes," she said, and walked out to find Sister Eileen.

The nun was at her desk, leaning over a sheet of paper with no folders or bookmarks in sight. It looked like she was writing a good old-fashioned letter. Ilka recognized the funeral home logo on the paper.

The door was open, and she knocked on the doorframe. "May I have a moment?"

"Of course." Sister Eileen nodded and slipped the letter in a drawer. She hadn't talked about what had happened last night, so Ilka decided not to, either.

Ilka walked in and sat down across from the nun. "I need to ask you about something."

The sister nodded.

"Do you know if my father was against selling the business to the Oldham family? What I heard is that they tried to talk him into it many times, but he always refused."

If anyone had been on her father's side, Ilka felt, it would be Sister Eileen. They seemed to have been close, so surely she would have known what he'd wanted.

The nun folded her hands on the desk and leaned forward. "It would be wise to stick with Artie when it comes to business. He knows what he's doing, and he wants the best for us all." Then she leaned back, as if the final word had been spoken.

Ilka stood up and left. Frustrated, tired, and about to call home to ask her mother for advice, she grabbed Artie's cigarettes as she walked through the kitchen and out to the parking lot.

The police had finished in the garage; their car was gone. She lit a cigarette, and again she noticed the woman sitting on the bench. She strode over and joined her.

They sat for a while in silence while Ilka smoked. She finished off that cigarette and lit another; then she sank back. "I think you knew my father," she said, without looking at the woman. A few moments later, she added, "Do you think he wanted to sell his funeral home to Golden Slumbers?"

The woman didn't react at first, and Ilka thought the

woman might not have understood what she was asking about. Then she slowly shook her head. "Never." Her voice was barely above a whisper. "He would never sell to them."

Then she stood up abruptly and left before Ilka could ask any more questions.

Ilka smoked one more cigarette while looking the building over. A gigantic house filled with life and death, and suddenly it was all hers. She stood and went back inside.

15

Ilka returned to the conference room, where Phyllis Old-ham was standing by the window, speaking in a low voice with Artie. She heard them mention something about the harbor and charity, but they stopped talking when they saw her.

"I'm sorry," she said to them. Mrs. Oldham's forehead twitched; Artie slowly turned away from the window. "The deal is off. I appreciate the work you two have put into this, but I can't sign something my father opposed."

A voice in her head yelled at her: *You didn't even know him; what the hell are you doing?* They both looked at her in disapproval.

"I'm going up to pack and return to Denmark. The estate will be...how do you say, finished by an official. Then what-ever happens will happen." She asked Artie to tell Sister Eileen to pack her things, thinking that if the IRS showed up and closed the funeral home, they might as well be prepared.

Before they could say a word, she left the room, ran up the steps, and slammed the door behind her. Her first thought was to call her lawyer.

For a moment, she closed her eyes and rested her head against the doorframe. She didn't even know if there were executors to administer estates in the US, but she didn't want anything more to do with this. The moment she'd found out what was going on, she should have refused to get involved, should have said she knew nothing about the funeral home business. Or her father, for that matter. Her mother had, of course, been right; she shouldn't even have come here. But she'd never been much for doing the smart thing, she reminded herself. She'd tried. And now she was giving up. It was simply too much for her, inheriting a funeral home in Racine. And even more too much to manage it and make decisions that ran against her father's wishes.

She fished her phone out of her bag and called her mother.

"Hi," she said, trying to sound calm and composed. "It's going fine. I'm coming home now. I just need to find out if I can catch a plane today, or if I have to wait until tomorrow. I'll finish packing; then I'll leave for the airport. No, nothing's wrong. But you were right—I'm not going to get bogged down in all this. I'm having an executor take over. Yes! I'm sure. Everything is fine. And I'll take care of the photo shoots starting Monday; don't worry about finding someone else."

Ilka heard the relief in her mother's voice, now that she was coming home without anything catastrophic happening. Knowing that Ilka hadn't ended up in an American prison undoubtedly kept her mother from asking more questions. Ilka promised to call again when she knew her arrival time in Copenhagen. It felt great to hear her mother say she and Hanne would pick her up at the airport.

She sat on the bed and glanced around the room. Less than two hours remained until the IRS deadline, and she hadn't even begun looking through her father's closets and all the boxes pushed up against the wall. Someone showing up and putting big locks on all the doors sounded like an exaggeration, but you never knew. When her hairdresser went bankrupt several years ago, all the employees in the chain's other shops had been ordered to close and leave without taking so much as a hairpin with them.

She had to get her father's things out of the house, but all she had to pack with was her small suitcase. At first Ilka considered dragging all the boxes downstairs, but where would she put them? They would still be on the funeral home property out in the parking lot. She would have to sort things out lightning quick and do the best she could.

The clock was ticking, and she felt a bit desperate, but finally she pulled herself together and went downstairs to look for boxes or something to pack with. She hated the thought of running into Artie. That asshole had known all along that her father didn't want to sell to the Oldhams, and yet he worked his tail off to do just that. Presumably he'd thought he could push the transfer agreement through before she found out how her father had felt.

She hurried past the office and arrangement room without seeing anyone. Phyllis Oldham had left, but her heavy perfume—cinnamon and something that nauseated Ilka—still hung in the air. The door into the preparation room was closed, but she could hear the fan running. Quickly she punched in the code to the garage, and for a moment she stood and looked around. A low shelf filled with black file boxes ran along the entire wall behind the hearse. For a second she thought about emptying and using them, but they wouldn't be able to hold much. She checked the high shelf on the other wall. Coffin liners, blankets. Farther down the shelf stood boxes of masks and plastic gloves. On one of the lower shelves, she found a large box with body bags. Ilka grabbed two of them and ran back upstairs.

At ten thirty, she started pulling drawers out of her father's desk. She scooped up all the letters; the most important thing was to rescue his personal papers. Of course, there could be other things with sentimental value, but they would have to wait. She had to get hold of everything that might explain why he had abandoned her and her mother.

She ignored a stack of old order books in one of the drawers. There were also calendars marked with birthdays of people she'd never heard of. The next drawer: opened envelopes containing letters. All addressed to him, some with a feminine cursive script, others with heavy block letters. She stuck them in a body bag, to be read when she got home. Underneath was a folder with children's drawings by Leslie and Amber. She laid them aside. Her half sisters would probably be happy to have them, or at least to know their father had saved them. She would drive by and drop them off before flying back to Denmark.

The bottom drawer was filled with scattered bundles of old bills and receipts. Something for the IRS to play around with. *Leave them*, she told herself.

It didn't take her long to decide about the few clothes that hadn't been given to the sister's parish. While sorting through them, it had felt wrong to empty out the whole closet. She left the few suits and shirts there.

Someone knocked, and she turned around. "Yes!"

Artie carefully opened the door. "May I come in?"

Should she tell him to leave, or what? Finally, Ilka nodded.

He glanced around the room before stepping inside and sitting on the bed, next to a pile of her clothes.

"I want to apologize," he said, his tone signaling unconditional surrender. "I totally understand why you got angry. It did come out sounding all wrong. It's true, Paul had several run-ins with the Oldhams over the years, and of course I should have let you in on that. I just didn't feel we had time to go over what happened so long ago. Like I already told you, I didn't know the business was in such bad shape before your dad's lawyer contacted me. I didn't know he owed the IRS so much, and I didn't know we were so close to bankruptcy. You can take this however you want, but I think I panicked. I've always had a good working relationship with the people at Golden Slumbers, and Paul could be stubborn as a mule. So when I contacted them, I felt I was trying to move things along, not acting against his wishes."

He leaned forward with his hands folded. "Of course you're the one who decides what will happen, now that you've inherited the business. But if that money isn't paid before the deadline, I'm out of work and the sister has no place to live. Shouldn't we try to work together and see what we can come up with? And you know what? It wouldn't be like Paul to throw Sister Eileen out with two hours' warning."

"Just like it wouldn't be like my father to sell the business, and you knew that. But you let me believe it was something he started."

The slow anger building inside her was about to explode again, and she did nothing to hold it back. She glared at him. "I've had enough of being a naïve fool. You could have fucking explained how things were. We could have talked about it, but instead I'm running around picking up dead people and talking to other people who just lost a relative. What the hell are you two thinking? You didn't tell me anything, to make me feel we could solve everything together. Honestly, I think you'd rather have done it all without me. And that's okay, but then don't fucking get me involved."

Sweat ran down her back, a stream of rage. "Everything just roars along over my head. And I won't be part of it. When I'm packed, I'm going to call my father's lawyer. He'll have to take over from now on."

"I have the sixty thousand dollars we need," Artie said, without a word about the shelling he'd just taken. "You can have the money as a down payment on the house."

Ilka shook her head. "Stick that money right up your ass. I'm going home to Denmark."

Artie stood up. "So what do you plan on doing with Mike Gilbert, Ed McKenna, Mrs. Norton? You want to cancel the old lady's funeral service tomorrow? Who's going to take care of Mike and Ed? What about all the relatives counting on us? And all the people we have deals with? Do we just say the hell with them? This doesn't just affect you, us. But if that's how you want it, great."

He walked out and slammed the door.

Ilka stared at the door, speechless. She hadn't given a

single thought to the 150 people who had cared about old Mrs. Norton and were coming tomorrow to say good-bye to her. She recalled the grandchild crying as he stood up and accused them of being cold and unfeeling.

She felt dizzy when she closed her eyes for a moment. It was as if she'd been ambushed, as if the ground beneath her kept shifting; she couldn't find her feet. She looked all around at the terrible mess she'd made of the small room; then she decided to go down and find Artie.

He was sitting on the steps near the carport with a cigarette and a Red Bull. He didn't even look up when she sat down beside him.

"What do we need for the funeral service tomorrow?" She took the cigarette he shook out of his pack.

"So you want the money after all?"

She nodded. "I don't think Sister Eileen can pack in such a short time." It was a quarter past eleven.

He crushed his cigarette with the heel of his shoe. "If we do this, it'll be a new situation. Do we need to sit down and talk this through before we decide if it's the right thing to do?" Ilka didn't hear even the faintest hint of sarcasm in his voice. She shook her head.

"I need a time-out to get a good picture of the situation and to find out how much money my father owes."

She told him about the call from the funeral home chain. "Golden Slumbers isn't the only one interested."

Artie set his beer down. "When did they call?"

"This morning."

"Did you promise them anything? Did you set up a meeting?"

Ilka shook her head. "I told them we already had a deal. But we could contact them and hear their offer. I don't know who it was, but surely we can find them."

She could tell he wasn't happy about that, but he let it go. "I'd better get to the bank so we don't miss the deadline." He started over to his car.

"Okay, and I'll let the sister know she doesn't need to pack anyway."

Ilka watched him go. His reaction to the call from the funeral home chain puzzled her. Again, she had the feeling he was trying to steer things to his advantage instead of following the path her father had laid out. Or at least selling the business the way her father would have.

Ilka had just stood up when a police car turned in and parked. She glanced at her watch; Artie had left for the bank no more than ten minutes ago; they still had time, so it couldn't be someone telling her to leave. Then she recognized the two officers, Thomas and Doonan. She walked over to them.

"We need to talk," Officer Thomas said.

Ilka nodded and asked them to follow her, but he pointed across the street and explained that the school had a surveillance camera. "We've just checked the recording."

Ilka looked over at the school, right across from the entrance to the funeral home parking lot. The bench on which the mysterious woman had sat was beside the entrance. She spoke hesitantly, unsure of where they were going with this. "Okay."

"Last night at three twenty-two, Howard Oldham walked across the street to the back of your house," Officer Doonan said, as if he were reading from a report. "The recording doesn't show him leaving the property."

He paused for a moment, giving her time to grasp the situation. He smelled of aftershave, and she looked directly at him so long that he finally lowered his eyes. "We've tried to contact him, so far without any luck." He looked up at her again with a glint in his eye that she couldn't read. "So that's why we have to ask if you can tell us what Howard Oldham was doing here last night."

Ilka gave him a puzzled look before shaking her head. "If you think he was with me, you're wrong; he wasn't. I haven't seen him either."

Officer Thomas's hands were in the side pockets of his jacket, as if that helped him rest his sizable body. "You're sure about that?" He looked at her expectantly.

She stared back at him as if he was joking. True, she had a healthy and natural appetite for men, but Howard Oldham wasn't on her to-do list.

"If that's the case, it's going to be interesting to find out why he was on your property last night."

Once again she felt like she was on shaky ground, and she wished Artie was there. She simply nodded when he said they would know more when they had Howard Oldham's DNA and compared it to what was found in the garage.

"Do you think he might have killed Mike Gilbert?" she asked. In her mind's eye, she saw the well-dressed undertaker. The nice suit, tie, the folded handkerchief in his breast pocket.

"No comment on that," Doonan said, a bit sharply. "We're interested only in his possible connection to what happened in the garage."

Ilka nodded wearily. She couldn't imagine what could make that gentlemanly man break in and haul a dead man out of the refrigerator.

"I'll have to ask you not to tell anyone who we've seen on the recording," Officer Thomas said, his voice leaving no doubt that this was an order.

She nodded again, and soon the two policemen were driving away for the second time that morning. She watched them disappear, then went over to Sister Eileen's door.

"I don't have the strength to carry the furniture out," the pale, red-eyed woman said after letting Ilka inside. "That little bureau was my mother's; I would be terribly unhappy if I can't get it out before the deadline."

"You don't need to pack; we're staying. Artie and I have found a solution. The IRS is being paid now, and as soon as he comes back I want all three of us to meet in my father's office."

A large suitcase was standing in the living room, and two travel bags were almost full. A stack of newspapers lay on the table; the sister had been packing her porcelain. Ilka recognized two pairs of shoes on the floor, identical to the practical ones she wore, and a pair of Adidas, which was so far from the nun's usual style that Ilka thought she must have borrowed them.

"So shall I unpack?" She sounded confused. She looked over at the full suitcase.

Ilka nodded and tried to smile.

16

Ilka had set out the cups and filled a bowl with chocolates. The coffee was almost finished brewing out in the kitchen when Sister Eileen and Artie walked in.

"I paid, and I just got a receipt from the IRS that confirms it," he said. He collapsed onto a chair on the other side of the desk. "So this is when we breathe a sigh of relief."

Was it really so easy? Ilka wondered. Throw a little money at them and everyone was happy. For the moment, maybe.

She poured the coffee ceremoniously and pushed the chocolates over to them. She'd taken a notebook from the shelf, and now she pulled her father's oversize office chair closer to the desk. "I think it's time to review the situation." She considered thanking Artie officially, but honestly, she thought, she had done just as much to save the day by letting him pay the sixty thousand dollars. She concentrated on what they needed to discuss.

"We have Mrs. Norton's funeral service tomorrow. What do we need for that?" She looked across the desk.

"The coffin was supposed to come today, but I haven't checked to see if it's been delivered," Artie said.

"But she's already in a coffin," Ilka said. She was in the cold room beside Ed McKenna and the dog.

"She's not in the one we ordered. I had to lay her in another one until it came. I finished working on her; she's ready. I was thinking that later we could use the coffin for Mike Gilbert, so I used the cheapest one we have in storage. We need to move her over into the right coffin today, so it'll be ready tomorrow morning, in case the family shows up early to decorate."

"Did they arrange for music?" he asked Sister Eileen. She shook her head.

"I informed them that they can use CDs or connect to an iPhone over our sound system," she said. She added that a choir would be singing at the chapel.

"What should we do if the coffin doesn't arrive?" Ilka asked. "Do we have another one we can put her in?"

Artie shook his head. "They've paid for a glossy black coffin with glitter. If that's not what she's in, we'll have to give a refund. And anyway, it's too late to tell them we can't deliver, so that coffin has to come. It might be a good idea for you to call the supplier, if you don't already have a tracking number. Then we can follow it on the Net and see how far away it is."

Sister Eileen said nothing, even though she was the one who dealt with the suppliers.

"What about one of the coffins we have in storage?" Ilka suggested. "One is light blue; another is white. And we have that big black one that was in the garage. Is it in the storage room now?"

"We can't use that one; it was delivered by mistake and will be picked back up. It's way too expensive to keep."

Ilka didn't answer, but she wrote: "Find coffin."

"We're low on formaldehyde," Artie said.

"Let's finish this first," Ilka said. "What else do we need for tomorrow?"

"Flowers are to be delivered, and there will be catering," the nun said. "I've ordered both."

"But the Norton family is bringing the flowers," Ilka reminded her.

"There are always flowers in the chapel and out in the foyer during funeral services," the sister calmly answered. "Those are the flowers I ordered."

Ilka nodded and made a note of it.

Sister Eileen hadn't touched the coffee or the chocolates, and suddenly Ilka remembered that she usually drank tea. How could she have forgotten?

"I've spoken with Ed McKenna's daughter," the nun continued. "She's coming to see her father this weekend. It sounds like she wants to take him home to Albany, which means we'll need a zinc coffin."

Ilka lifted an eyebrow. "For the plane," Artie explained. "When the deceased are flown, they have to be in zinc coffins."

Ilka nodded thoughtfully when he added that there were many on domestic flights.

"The distances are too long to drive," he said. "But there are strict rules for transporting them, of course. The coffins have to be zinc lined and contain absorbent material. We use

151

charcoal powder. And then there must be a pressure equalizer. And the deceased must be embalmed. And usually the coffin has to be wrapped so the other passengers can't see there's a dead body on board."

Suddenly he seemed to take her wanting to be fully informed very literally.

"If there isn't anything more, I'd like to unpack my things now," Sister Eileen said, a bit sharply. She stood without waiting for an answer.

Artie was also on his feet. He wanted to take care of Mike Gilbert so his mother could view him when she came.

"How much formaldehyde?" Ilka yelled after him.

For a moment, she sat alone, staring into space before slowly rising and walking over to find the file with the Nortons' funeral service notes. After laying it on the table, she walked out to the sister's desk in the reception area. A calendar lay open on the thick green desk mat; beside it lay a black leather-bound telephone book with JENSEN FUNERAL HOME printed on it.

Ilka found the order book in the top drawer. It wasn't difficult to locate the coffin supplier where most of the sister's orders were made. She cleared her throat and dialed, with the order number on Mrs. Norton's coffin in hand.

"Why do you say you can't deliver coffins to us?" she said, baffled by what she'd been told. "You just received our order. You could have said you don't want to do business with us anymore when we sent the order, to avoid this terrible situation we're in. The *family* is in. We're holding a funeral service tomorrow, and the relatives expect to see the deceased in the coffin they ordered. No, I will not listen! You listen. It's unprofessional and horrible, what you're doing.

Maybe it's right that we've exceeded our credit and you've had to send several reminders. But as you might know, Paul Jensen is dead and I've taken over and I'm trying the best I can to finish the agreements the funeral home has made. Of course we will pay what we owe you, but you must deliver the coffin we need now. And I'd like to—"

Ilka didn't know when they'd hung up; all she knew was that she was listening to static. She looked up and saw Sister Eileen turn around in the doorway—hadn't she gone over to unpack? How long had she been listening? She didn't care for the nun observing her like that.

She found two more coffin suppliers in the order book and made a call. "Yes, we're prepared to pay extra to have FedEx deliver it today."

Her tense shoulders relaxed, and she leaned back in her chair. The supplier asked for the name and address of their funeral home.

"Jensen Funeral Home," she began, but was interrupted before she could give their address.

"Unfortunately you what?" This time Ilka tried to control herself and sound friendly. "I can assure you we'll pay what we owe you. We're in the middle of a sort of generational change here; we're putting in new systems to stop this type of error."

Generational change my ass, she thought. She briefly debated with herself whether she should continue this way until she found a supplier who didn't already know them.

"Yes," she said, "please send a bill on what we owe. Have a nice day."

After trying two more suppliers, she gave up in anger. She went out and hammered on the preparation room door until some sort of electric machinery was shut off and Artie opened up.

She couldn't help noticing the naked body on the steel table by the wall. She stiffened for a moment, but then she pulled herself together and walked inside. "It can't be true that we owe money to every single coffin supplier in North America, can it? I can't buy a coffin anywhere."

Artie shut the door behind her. He walked over and turned down the Beach Boys; then he glanced at the steel table as if he should be protecting the body. He wore a green apron and an elastic band around his longish hair. He struggled to take off his mask, which was tangled up in his glasses.

"That sounds about right," he said, after the mask was finally off. He stunk, and Ilka instinctively backed off a few steps. "You probably should've let the sister call around. She can usually finagle a coffin out of them, even though they've shut us off."

"You could have told me that. What do we do now?"

He shrugged. "You're the boss!" His eyes twinkled a bit.

Ilka stared at him in anger, then turned on her heel. She was determined to get hold of a coffin, even if she had to nail one together herself and paint it black and spread glitter over it.

"They sell coffins over at Costco," he yelled at her back. "The closest one is in Pleasant Prairie. Just follow Lake Michigan down to Kenosha. You'll hit Highway 50, and then it's straight west from there. Really, though, I doubt if you can get them to deliver today, in time for tomorrow morning."

She turned at the door, tired now. "And what's Costco?"

"It's a warehouse that sells just about everything, most of it in bulk. They're about to drive the coffin suppliers out of business anyway, with their prices. You just have to pay an annual membership fee to shop there."

"Fine." Ilka imagined people at the warehouse, shopping for giant packages of toilet paper, paper towels, and coffins.

17

She drove through a landscape of open fields, lakes, and lush forests. She was just as stubborn as she was mad; all she could see was the white stripes on the road and the notepad on Sister Eileen's desk where she had crossed off the names of coffin suppliers one by one as they rejected her. In fact, she was enraged at how they had treated her. At the very least they could have given her a chance to make things right. They'd regret turning her down!

She stomped on the brakes when a car passed and nearly swiped her bumper as they swerved back in the right lane. The hearse rocked heavily.

"*Røvhul!*" she yelled, as loud as she could. Asshole! Not that the driver heard her, or understood her even if he had. It just felt good. If she stayed in Racine long enough to arrange more funerals, none of those fucking suppliers would get so much as one single order from her.

"Maybe it's a real idea to go organic," she muttered to herself. Just like in Denmark, surely someone over here was making coffins out of recycled material or paper, in that ashes-to-ashes, dust-to-dust way in which coffins decomposed in a relatively short time. She'd be the first funeral director in town to think environmentally. That would get the Oldhams' attention.

Her thoughts were in a jumble as she pulled into an enormous, almost empty parking lot. She chose a space close to the main entrance. Banners announcing the weekly bargains hung from both sides of the sliding doors, and pallets with gallon jugs of laundry detergent and stacks of white plastic lawn chairs stood just inside. She stopped for a moment to get her bearings. The warehouse had an optician and a photo center with good offers on tripods for various cameras. Ilka walked over to ask a young man behind the vision center counter, which was crowded with glasses and offers on vision tests, but on the way, she noticed ends of coffins sticking out from a small niche in the wall.

Seven hundred ninety-nine dollars and ninety-nine cents. And the price was the same regardless of color—dusty rose, silver, or marine blue—but there were differences in how showy they were. Two of them boasted large rosettes in all the corners and a broad, gilded piece of trim—plastic, no doubt, Ilka thought. She looked at the price again. It was a hell of a lot cheaper than the ones from the suppliers—about a tenth of the price of some of them.

She walked over and read a sign on the wall between the models on display: ALL COFFINS HAVE THE SAME FUNCTION. THEY ARE THE FINAL RESTING PLACE FOR THOSE YOU HOLD DEAR.

CHOOSING A COFFIN IS A VERY PERSONAL DECISION. FAMILIES SHOULD CHOOSE A COFFIN BASED ON THEIR OWN PREFERENCES AND THE PERSONALITY OF THEIR LOVED ONE. Beside the sign was a plastic holder with order forms.

That's certainly good to know, Ilka thought, shaking her head. None of the models came even close to being black. But they all had a two-piece lid for viewing, and apparently, a coffin liner, pillow, and blanket were included. So far, so good.

She pulled out an order form. To her relief, the coffins came in several colors, including gold. There was also one in black. She read the instructions:

1. Choose a coffin in our selection.
2. Fill out Costco's Purchase Order.
3. Take to the cashier for payment.
4. Delivery time: 48 hours.

"Shit," Ilka said. She stuck the order form in her pocket; then she set off to find someone to help her.

"No, not at all," she assured the elderly gray-haired employee. Frank had reluctantly agreed to check returns storage to see if a black coffin had been returned, and he had come back with a discouraged look on his face. "One small scratch on one side doesn't matter. But does it have glitter? Okay, okay, that doesn't matter either. I'll take it without."

Ilka had gone through three employees before ending up with Frank, the returns manager. The first two she'd talked to had told her she couldn't get a black coffin delivered immediately; it was out of the question, even if they had them in stock. That's not how things worked. The coffin had to be ordered and would be delivered. And the third employee got so sick and tired of Ilka that she finally said the only chance Ilka had of leaving there with a coffin was if they happened to have one that had been returned. But it probably had been damaged during transport.

"Fine," Ilka had said. That's when Frank came into the picture. He refused outright to sell her a damaged coffin. He wasn't going to risk her complaining afterward and him ending up with having to supply her with a replacement.

"That won't happen," she said, but he wouldn't budge. She persisted. He kept saying no. But finally, Ilka talked him into checking to see if there even *was* a black coffin in return storage.

"I'll pay you right now; I'll give up my right to return the product," she said.

"You can't get a truck to deliver it today anyway," he said.

"I can take it with me," she replied quickly, and before he could say more, she added, "This is my last chance, and I will be so very grateful to you. My father is dead, and I've come all the way from Denmark to bury him. Yes, Denmark. Yes, like kringles. I never have, no, not with cranberries. We don't have nearly as many kinds in Denmark; we just sprinkle them with powdered sugar and hazelnut flakes. No, at least *I* don't think they taste plain."

He kept on about the kringles for a while, but finally he asked why she didn't just wait until Monday, when a new coffin could be delivered.

"I have to leave Sunday. Monday morning my mother is having some very important tests taken at the hospital. She's a terminal cancer patient, and her medicine is making her dizzy and confused. I have to be there for her.

"The thing is," she added, again before he could butt in, "she's too sick to come over here and be at my father's funeral. It's so terribly sad; none of us could bear the thought that there wouldn't be any services for him because I couldn't get hold of a coffin."

At last, he gave in. But only if she could arrange for the transportation of the damaged coffin to wherever she wanted it dropped off.

"That's no problem," she said.

He looked at her quizzically for a moment, but then he nodded and checked his watch.

"Well then, let's go get this taken care of." He ushered her over toward customer service. Two of the employees Ilka had spoken with were standing by some tall shelving, eyeing them as Ilka strode along behind Frank. She already had a credit card out by the time they reached customer service. Frank gave a number to a coworker at the desk; then he handed Ilka two forms to fill out and sign: her membership application and the other acknowledging that she couldn't return the item she was buying.

She signed and stood for an ID photo for her membership card. Frank hadn't told the man behind the counter what he had sold her, she was sure of that, so she didn't say anything either, just took the receipt and her new card and then nodded when the man told her to have a nice day.

"Give me ten minutes. I'll go back in and get it ready for you to pick up," Frank said, adding that he would help her load it in her vehicle.

Ilka thanked him without commenting on what he said

about helping. She walked back to the hearse. The parking lot was much fuller now, but according to her watch, she'd been in the warehouse for almost two hours.

There wasn't much room between two trucks unloading at the docks. She backed in, and just as she got out of the hearse, she saw Frank bringing the coffin over on a forklift. Ilka waved at him and asked if she should drive forward for better access to the rear door.

"Where the hell did that come from?" he said when he spotted the hearse.

"It's my father's; he was an undertaker. He went bankrupt just before he died."

She could hear how suspicious that sounded, so she opened the door at once, then tried to distract him. "I want you to know how incredibly grateful I am for your help and your understanding of my difficult situation. And I know my mother will be, too, knowing that my father got a dignified burial." She unlocked the wheels of the rollers to push it over to the coffin.

"Wait just a second here," Frank said, rubbing his full gray beard. "You're not thinking about using this coffin in a funeral home business, are you? And I end up getting complaints and demands for replacement because it's damaged?"

"No, this is for my personal use. My father will be driven to the crematorium in it tomorrow."

Frank helped her get the coffin on the rollers and shove it in the back of the hearse. She slammed the rear door shut.

"Which crematorium did you book?" he asked.

Ilka pulled a hundred-dollar bill out of her purse and handed it to him. "Thank you so much for your help. I

161

can't tell you how important this is to me." She meant every word she said, but then he startled her when he stepped back abruptly.

"I can't take that sort of money," he whispered, as if he suddenly was afraid someone was listening.

"It's okay," Ilka quickly assured him. "It's a donation to the church you support."

"What the hell makes you think I support a church?" It was his turn to look startled.

"People with a heart like yours always support a church." She left it at that and thanked him again before he could say another word. He took the bill and watched her drive away.

18

Ilka had just parked the hearse in the garage when Sister Eileen came out to tell her that Shelby Gilbert was there with photos of her son.

"Can you give them to Artie?" Ilka asked, as she was about to unload the coffin.

"I think she needs to talk. Your father probably spent more time talking to people than anything. It's important for relatives to be able to talk about those they've lost. And you are like your father; you're good at that." Ilka wasn't one hundred percent sure the nun meant that last remark.

"Of course," she said. On the way into the house she glanced down at herself; her blouse and dark blue jeans would have to do. After all, they hadn't scheduled a meeting.

In the arrangement room, Mike's mother sat at the table with an open photo album beside her coffee cup. Ilka noticed the picture of her son, smiling broadly at the camera.

"I just came from the police station. They say they'll find out who did it. But who does these kinds of things?"

She was hurting badly. Ilka walked over and gave her a hug before sitting down across from her and pouring herself a cup of coffee.

"How could anyone hate him so much? And after so many years?" Shelby looked imploringly at Ilka, then shook her head. They sat for a moment in silence; then she twined her fingers together in her lap and fidgeted; it looked like she was working up the nerve to say something.

"I didn't tell the police everything. I didn't know if it could harm my son. But after what happened last night, I think I might have to."

Ilka scooted forward and laid her hands on the table. "What do you mean?"

Shelby squirmed in her chair. When she finally spoke, she stared at Ilka, her eyes radiating pain and something else Ilka couldn't put her finger on.

"My son was paid to leave town. I didn't know about it back then. I thought he left because he was ashamed. Everyone thought that. But someone gave him money. A lot of money. So he could start a new life. He told me that the last time I talked to him. He'd changed his name to Mike Miller."

She hid her face in her hands and breathed deeply to calm herself down. Ilka reached over the table, but Shelby didn't take her hand.

"I hate this town," she whispered, spitting each word out. "I regret every single day that I went out on the evening I met my kids' father. We were both going to Wisconsin Parkside. I hadn't noticed him before, but all of a sudden, he was standing there, and, well…"

A few moments later she explained she came from Chicago, where her parents and sister still lived. "But Tommy was from Racine, and when I got pregnant we bought the house here and had two kids. Emma was a year and a half when he took off. He ended up somewhere in Ohio."

She breathed deeply again. "When Mike left, I thought for a while he'd moved in with his dad. But when I finally got hold of Tommy's phone number and called, he said he hadn't heard from Mike. And Mike wasn't welcome, either, after what he'd done. It was in all the papers."

"But you stayed here after he left you?"

Shelby nodded. "I had the house. And where could I move to? Back home with my parents?" Her lips quivered, partly from bitterness. Ilka shook her head.

"And I couldn't move when Mike disappeared, either; he wouldn't know where to find us. I feel like I've been tied to this place."

They sat for a moment in silence. "Who paid your son to disappear?" Ilka asked. "Did he say?"

Mike's mother shook her head. "I don't know. But I've always been sure he didn't kill her. He was so happy. No matter what I thought about Ashley Simpson, she made my son happy. Besides his afternoon job at the shop, Mike worked three evenings a week, at this Italian restaurant down by the harbor that closed several years ago. When he came home the evening it happened, he was in a good mood; he acted completely normal. He might even have been in a better mood than usual. They'd given him permission to bring Ashley along to the restaurant's Thanksgiving dinner, and already he was talking about what he was going to wear, even though it wasn't for another week and a half."

She shook her head. "The next day he went to school, just like always. But he was home in less than an hour, down in the living room. White as a sheet. He couldn't tell me what happened. I'd just had a shower, and I was on my way out the door; I had to go to work. Back then I was working full-time sorting mail. I still work there."

By now the coffee was cold, and Ilka offered her another cup, but she declined.

"He broke down, completely. He insisted on going to the police, telling them he and Ashley had been together the day before. I tried to talk him out of it—what good would it do? But he wouldn't listen. He said someone pushed her, because she hadn't been out on the ice. She was up in the fisherman's cabin, where they'd been together. It wasn't any accident."

Shelby shook her head again, as if the rest of the story wasn't important. But she continued. "It was like the whole town decided it was him, even though everyone knew there were others besides Mike, then and before."

After waiting several moments, Ilka said, "What others?"

"Like they say, she got around." Shelby spoke quietly, as if she wasn't sure she should let Ilka in on the town's gossip back then. "There were stories about the men Ashley attracted. And it wasn't just teenagers. They say she went after older men, and men with money. And yet she wanted my Mike. I didn't understand what she was up to, but maybe she really did like him."

Ilka leaned a bit farther forward. "Are you saying she was doing it for money?"

Shelby straightened up, shocked now. "No, definitely not. I just think she liked the power she had over men who fell in love with her."

Jealousy, Ilka thought. If the young girl had been easy, it wouldn't have been the first time in history that a boyfriend or girlfriend lost their head.

"If you only knew how much hate there is in this town," Mike's mother said. She folded her hands in her lap again. When people heard that Mike had been the last one Ashley was with, they broke out all the windows in their house, she explained. "People threatened us; they wrote the most horrible things on the outside of our house. At first, Emma didn't dare go out alone. But after her brother left, things settled down, thank God. Like people were satisfied with running him out of town. We weren't welcome in our own church, either."

She held her head and breathed deeply, all the way down into her stomach. "I can't stand thinking about someone who hated my son so much, just walking around out there. How could anyone kill him? And last night, how could they..."

Ilka felt the woman's loneliness, an icy chill slinking across the table "How did Ashley's family react back then?"

"They were angry and heartbroken, of course. Her mother died a few years ago, but the police have talked to her father. He moved to a nearby town five or six years ago, when he and his wife divorced. She had a brother, but he left Racine a long time before this happened. The police officer said they're trying to find him."

Mike's mother stared blankly for a moment; then she laid her hand on the photo album. "Artie promised I could see my son. I brought along the pictures he asked for."

Ilka stood up. She was relieved the conversation was over, but Shelby's story also confused her. "I'll tell him you're ready."

The woman nodded, but she seemed uneasy. Her eyes darted toward the door, as if she didn't feel quite ready after all.

"Here, please, have one." Ilka slid the bowl of chocolates across the table. As if that helped. "He'll be here in a moment."

She hurried out the door. She felt like a coward.

19

Ilka kept knocking on the door of the preparation room until Artie finally came out. "I can't let anyone view Mike right now," he said. "He hasn't been embalmed, so he's in no shape for her to see."

"Then you'll have to go out and tell her. You had an agreement." Ilka wheeled and walked away, but she heard Artie follow. "She has the photos you asked for. How do you think she feels about going in there to look at him? She's pulled herself together to do it, and after what happened last night it's probably not easier for her."

"Okay, but—"

"If you want to send her home again, it's you who has to tell her."

"Give me a second here." He walked over and washed his hands; then he took off his apron.

Ilka's eyes widened. "Do you plan on talking to her

wearing that?" She pointed at his Hawaiian shirt, the blazing colors, the parrots.

Artie ignored her and walked out, leaving her speechless.

Ilka stayed in the background as he gave Shelby a hug. "I'm so sorry about what happened last night," he said, his arm still around her shoulder. "Believe me, it hurts to see you put through this; it was totally disgusting. And I'm sorry that someone could break into our building. We've had some problems with our alarm system, but of course this kind of thing shouldn't be possible."

He apologized again. Ilka had the feeling it wasn't all about Paul's daughter screwing up by opening the window so the cat could come in. Something else was going on. Maybe he was afraid Shelby might sue them for not taking better care of her deceased son; if she did begin thinking that way, it could turn out to be horribly expensive for them. Ilka let Artie keep talking. But then she heard Shelby wave off his apologies.

"The person who dishonored Mike's body would have broken in even if you had bars on all the windows and doors. This happened because someone in this town still wants revenge."

"I know what I promised you," Artie said. He explained carefully that he couldn't let her see her son after all. "Everything's been delayed; we had to call the police after what happened last night."

"You can at least let me see his feet," she said. "That's enough. He has two toes on his left foot grown together. I know you all say it's my son in there, but I need to see it with my own eyes. I hope you understand."

Artie nodded. "Of course. Just give me a minute. If you two would just step in there, I'll bring him in."

He pointed at the large chapel used for funeral services. It looked like a lecture hall, with rows of chairs filling the room, though the first row was filled with plush sofas. The entire room was in beige, even the ceiling and the soft carpet. Muted and austere in a way that couldn't offend anyone or clash with any style or religious belief. The acoustics were good, thanks to a carpet so thick that you sank into it as you walked.

Ilka followed Mike's mother inside and turned on the light. The vases were empty, and the pleated floor-length curtains were closed behind the catafalque that supported the coffins. A lectern stood to the right of the catafalque, and loudspeakers on stands were spread around the room so everyone could hear relatives talk about the person they had lost.

Jensen Funeral Home went along with any kind of funeral service the relatives wanted, so long as it didn't involve alcohol or anything unseemly. According to Artie, one time there had been karaoke at the lectern, because it had been the great passion of the deceased. It had been nearly impossible to stop once it got going, because there was always one more person who wanted the microphone.

The door opened behind them, and Artie rolled the stretcher in. Mike was covered with a white sheet. The stretcher's wheels left tracks in the carpet. Ilka couldn't help but notice Shelby's expression tighten as he approached the catafalque. She stepped forward and laid a hand on the woman's back, then asked her if she was okay.

Shelby nodded. Her face was like stone, her fists

clenched, but her eyes followed Artie as he parked the stretcher between the sofas and the catafalque.

He nodded and told her to take her time.

"I'm ready," she said, and she walked over and stood at the end where her son's feet stuck up.

Artie took hold of the sheet; then he waited until she gave him a small nod. He lifted the sheet, and Mike's feet and lower legs appeared.

It took her only a moment to confirm what she already knew. She turned and collapsed into Artie's arms.

Ilka had kept in the background, but now she stepped forward and pulled the sheet back over Mike's feet. She thought about pushing the stretcher out again, but she decided that Shelby should be allowed to leave the room before her son. When and only when she was ready to leave.

She went out into the hallway to give the mother time. Ilka needed time herself, to gather her thoughts. Though she tried not to worry too much about the problems with coffin suppliers, she wasn't used to giving in and letting herself be patronized. She took it personally that no one was willing to be helpful. On the other hand, she did have the coffin for tomorrow; she didn't need to worry about that. But it exasperated her that they had simply shut her off.

Stop it, she told herself. Artie and Shelby came out, and Artie asked if there was anything she wanted her son to have with him in the coffin.

"Think it over," he said as they stood in the doorway. "Don't go out and buy something. It's more like if there's anything at home that you know meant something to him. Or to you."

Shelby promised to think about it and let them know. "I

couldn't bring myself to throw anything of his away after he left; it's all up in the attic, but I haven't looked at it since then. I'll come over tomorrow if I find anything."

"And if you don't have any clothes for him, we'll take care of it," Artie added quickly. He hugged her one last time.

She nodded and thanked them; then she glanced again at the open door to the room where the stretcher still stood before walking out.

20

Back in her father's room, Ilka checked her phone. She had two messages, both from her mother. The first one: *"Let us know when you land. Will pick you up at the airport."*

The next message was a bit more demanding: *"You have three jobs Monday, and the entire week is filled up. The first job is nine o'clock Monday morning at Linde School in Virum."*

Ilka plopped down on her father's bed and closed her eyes for a moment. Earlier that day, she had been more than ready to go home. Turn her back on everything and pick up where she had left off. If she had followed that plan, she might even have been sitting on a plane right now. But that was no longer an option.

Insulted? Vindictive? Enraged? Ilka wasn't sure how she felt. Maybe she was just offended on her father's behalf, but pride and vanity were involved, too. She was not going

174

to take the coffin suppliers' rejections lying down. Yet she didn't feel at all like they had won the first battle. On the contrary. And it would suit her fine if they found out she could manage without them. Then there was Shelby. Ilka had to make sure she got to say good-bye to her son in a dignified manner. And finally, of course, there were all her father's things. And the two half sisters she'd found out about. She was anxious to meet them, and she had in fact expected they'd stop by to say hello, but maybe they thought she needed time to settle in. As if she'd had time for that.

She smiled and glanced around the room, which was a complete mess. Almost everything lay in piles, and the two body bags she had begun filling had to be emptied again. What would Erik say if he could see her now? "Pack your stuff and go home," or "Get everything under control and figure out what you want."

To try to get herself going, Ilka filled several supermarket plastic sacks with things she was sure would be thrown out. She went downstairs with one in each hand and walked out behind the house to the big Dumpsters. She opened the door and tossed the two sacks inside, but as she was about to slam the door shut, something caught her eye. A jacket sleeve stuck up between the bags over in the far corner of the Dumpster.

Ilka stood on tiptoe and leaned over to grab the corner of the topmost sack. To her surprise she saw the bags of her father's clothes she had packed for Sister Eileen to give to her parish, hidden under trash sacks. But the nun had said she would take the clothes to the parish herself, so...

Ilka stared at the sacks for a moment; then she leaned back and slammed the Dumpster door shut.

Back in the bedroom, she gathered up the drawings her half sisters had made for their father. She would drive out later and give them to the two women, use them as an excuse for showing up and introducing herself. She was nervous but curious—would she see any of herself in them? Or something of their common father?

"Couldn't leave after all," she wrote to her mother. "Something has come up I have to take care of. Could you handle my jobs? Get Hanne to help set them up."

Her mother had helped several times when Ilka had been on a tight schedule, so she knew the routine on photo shots, how the school students were to be placed. Granted, she'd never actually taken the photos, but that was the easiest part. All she had to do was press the camera's button, Ilka had explained.

Before sending her message, she checked her watch. Her mother was probably asleep and wouldn't see this for another eight hours. Ilka would be asleep then, and her mother would realize it was too late to find someone to do the jobs. Ilka knew she was conscientious; she would step in when she saw there were no other options.

The sun was about to go down, and Ilka felt restless. With a hint of a smile on his lips, Artie had helped her unload the Costco coffin out of the hearse. He decided to cover the scratches with black shoe polish; he doubted the family would notice. Fortunately, the damaged side of the coffin would be turned away from everyone.

There wasn't anything more Ilka could do to prepare for the next day's service, and besides, she was hungry. And in need of company, of a normal conversation that didn't include coffins, dead people, and complicated inheritances. She rose from the bed and picked her sweater up off the floor; then she went back downstairs to ask Artie if he wanted to go to Oh Dennis! for a bite to eat.

The preparation room door was open a crack, but she couldn't hear the fan. The Beach Boys were, however, at top volume, with Artie humming along. She stepped inside. Mike lay on the table in the middle of the room. Artie was leaning over his face, concentrating on brushing another layer onto the crushed cheekbone. Then he studied the face below him before using his brush on the cheek again.

The easygoing California summer surfer music contrasted sharply with the strange sight before Ilka, but in a way, Artie's movements were so gentle that it didn't seem grotesque.

Ilka cleared her throat loudly so as not to scare him to death; then she asked if she could come in.

He glanced up and nodded a bit absentmindedly before focusing again on the face. Mike's body was still covered by the sheet; only the face was visible. He lifted a small putty knife out of a bottle of something that reminded Ilka of modeling wax. Then he pressed a small clump of the material into the part of the sunken cheek he'd been brushing and carefully smoothed it out. He leaned closer in and compared the damaged and undamaged cheekbones; then he added more wax and rounded it off to make them look identical.

Ilka was fascinated by his work. He concentrated on applying layer upon layer, and Mike's cheek and eye socket soon were as prominent as they had been before someone had destroyed them.

"Are you hungry?" she asked. "I can pick up something if you want to finish here."

He glanced up at her as if he'd forgotten she'd come in; then he shook his head. "I'm okay, but thanks."

He concentrated as if he were creating a work of art, and in a way, he was. Ilka noticed the cans of Red Bull lined up on the table by the wall. One of them was open; three others sat there waiting.

"Text me if you change your mind, or if you want a beer when you finish. I'm going out and see if anyone in this town has discovered it's Friday, the day before the weekend." She left him to his work.

The food wasn't exactly a gourmet delight, though there was lots of it. The spareribs that had filled Ilka's plate were gnawed to the bone, though, by the time the waitress returned to her table and asked if she wanted coffee and cheesecake. Ilka answered with a question of her own: Where do you go on a Friday evening if you're looking for some company?

Ilka nodded as the young woman told her to drive down the main street and cross the small canal; a little bit farther down, on the right side, was a bar with live music. If she liked that sort of thing.

"But there are other bars," the girl said. She pointed up the street, away from the square. "I think they have music there, too; I'm not sure."

Ilka paid her bill and decided to try the bar across the canal. If it wasn't her type of place, she could check out another bar on the way home.

21

At least there was live music. A group of men about her age was standing around when Ilka walked inside. So far, so good. She squeezed her way through.

It was only a little past nine, but most of the tables were already taken, and the dim bar with the low-hanging lamps was lively. The only other light was a grainy yellow glare from above the bottles behind the bar and a colored string of lights nailed up along the edge, like an elaborate drapery.

Some people were rolling dice, and at a table up next to the stage, a group of women sang loudly. Western hats and boots; the guy standing there with his guitar was going for it, Ilka thought, as she pulled out an empty bar stool and sat down. He sang well, and the vibes in the bar were good. She glanced around while waiting for the bartender in the plaid flannel shirt to notice her.

"Root beer," she said, when he came over.

The men behind her burst out laughing at something she didn't hear. They ordered more beer. More people came in; greetings were being yelled all around her. Everybody seemed to know one another, from the conversations going on. "How's Greg doing?" "Is your mother okay now?" "Did Jenny have her kid?" Where in the world were all these people in the daytime? Not on the street; that was for sure.

Applause, more music. Several people also said hi to Ilka as they walked by or came up to the bar to order.

"Are you new in town?" someone behind her suddenly asked. She turned and stared straight into the face of a guy at least ten years younger than her. Dark hair, blue eyes. Handsome.

She nodded when he asked if he could sit down, but she said no thanks when he offered to buy her a beer. Though every seat around her was taken, he pulled up another bar stool from somewhere. His name was Larry; he'd moved to town to work at Johnson Wax, whose headquarters were located here. He was born and raised in Chicago, had gone to college there also.

Ilka listened with half an ear, nodding occasionally while trying to place the scent he had on. Masculine and yet light. Nice. She didn't hear his question, which he repeated when she didn't answer.

"No, I'm just visiting," she said. She told him she was from Denmark and would be going back. Soon.

"So have you seen anything while you've been here? Sailing is good on Lake Michigan, and there are some beautiful lakes in the area. I'll show you around this weekend if you like."

Either he was terribly lonesome or he was trying to score.

The latter was preferable. Ilka turned to get a better look at him. His hair hung just over his eyes, but not enough that it seemed deliberate. He just needed a haircut. A point in his favor. Dark blue long-sleeved T-shirt and jeans, no problems there.

"That sounds nice," she said, and she ordered a beer for him while looking at her root beer, which she hadn't touched.

The cowboy singer was on break; they were playing Taylor Swift over the house speakers. The women up front sang along. The bar was full now, every table was taken, and crowds of people were standing behind them. Ilka pulled her chair closer to Larry, their legs slipped in between each other's.

"How long have you lived here?" she asked. Someone walked by and nudged her leg against his; she kept it there. She leaned forward slightly to hear him better.

"Two years." His cheek happened to brush against hers.

The singer was back onstage, and the music seemed louder than before.

"Let's go outside," she suggested. "I can't hear a thing in here."

He hesitated for a moment when they stood up, as if he'd lost his nerve when he saw she was taller than him. Quite a bit taller. But he grabbed his beer and followed her anyway.

While elbowing their way to the door, Ilka couldn't help wondering if anyone here had something to do with the writing on Shelby's house. This was a small town; somebody here must at least know something, she thought, though everyone seemed friendly and nice enough.

"Denmark, you said?" Larry asked, as they walked down toward the canal. There were a few small sheds on the wharf; motorboats filled one side. "Have you checked out any of the Danish bakeries here? My boss speaks a little Danish. Helmersen's his name; his wife runs one of the bakeries with her brothers. I think she works behind the counter; the brothers do the baking."

His arm was around her as they walked, and when they reached the first shed, Ilka turned and kissed him. She maneuvered him over to the other side of the shed, out of sight, and he put his arms around her.

He mumbled something about the Danish Vikings and how nice she was, but she shushed him. No more talk. He kissed her harder and got rougher with his hands, and before she managed to unbutton his pants, he took over. No more thoughts about the coffin suppliers, debt, the funeral service that still could turn into a nightmare if the family discovered she'd cheated them on the expensive prepaid coffin. No more funeral home business and old murder cases. No more photo shoots and responsibilities. She nipped at his earlobe and held on to him as all thoughts disappeared.

"Thanks," she said after it was over, as if they'd just wound up some business.

"My pleasure." He held her face and kissed her on the forehead. "You want to go back and have a beer?"

Ilka smiled and shook her head. "I've got to get home." She said she had to get up early the next morning.

He studied her for a moment. "Would you give me your phone number?" He smiled a bit awkwardly.

She shook her head as she straightened her clothes.

"So will I see you again before you leave?"

"Sorry, I don't think so," she said, then added that it had been nice.

She kissed him and laid her cheek against his, breathed in his scent. When they reached the street, she walked away, but she noticed him turning to look back a few times before going into the bar.

Ilka smiled as she drove back home. He couldn't be a day over thirty, and he had made her evening. For a moment, she wondered if it was dumb of her not to get his number, but no. Once was enough.

As she moved through the deserted town, she realized that for the first time since she'd arrived in Racine, her head wasn't buzzing in confusion and wrestling with decisions to be made.

22

Ilka woke up to someone knocking on her door. At first
she was afraid she'd slept late, but then she saw it was
only eight thirty. She'd set her alarm for nine.

"Okay," she yelled. "Just a second."

"We have a decision to make," Sister Eileen said from
outside. "We have a problem."

Why doesn't that fucking surprise me? Ilka thought. She
was pulling her pants on when the sister knocked again.

"*Jeg gider ikke flere problemer,*" she yelled. She didn't want
any more problems. Several messages had come in from her
mother, she saw. She tossed her phone onto the bed and
opened the door. Sister Eileen was holding a sheet of paper,
which she handed to her. "Joanne had agreed to bring the
flowers at eight thirty, so I could decorate before the Nortons and the caterers arrive. But she brought this instead."

She nodded at the sheet of paper. "It's a final bill. She

refuses to work for us anymore. She says she doesn't think we will pay her what we owe, so now it's over."

Ilka glanced at the statement. They owed more than twenty-eight hundred dollars.

"I've informed Artie about this, and he has promised to take care of the flowers for today. He'll bring them with him when he arrives. But we still have a problem."

"Why is she stopping right now?" Ilka asked after checking the dates. Deliveries had been made up to last weekend; they had begun all the way back in June. They'd been receiving flowers on credit for more than three months, almost four. And it wasn't even close to the first of the month, so why deliver the bill now? Something must have happened.

The sister shrugged. "We've always had a fine working relationship with Joanne, even back when her sister ran the shop. They've delivered flowers for us for all the years I've been working here. Your father wouldn't dream of ordering from anywhere else."

Ilka was angry now, and she decided to go down later to confront them and hash out some sort of installment agreement. "And Artie knows what flowers we need? They're going to take care of the coffin decorations from her own garden; it's just the room that needs decorating."

The nun confirmed that Artie was aware of all this.

"Is there anything else to be delivered for the funeral service today?" Ilka asked. She was counting on the family arriving at eleven, and if there were any more unpleasant surprises in store, she wanted to be prepared.

"The food. But it's coming. I ordered hors d'oeuvres, and I called yesterday to make sure everything was going according to plan. And it was."

"And we can count on that?"

"I hope so." She turned and walked back down the stairs so quietly that Ilka wasn't sure her feet touched the steps.

Ilka took a quick shower, and when she returned to her room, she opened her father's closet to look over what was left inside. She hadn't had time to wash her clothes, and besides, nothing she'd brought was appropriate for the funeral service of an elderly lady.

She slipped a white shirt off a hanger and glanced over at the two dark jackets. One of them looked new. It fit her across the back, but the sleeves were too short. The same was true for the other jacket. Along with the shirt, she tossed one of them over on the bed and tried on the black gabardine pants, complete with pleats and tucked pockets—the uniform of a funeral director. Unlike the jacket, the pants were long enough; her father had been tall. With a belt, they were okay, though she wasn't going to get a lot of compliments on her great ass when she wore them. Considering the occasion, that was probably the last thing anyone would notice anyway.

Before going downstairs, she shook her head and ran her hands through her straight hair to make it look fuller. She'd forgotten her hair dryer, or rather, she hadn't even considered taking it along. A quick application of mascara, and that was that.

She turned on the standing lamps in the two rooms that made up the chapel; a folding door had been opened and now the room was twice as big as it had been the day before, when Shelby had been there. There was room for 175 people, but they were expecting between 100 and 150 to show up. The Nortons had ordered food for 160, just to be safe. Ilka was a bit nervous that the caterer might pull the same stunt as Joanne had. She was on her way to the office to call them and double-check when Artie showed up, struggling to get inside.

"Could you give me a hand here?" he asked.

"What the hell is this?" He was carrying a jumble of flowers and wide satin ribbons.

"Time to decorate," he said, nodding at the closed door to the chapel, where Sister Eileen had brought in more chairs for the service.

Ilka stared for a moment; then slowly she understood where the flowers had come from. This was the moment to decide whether it was better not to ask so later on she could deny any knowledge of it.

She opened the door for him, and Artie managed to get to the table and dump the flowers. He pulled a pair of scissors out of his back pocket and started clipping the silk ribbons tied around the bouquets, tossing the ribbons on the floor one after the other; then he cut the strings holding the flowers together until they were strewn all over the table.

"Nobody's going to miss them," he said, even though Ilka hadn't said a word. "They come from the common grave; there are so many that no one's going to notice."

Ilka shook her head and turned around. Sister Eileen walked in with a jug of water and started filling the vases. She didn't so much as lift an eyebrow, though she glanced at the flower table and announced tersely that she would begin decorating.

"Hello," a voice called from out in the hallway.

Ilka immediately kicked all the ribbons under the floor-length tablecloth; then she walked to the door, where she was met by a young man in a light blue shirt and black pants. The insignia embroidered onto his shirt pocket looked like a delivery boy holding a dish.

"Hello," she said, closing the door behind her.

"Where do I put the food?"

You actually showed up! she almost cried out. But instead she simply smiled and showed him out to the kitchen. When he saw the table she pointed at, he shook his head. "Usually we put food on long tables; are they ready?"

Ilka tried to think where the long tables might be, when Sister Eileen came out and took over.

"They're out in the front hall." She followed him out toward the stairway. "When we receive funeral guests, we take them directly in to the service, so it won't be open out here until the service is finished. That should give you enough time to set up."

Once again Ilka sensed the nun was deliberately not letting her in on procedures in the funeral home. As if she didn't think it was worth the effort. Or maybe she wanted Ilka to remain an outsider. She watched the sister show the boy exactly where she wanted the various dishes placed. But that wasn't what was gnawing at her.

Ilka had the feeling Sister Eileen was keeping something to herself. It was hard to put a finger on what it was. It just seemed that she kept Ilka at a distance most of the time. And then suddenly she could be pleasant and helpful.

For a moment, she thought about insisting on participating in the planning, to show she wouldn't be brushed aside, but then she looked at the clock. The funeral service would begin in less than half an hour, and the relatives were already getting things ready in the chapel.

Ilka stayed in the background while the family made the final preparations. She watched Helen arrange the pillows, shift the Kleenex boxes at the end of every row by a few inches, and light all the candles, even though sunlight streamed through the windows. She also took care of the flowers, while the two brothers stood with arms crossed, speaking softly to each other. Ilka tensed up when they started walking over to where their mother lay. She wished she were invisible.

She held her breath while the brothers approached the coffin. The upper half was open, and the elderly woman was visible from the waist up, her hands folded and her eyes closed. As usual with corpses, the skin on her face was smooth, almost like that of a little girl.

Ilka stared at the floor while they circled the coffin. After a few minutes, she looked up and breathed out through nearly closed lips. They hadn't noticed any scratches; the shoe polish had worked. The only thing bothering them was the missing easel for the life board they'd ordered.

She pretended not to have eavesdropped. First and foremost because she didn't know what a life board was, and therefore couldn't tell them where it and the easel could be. It dawned on her that it was something Mrs. Norton had told Ilka's father she wanted, back when she had preordered her funeral. When they had gone through all the details after the first meeting, the sister had been assigned to take care of it.

Knowing she would have to confront the nun about

something that should have been taken care of felt great— but only for a few seconds. The sister appeared with the life board and easel. It was a long sheet of cardboard, the size of the mirror on the back of the closet door in her father's room, with photos of the deceased illustrating her life story. A black-and-white photo of a young Mrs. Norton with big curls and a sugary smile, then a grinning young college graduate wearing the coveted square graduate cap. Then a happy wedding photo. Then a large leap in years to an older lady smiling pleasantly at the camera. An entire life in four photos. It almost looked to Ilka like a poster for someone running for office, promising voters a long and prosperous life. Then a sharp odor of food interrupted her thoughts, and she turned to the door, where Mrs. Norton's grandchild walked in holding a full plate in each hand.

It wasn't until he pushed aside the box of Kleenex on the small table between the sofas that Ilka realized what she smelled: a combination of macaroni and cheese and pecan pie, a dessert his grandmother had loved to make. Still warm, Ilka discovered, when she walked over to the boy and asked if she could help.

"I want Grandma to have this in her coffin. Mom helped me, but she says it can't go in until the guests leave. But she'll forget it for sure; she's more worried about whether there's enough food for everybody."

"I'll make sure we remember," Ilka said. She was just beginning to enjoy how everything was going as it should, when she noticed the younger brother prowling around the back of the coffin, again with a critical eye. He stepped back and took a good look; then he walked around to the head of the coffin. Again he stepped back, as if the light wasn't exactly right where he was standing. He kept to the front of the podium; it couldn't be the scratches he was looking at, Ilka thought, as she listened distractedly to the grandson.

"The plates are ovenproof, but Mom says we don't need to tell the guy who's burning the coffin."

"Don't worry about that," Ilka murmured. Joe was at the back of the coffin again, and he called over his older brother. They began scowling in Ilka's direction. She couldn't hear what they were saying, but she was certain they were discussing how big a refund they should demand if they could prove the coffin was damaged or the wrong color.

"You're right; it's not the right coffin." The older brother spoke so loudly that Ilka couldn't help hearing. Ilka was beginning to catch on; the older brother was less conflict shy, while the younger brother was the brains of the outfit. They walked toward her.

"There's no glitter in the paint. It's glossy, but it doesn't glitter."

They spoke almost in unison, and Ilka reacted by taking a step back and bumping into Artie, who had parked himself behind her without her noticing.

"It doesn't, no," he said. "It's not exactly what your mother ordered, which isn't available anymore. This coffin, though, is a jet-black limousine. It's the replacement model, more exclusive, like the name suggests. That's also the reason it's much more expensive."

The older brother butted in. "We're not paying one penny more. You didn't warn us about any extra expenses. And we're not paying just because a model was discontinued. It's not our fault!"

"No, though a lot of people insure themselves against things like this, so they don't have to worry."

The brother was about to protest, but Artie beat him to it. "But of course you don't have to pay the difference." He laid a hand on Steve's shoulder, as if they were old friends. "It's part of our service. With us you don't have to worry about expensive insurance to guard against extra costs. And no one who preorders their burial in this funeral home will ever see us compromise on quality, even when prices go up. In fact, we try to give our customers more than what they pay for."

Ilka realized she'd been holding her breath again during this whole conversation. Not so much because of what Artie had been rattling on about, but because he spoke in an entirely different manner: Everything sounded so convincing. She hadn't known he had this in him. Impressed with how he had saved the day, she turned to him and nodded in acknowledgment before heading for the door. It felt like the room was closing in on her; she needed some air, but just as she reached the hallway, she was called back.

"Is there a hook for Mother's dogs, to hang the leashes on?" Helen had just finished placing flowers on the floor around the coffin.

"Not a real hook, no," Ilka said. "But I was thinking you would have the dogs with you in the first row, and you can fasten the leashes to the sofa's leg. Or will your mother's dogs be too close to the coffin that way?"

"Oh no!" Helen said. "We want the dogs up front. That's what Mom would have wanted."

"Fine, then we'll do it that way." Ilka was about to leave again when she ran into the choir, seven men and three women from the seniors' club, who wanted to know where to stand.

Suddenly Ilka realized she hadn't seen anything of Sister Eileen since she'd brought in the life board. And now, as guests were beginning to arrive, she was still nowhere in sight.

"Just a moment," Ilka said, walking away without answering them. The nun wasn't in the reception area or the front hall, where the food was set out.

On the way to the small kitchen Ilka glanced into the arrangement room and her father's office—empty. Back in the hallway now, she was heading for the garage when the door opened and Sister Eileen entered.

"The guests are arriving," Ilka said. She was annoyed; she hadn't yet asked about the clothes in the Dumpster, either. Couldn't bring herself to. She was afraid of being too pushy. Though it might just be a question of learning something about the way nuns like her live, Ilka thought. Maybe she'd been praying over in her apartment, or whatever the proper thing to do was. "I would appreciate it if you could go in and welcome them. The choir is here too. Could you show them where to go?" she added as she headed back to the chapel.

The people attending the services streamed in, and a low murmur slowly spread throughout the chapel. Ilka made her way into a corner behind the open folding doors. Artie was in the middle of the crowd; she sensed he was giving some final tips to the family, who had wanted to arrange the funeral service. He nodded when Steve signaled he was ready to start the music. The choir would sing after the two brothers each spoke about their mother.

Ilka noticed the grandson sitting on the plush sofa. One of his grandmother's dachshunds was on his lap; the other sat at his feet. The chapel was almost full; people were speaking in hushed tones. Most of them were older, but there were also many close to Helen's and her brothers' ages.

"Thanks," Ilka said, when Artie came over and stood beside her. Soft music poured out of the speakers, and the voices fell silent. For a moment, everyone listened to the music; then the two brothers stood and walked up to the podium to welcome everyone.

When one of the brothers began his speech, Ilka looked over at the table with the long tablecloth. One of the broad satin ribbons from the stolen flowers stuck out, a scarlet ribbon, and part of a woman's name—not the name of the deceased lying in the coffin—stood out in gold.

"Come on," Artie said, pulling her away. "They'll handle the rest themselves. And Sister Eileen will take care of the food; it's all been put out."

She followed him out back under the carport. He lit a cigarette and blew the smoke out slowly.

"I think Sister Eileen threw my father's clothes away instead of giving them to her parish, like we talked about," Ilka said. She sat down on the steps.

He looked surprised. "Why would she do that?"

Ilka shrugged. "I don't understand it either. She even offered to take them herself, when I said I would deliver them."

He crushed out his cigarette, then walked over and threw the butt in the Dumpster. It was as if what she'd said didn't really interest him.

"And what got into you back there at the coffin?" she asked. "Have you been smoking weed or something?"

When he didn't answer, Ilka realized she'd put her finger on the real reason for his bravado in front of the Norton family. "Damn, Artie, what if they'd noticed it?" She was serious now.

"The only thing they noticed was the coffin model wasn't what they'd ordered."

Ilka nodded. After a few moments, she shrugged. "You handled that great. But what if someone had found out about the flowers? It would have ruined our image!"

He gazed at her a second longer than necessary before saying, "Sweetheart, we don't have an image. Not anymore!"

The choir began singing.

23

The coffee had just finished dripping through the filter, and Ilka had brought two cups out to the steps where Artie was smoking another cigarette, just as Shelby came marching across the parking lot. Her face was ashen, her lips pursed in anger. She carried a pair of pants and a shirt over her shoulder.

Ilka had hoped that Shelby wouldn't show up until the people attending the funeral service had left. It would have been best given the present situation—Artie wouldn't have been stoned any longer, hopefully—and Ilka needed a breather. The past days had simply been too much pressure.

"I'll kill him," Shelby said, when she reached them. She threw the clothes at Artie, who was on his feet now. "I'll wring his neck; I'll cut him up into pieces."

Ilka handed one cup of coffee to her, the other to Artie.

"Shelby, what happened?" Artie said, trying to placate

her. He pushed his hair back so it wouldn't fall into the steaming cup of coffee.

"I'll tell you what happened!" she yelled as she looked for a place to sit.

Ilka took her elbow. "Come in; let's go sit down."

She gestured at Artie in no uncertain terms for him to follow.

"I just came from the police station," she said, after she and her coffee had been settled in the plush chair in the arrangement room. Ilka and Artie sat across from her.

"It's Howard Oldham! You already know he was on the tape of the school's surveillance camera that night; the police said so. And he admitted doing it, but you'll never guess what made him break in and do the horrible thing he did to my son."

She made it sound as if an undertaker from the town's leading funeral home breaking into a competitor's business, pulling a corpse out of the refrigerator, and urinating on it was a minor detail compared to what she was about to say.

Artie set his coffee down and hunched over a bit. He looked frozen. Through the thin walls they could hear singing from the funeral service.

Shelby looked back and forth between the two of them.

"No, you're right," Ilka said. "We'll never guess."

She didn't seem to have heard Ilka; she was too outraged to deal with what was about to burst from inside her. Her anger stood in total contrast to her small, delicate body. "He was wild about her. Howard Oldham claims that Ashley was his great love. The police told me he broke down; they had to postpone the questioning because he wasn't able to speak."

Tears appeared in her eyes. "He says my son stole her from him. That Mike ruined his life. Howard claims that if it hadn't been for Mike, he would have been engaged to her."

Artie was confused. "Are you saying he and Ashley had a relationship before she met your son? He must've been twice her age."

"It's not like that's never happened before," Ilka said. She was thinking of the center of Copenhagen on Friday nights, where men in their forties and fifties puffed themselves up like roosters, drinking cocktails, with teenage girls all over them.

"I don't know if they actually had a relationship," Shelby said. "But he was courting her, per the police report. They let me see it down at the station. He must have thought their age difference wouldn't be important if he could just show her he was serious. Something must've gone on between them, anyway."

Artie began nodding, as if something was dawning on him. "Ashley Simpson's dad was a chauffeur for the Oldhams. Not for the funeral home, but the private chauffeur for Douglas Oldham, the old undertaker." He explained that Ashley had lived in the chauffeur's quarters with her brother and parents. "It's behind the Oldhams' house, farther out on the coast road. I remember hearing the old man couldn't keep his hands off the daughter. But I thought they meant Douglas Oldham. I only met him a few times. He killed himself a year after all this happened. Or maybe he just got sick? There were a lot of rumors flying around back then."

Shelby looked fragile and pale as she sat slumped over,

staring down at the table seemingly without seeing the coffee or her folded hands in front of her. She shook her head weakly. "It never would have happened. What would she do with an old man? She was just a big kid. Even if Mike hadn't fallen in love with her, she wouldn't have hooked up with a man old enough to be her father. Would she?"

She looked up, confused and in despair.

"But was it Howard Oldham who paid your son to leave town?" Ilka asked. So it was jealousy, just as she had guessed.

"Paid?" Artie said, still looking at Shelby. "What's that about? Paid for what?"

She straightened up a bit. "My son was paid to leave town. He was given a lot of money to start a new life. A lot. Someone bought him."

Artie stared straight ahead in thought. "Which made it look like he ran away." He nodded.

"Like he was guilty." Shelby spit the words out. She drew herself up, tried to get a grip. "But the money didn't come from Howard. The Oldham family was questioned, because they knew Ashley and her father, and maybe they knew something, but Howard wasn't even in town back then. He was in Minneapolis, taking extra courses to add to his undertaker degree."

She paused a moment before explaining that it was his alibi, not being in Racine during the three weeks between Ashley's death and Mike's disappearance. "He didn't kill her, and he wasn't around when Mike was paid either."

"No one can be sure he wasn't home some of those days, can they?" Ilka said. "It was a long period. It almost sounds too good to be true, gone the entire three weeks. Very convenient."

"He was gone for four weeks, in fact," Shelby said.

Artie nodded at Ilka. "He fabricated the alibi, you're thinking."

"That's what I said too, down at the police station," Shelby said. "But they reopened the old case, and the alibi is good. He enrolled in the continuing education half a year before all this happened, and he had no absences from class. And besides, it's written in the witness statements that his reaction clearly showed he had no knowledge of what had happened. Back then, though, he didn't mention his relationship with Ashley. The police just found out about that."

They sat in silence as the magnitude of his confession sank in. A grown man, Ilka thought. How could he let himself break in and pull a body out of the refrigerator and piss in hate—over twelve years of hate—on it?

"And he wasn't the man who killed my son," she finally continued. "He also has an alibi for the evening that Mike came back."

"That's even more convenient." Artie sounded suspicious. He seemed to be completely sober now; his eyes were clear and focused, as was his anger.

"The police have arrested the two Oldham sons," she said. "They're suspected of doing the dirty work for their uncle. The officer couldn't tell me more, but obviously they deny having had any contact with Mike after he came back. But why would they admit it if they did?"

"*Hold da kæft!*" Ilka said. Unbelievable! She sat back in her chair. Everything began swirling in her head: names, dates, people she didn't know. None of it made sense to her. She needed to take a walk, be by herself for a while.

She turned and glanced across the parking lot. People

who had attended the funeral service were beginning to drift outside in small, scattered groups, and she thought about Mrs. Norton's favorite dishes, which were to be placed inside the coffin before it was taken to the crematorium.

"Please excuse me," she said. She bumped into the table when she rose, spilling coffee. "There's something I have to take care of."

The grandson was standing alone by the coffin when Ilka walked in. She heard voices out in the front hall; a few people must still have been eating canapés.

Pete stood with his back to her. The two small, ovenproof dishes were still on the small table, and the two dachshunds were curled up, each at one end of the sofa. There was something comforting about the silence. Peaceful, Ilka thought.

He turned and watched her approach. "My uncle thinks it's stupid, about the food." He glanced over at the table. "Grandma doesn't know we're doing this."

Ilka smiled. "Don't you think she does?"

He wasn't sure if she was serious. "Isn't it a little bit yucky?"

"Well, yeah. It's a little bit yucky. But so what? No one will know, and if it feels right to you, I think she should take it along with her."

"Maybe we're not supposed to do it?"

"Maybe not, but we can just not ask anyone about it."

"But aren't you the one who decides?" He looked at her suspiciously.

Ilka nodded. "Yes, but you didn't ask me, either. You just said this is what you want to do. And rule number one is that the nearest relatives should decide how they want to send someone off. I think this is very thoughtful of you, to give your grandmother a few of her favorite dishes on her last journey. That's how they did it a very long time ago. They gave the dead something to eat for their journey."

Ilka should have stuck a bottle of red wine in Erik's coffin; she just hadn't thought of it.

She opened the bottom half of the lid and told him he could put the food down there, that no one would discover it.

As soon as the boy grabbed the two plates, the dachshunds jumped up and began barking, shrilly and very loudly. They wagged their tails and danced around Pete's legs. "I could just…" He nodded down at the dogs.

Ilka laughed. Not because she thought dachshunds were particularly lovable, but the glint in the grandson's eyes told her this wasn't the first time the two small, dark-brown wiener dogs had begged their way into his heart. He had already surrendered, and there was something proper, something touching, about him shifting his attention from death to what was still a part of life.

"What do you think your grandmother would do?" she asked, but he'd already set the goodies on the floor. Two minutes later they were licked so clean that you couldn't see the plates had been used.

"What's going to happen with the dogs?" Ilka asked as they walked out into the front hall. His mother was putting her coat on.

"They're going to stay with us."

Helen had red splotches on her cheeks. She smiled at her son. "It went so well." She shook Ilka's hand. "Everything was like Mother would have wanted. And there were no problems whatsoever. I am so grateful to you. Should we take the flowers with us, or will you take care of them?"

"If you don't want to take them with you, we'll make sure they are laid on the coffin after it's closed." Ilka spoke with such authority that she surprised even herself. It struck her again that only a few days ago, all she knew about the funeral home business was what she had picked up as a child, but now here she was, talking as if she were running everything. Which, in a way, she was. At least on paper.

She shook her head and watched Helen walk to the car with her arm around her son, the two dogs running at their feet.

24

Shelby had left by the time Ilka returned, so she kicked off her shoes, shrugged out of her father's stiff jacket, and hung it back in the closet along with the pants. She'd just pulled a sweater over her head when someone knocked on the door. At first, she thought about hiding somewhere, but they knocked again. When she opened the door, Sister Eileen was standing outside holding a small tray with tea and a bowl of cookies that had been left over from the funeral service.

"Something to eat and drink?" The nun held the tray out and looked at Ilka exactly the way her mother did whenever she thought her daughter was working too hard.

"Thank you." She was surprised, and suddenly she felt hungry.

"There's also a plate of canapés downstairs. I wrapped them up and put them in the refrigerator."

Ilka eyed Sister Eileen, who politely stood out in the hall. Nothing about her smile gave the impression she was holding anything back from Ilka. She looked friendly and considerate. Maybe Ilka was only imagining this mistrust.

She took the tray. "Thank you so much. I really am hungry, in fact."

Once again she considered asking about the clothes, but instead she pointed at the small pile of drawings beside the odd clay figure and homemade Father's Day card. "I've been thinking about driving out to my half sisters and giving those to them."

"That's very thoughtful of you," the nun said. She offered to find a bag for them.

"That's okay; there's not very much, only those things. Is there anything I can do to help downstairs before I go?"

Sister Eileen shook her head. She stood in the doorway, as if there was something else on her mind, but she didn't say anything. Ilka broke the awkward silence. "How did you end up in Racine, by the way? Was it because of your parish? You didn't grow up here, did you?"

She was just being friendly, making small talk so they could get to know each other better, but the nun's reaction was so dismissive that Ilka wondered if she had said something wrong.

"I've picked up downstairs, and the tables have been put away. I'm going to lock up and take the rest of the day off. If, that is, you don't need me for anything more."

She'd already turned to leave when Ilka quickly shook her head. "No, go ahead, take the day off. What time is Ed McKenna's daughter coming tomorrow?"

She answered from halfway down the stairs. "She won't

be here until twelve; there aren't so many flights during the weekend."

"Fine. We can sleep a little longer." Ilka smiled at her back.

She had tied a wide green satin ribbon around the drawings and put them aside. While going through the drawers, she had also found some photos of her father with her half sisters. And a brown envelope with several letters from them addressed to him. It looked like they were written while he was traveling in California. Naturally she had read all of them; no one would mind, she thought. The letters were mostly about things like the rabbits doing well, their homework was hard. And their mother had been in the hospital, but they had visited her, and she had come home after a few days. Even though their father had been gone only three weeks, the girls had dutifully written him every other day.

Ilka folded the letters up again. Surely he had written back? Nothing they had written seemed like answers to any questions he might have asked. They were just small, childlike updates. She guessed that some of the drawings had been sent with the letters.

On the way to her father's family, she tried not to think too much about meeting them. She tried to convince herself there was no reason to be nervous. And she wasn't, not really. And yet. Should she have called, given them the chance to prepare for her?

She still hadn't heard from them. It struck her that they might be angry about her inheriting the funeral home business. They might feel she had taken something from them. But they could just come right out and say it. They could have it. Right now. Maybe that was why she was a bit nervous: They hadn't reacted.

She thought about the wheelchair. Possibly they assumed she would come to them. Maybe they couldn't understand why she hadn't already contacted them. But she was the stranger, the guest. She was the one to be welcomed.

Stop it, she told herself. Though it felt like an eternity, she hadn't even been in town for a week, and they'd had plenty to do after her father's death. Of course they had.

She drove under the viaduct, above which the wide freeway ran north. She thought of something else: Her half sisters must resemble her, surely? Did they share some of the same features? She hoped for their sake they hadn't inherited her father's height like she had. It had been hard to see the evening she'd caught a glimpse of Leslie on the porch. From a distance, she'd looked very feminine. Not a skyscraper, like the boys in Ilka's class at school had called her, when they weren't asking if her parents had forgotten the *B* when they named her—Bilka, the name of the Danish hypermarket chain. All through the lower classes at school, she was called Bilka. But that stopped one day when she lost her temper and grabbed a chair and smashed it over Jakob's head—he had been her worst tormentor. The chair leg broke his nose, but otherwise nothing happened. After that, no one had felt any need to comment on her name. Or her height, for that matter.

Leslie and Amber were two common names; no one would have teased the two girls. Her father must have turned into a lightweight after coming over here. Or else he hadn't seen the same strength in them that he'd claimed to have seen in her as a newborn baby. That was his explanation when she asked him about her ridiculous name. "You're a winner, Ilka, and they'll find that out sooner or later. A person has the advantage when the odds are against them, when they're the big surprise. When they're someone no one had seen coming, when they strike when it's least expected."

"Talk, talk, talk," Ilka muttered to herself. It annoyed her that her nerves were getting the upper hand. And what the hell for? She didn't need her father's new family. "I'll leave if I don't like them," she told her windshield.

Massive treetops drooped over the street where Ilka turned off a bit later. She was close now. A large American flag hanging from the gable end of a corner house nearly touched the ground, and there was a round plastic swimming pool under a square parasol on the front lawn. Kids' bikes were parked near the gate, and plastic toys were scattered around, as if some game had suddenly been interrupted. She drove past slowly, her eyes glued to her father's house. Even at a distance she could see the porch was deserted, but the front door was open, though barely.

She took a deep breath as she parked at the curb and shut the engine off. She sat and stared at nothing, then grabbed the bundle of drawings and letters. The small clay figure was in her pocket.

Before she shut the car door, she saw Mary Ann in the doorway, coming through in her wheelchair. Ilka hesitated before walking up the flagstone sidewalk to the house. She smiled as her father's wife, a frail, light-haired woman, wheeled across the porch to meet her.

"Hello," Ilka said when she reached the steps. "I'm Paul's daughter from Denmark." She started up the steps.

"Yes, I figured that, when you drove by the other day," Mary Ann said. She backed her wheelchair away from the steps so Ilka could pass.

Ilka shook her hand and smiled, and immediately the two sisters appeared in the doorway behind their mother. "I'm Ilka. Ilka Jensen."

She walked over to say hello to the sisters, one of whom had stepped behind the door. There was something familiar about the dark-haired woman. After stepping closer, to Ilka's surprise she saw it was the woman from the bench by the funeral home parking lot.

How about that, she thought. Then the blond older sister, the one she'd seen on the porch the other day, asked if she could help her with something.

For a second, Ilka wasn't sure why she had come, but then she remembered the things she'd brought along. She smiled when she realized the older sister must not know who she was.

"I'm your half sister." She added that she had been looking forward to meeting them, that she hadn't even known she had sisters. "It's so nice to meet you."

The blond sister—Leslie, according to Sister Eileen—stood behind her mother's wheelchair, and when no one spoke, the moment became so awkward that Ilka began to regret she'd come.

"I brought this along," she said. She showed them the bundle of drawings and letters. "I found them up in our father's room."

The dark-haired sister—Amber, she must be—seemed uncomfortable; obviously, she hadn't wanted to reveal who she was. Apparently the two other women weren't supposed to know she and Ilka had met. Leslie reached for the drawings.

"Thank you very much. That's very thoughtful of you."

Ilka gave them to her; then she fished the small clay figure out of her pocket. "And I found this." She held it so it sat in the palm of her hand. Leslie took it, too.

"We don't have any of your things here," she said. Then she walked back toward the front door.

Ilka was about to follow her, when Mary Ann quickly stuck out her hand and thanked her for stopping by.

Ilka stood for a moment and looked the three of them over. Her half sisters didn't resemble her, apart from being tall, though not as lanky as Ilka. In fact, Amber's figure had more than average female curves, which made her height less obvious. Ilka took a final glance at the younger sister; she looked a bit like a clumsy ox, she thought, rather ungenerously. Then, taking the hint, she started down the steps, but quickly turned around. "Would you like to get together for a cup of coffee one of these days?"

"Unfortunately we won't have time before you go home," Leslie said. Amber still hadn't said a word.

"Thank you for stopping by," Mary Ann repeated. "It was interesting to meet you."

Ilka started for the car again. She felt their eyes on her back, and she turned around again. "You're very welcome to stop by the funeral home," she said, staring directly at Amber. "There might be some of your father's things you'd like to have."

None of them reacted to her invitation, and she decided to give up, yet she took a few steps back toward them. "By the way, are there any plans for when my father's urn is to be interred?" This time she looked at Mary Ann, who simply shook her head and answered, "No."

Ilka nodded quickly and walked back to the car. For a moment, she stared out the windshield; then she pulled herself together and started the car.

Twilight seemed to have fallen during her short visit with her father's new family. Shadows had lengthened; the evening sunlight hung low over the treetops. Ilka turned on the windshield wipers when it began sprinkling. She drove slowly to the end of the street and was about to turn, when a gray squirrel darted over a low wooden fence. Over by the gate, a woman whacked a doormat against the fence; then she tossed it down by the front door, walked inside, and shut the door. Neighbors, people who had known her father, Ilka thought. It was hard for her to imagine the man she had known and missed all these years, living his life here. In a residential district, so dull that it reminded her of a stage set, and with a family as stiff as starch. So different from her own mother.

They hadn't given her one single opening. Not one sign of any interest in getting to know her. Obviously, they wanted nothing to do with her.

Ilka tried to put herself in their shoes. The sisters had just lost their father, a man who had been with them all their lives, and of course they were mourning him. She could see that. And maybe they hadn't known about her, either. But their total lack of interest in digging just a bit deeper into his past surprised her. And admittedly she had hoped his new family could help shed some light on what had happened back then. Why he had chosen to settle down in Racine. She had so many questions.

Ilka made a U-turn, and when she drove by their house again, the porch was empty and the front door shut. Maybe they preferred to look on his life as having begun with them.

"Have a great life, assholes," she said. She noticed her hands gripping the wheel, so hard that her knuckles hurt.

I was the first, she thought. As if that were a victory in and of itself, being the first child he had created. On the other hand, she was the one he had left. And the one he had cut off all contact with.

Ilka drove blindly now, noticing nothing. The monotone voice of the GPS guided her as she relived the loneliness and abandonment she'd felt for long periods of her childhood after he left.

She noticed a gas station up ahead, and on impulse she signaled to turn in. A moment later she was facing a freckled guy with wild red hair and a cap with the bill turned backward. Cash or credit card? "Cash," she said. "And a pack of Marlboro's."

She tossed the sack filled with bottles on the front seat, pulled out her phone, and checked the address.

25

Ilka parked her father's car and walked down to the house. At first, she thought Artie wasn't home. She walked up the stone sidewalk and called out several times, but no one answered. The lake was over to her right; she could sense it. A pleasing smell of freshwater and earth.

She laid the sack of beer and root beer down on a table carved out of a tree stump; then she went up and knocked on the front door. After waiting several moments, she knocked again and called out his name. Finally, she walked around to the side of the house facing the lake. It looked a lot nicer than what she had expected, with an outdoor kitchen against the wall, a large stove with a log still glowing. To top it off, he had the largest gas grill Ilka had ever seen. And the wooden sculptures, some abstract, others animals, meticulously carved so even the slightest details were visible. Impressive! She walked over and admired the works.

"Sorry." Artie appeared around the corner, out of breath. "Must have left my phone in the car. You been calling a long time?"

He wore a heavy sweater, and the tails of his Hawaiian shirt hung down in front. Judging from his rubber boots, he'd been down at the lake. He carried a rolled-up fishing net under his arm, with a bag over his shoulder. He threw everything on the ground beside the end of the house.

"Where are we going?" He walked over and unlocked his door. Then he noticed the beer Ilka had laid on the table. "What's going on? Are we celebrating something?"

She shook her head and explained that she'd just visited Mary Ann and her daughters.

"Say no more!" He lifted his palm up; then he fished a cigarette out of his shirt pocket underneath the sweater. "They weren't all that friendly, am I right?"

She nodded. That was one way to put it.

"I guess I've already explained they're not really interested in the business. Truth is, I don't think I ever saw the girls with their dad at work. Mary Ann was there a few times, but only to pick him up when they were going somewhere. That was before the accident, of course; she doesn't drive anymore. But the girls. I always got the feeling they were ashamed of what Paul did for a living. It wasn't dignified enough for them."

While he spoke, Ilka walked over to him, put her arms around him, and leaned down to kiss him. Her lips were nearly touching his before he stopped talking. He tasted of lake water and something sweet he'd eaten. Hard candy, she guessed.

He was startled. "Are you sure about this?" he murmured, but he allowed himself to be backed up and led into the house. With her hand on his chest, she tried to steer him around even though she'd never been inside his house. She backed him through the kitchen with big windows facing the lake, then through the living room. She sensed more than noticed the sofa and dining room table. The small TV on a box in the corner, low priority. Paintings on the wall, antlers. She felt his breath against her neck as her heart hammered away. And she felt the freedom to loosen the knot of anger that had built up since she'd left Mary Ann's big white house.

Artie managed to open the door at the end of the living room. "Are we sure this is a good idea?" he said, his words streaming directly into her mouth.

Ilka kissed him harder and began unbuckling his pants with one hand, her other hand still around his neck. That seemed to wake him up. He ripped his sweater off and helped her loosen his belt.

She sat down on the bed and pulled him down to her. Then she noticed he was still wearing his rubber boots. Her greedy hands got rid of the Hawaiian shirt in short order, and they both smiled when Artie stood up and took his pants and boots off. The bun of hair on top of his head was coming undone; it looked like something exploding. Ilka didn't bother taking off the white shirt she'd been wearing since the funeral service. Her father's shirt. Though that detail was the last thing on her mind at that moment. She stared as Artie pulled his boxers off and fell back onto the bed, muttering, "Jesus Christ!"

He spoke directly into her ear, asked if Danish girls usually took whatever they needed, whenever they felt like it.

She leaned over and pulled her jeans off as she assured him that it was completely normal, that there was nothing more to it than that.

He could have thrown her out. He could have invited her for a drink afterward. Or asked why the hell she hadn't at least called before showing up. But Artie Sorvino simply followed her out onto the front porch after they'd taken a quick shower and wrapped themselves up in thick blankets he pulled out of a reed basket in the hallway. Ilka handed him a can of beer and opened one of her root beers; he tossed a few cushions on the porch chairs and grabbed the lighter in the kitchen.

The sun had set; the darkness hid Lake Michigan. The only part of the lake that reached them was the roar of the waves rolling in over the rocky shore. And the smell.

She sensed him looking at her. Sensed that he was unsure what she expected from him. If it was affection she wanted.

Ilka pointed to a chair on the other side of the table, hoping it was enough to make him understand that this wasn't anything more than what they'd already done.

"What is it about that family?" she asked, after they sat down. "It's like they don't want to have anything to do with my father. Has it always been like that?"

She pulled the blanket tighter around her, though she enjoyed being outside this late.

Artie lit a cigarette and pushed the pack over to her, but she let it lie. He shook his head. "That's not how I see them, but you're right that Paul kept his private life and the business separate. Very separate. It wasn't something I thought about so much. That's just how it was."

He hesitated a moment. "A lot of people have problems with this business. Several very nice female acquaintances jumped ship on me when I told them what I did for a living. It's almost like people think that death disappears if you ignore it. Or that you can keep it at a distance by not talking about it."

"But the business must have been a big part of his life."

He nodded. "I think they had an agreement. He wouldn't bring the dead home into his private life. And he kept his private life away from the dead. That's how I always saw it. And it probably wasn't a bad way to do it. A business like ours can dominate your life."

Ilka set her bottle down and pulled her legs up.

"You might not want to hear this, but your dad was very caring toward Mary Ann and the girls. I thought he overprotected them, but I never told him that. If anyone so much as mentioned something like that, he'd turn around and walk off."

She stared into the flame of the small square electric candle in the lantern. It flickered mechanically, as if an invisible wind blew inside the glass and shook the wick. She didn't want to hear any more. It might have been naïve of her to expect them to greet her with open arms. If they'd felt that way, they would already have visited her. She thought about Amber, who clearly hadn't told the others she had sat for hours on the bench in front of her father's business. Maybe she had hoped Ilka would invite her in or take her up to her father's room, which still held so much of him.

Artie interrupted her thoughts. "That name of yours—is that a usual name in Denmark?" He opened another beer.

Ilka shook her head. "I'd be surprised if there is one other person so unlucky. My father named me for the horse that won the Derby in 1947. Ilka Nichols only won once. It was the year my grandfather took my father to the track for the first time. He talked my mother into giving me this idiotic name because he said it was the symbol of a winner and...how do you say, someone not like other people. Someone who fought and did okay against the odds. But the name has been more like a curse, when I think about what the racetrack meant for my father's life."

She had the feeling Artie was about to protest but then changed his mind. They sat for a while in silence.

"He couldn't have been more wrong." Ilka spoke quietly as she pulled the blanket around her legs. "I've never really fought for anything. I can't remember ever deciding to point myself in one direction. My life has been all these coincidences. My high school grades were good enough to get me whatever education I wanted. I took a year off after high school, and then I started law school, but after six months I found out I had cancer; they took out my womb and ovaries. The tumor was...bad; I didn't have a choice.

"I was sick for a long time; then when they finally said I was okay I celebrated by putting on my backpack and traveling. First stop Argentina. I worked with cattle; then I went to Australia. I was gone for a year and a half, and when I got home my mother had moved in with another woman. That surprised me, but it was good for her. Then I met Erik, so instead of going back to law school I started working for him. As a school photographer, can you believe that!"

Ilka took a drink of root beer. She'd been aware for a while that she was running off at the mouth, but she didn't care. She needed to talk, and he was a good listener. He opened another beer.

"Maybe it's true that everyone has a soul mate. Erik was mine. After losing my father, it felt like I finally came home. He was fifteen years older than me, and I thought we'd be together forever. I took over his business when he died. I never took any photography courses, but he taught me what I needed to know. And I'm happy."

She folded her hands. That last sentence sounded forced to her, but she meant it. She would never have chosen to be a school photographer, but now there wasn't anything else she would rather do.

"And now it's happened again," Artie said. "Now circumstances have made you a funeral home director."

Again, Ilka felt his eyes on her. She shook her head, though she wasn't sure he could see. "No. I could have chosen to stay home; I could have let my lawyer handle everything. I told my mother I had to be here personally, though it wasn't true. I'd needed to meet my father. Even though he wasn't around anymore, this was my last chance to get closer to him. Missing him has been way too big a part of my life. Maybe I didn't even know how much. And really, it's not that he wasn't around when I grew up; it's more that I never understood why he left."

Artie wouldn't let it go. "But now you *are* a director."

"Like hell I am. I'm just a daughter trying to sell her father's business so his reputation won't be damaged too much." She snorted. "All right, that's not exactly true. It's probably more that I'm trying to pick up the pieces of a life I never really understood."

Her phone rang several times before Artie suggested she answer.

"Aren't you asleep?" Ilka said when she heard her mother's voice. "Is something wrong?"

"What's going on over there? I have a bad feeling about this. I can't sleep. I'm worried."

"That's so nice of you, Mom." Instead of being annoyed, she suddenly felt warm inside. Her mother had been through a hell of a lot, too, when it came to Paul Jensen. "Everything's fine. I just need to take care of the last details before I can come home. And I would be very grateful if you'll do the jobs for me. Of course I'll pay you."

"Come on! Money doesn't matter; you know that, dear. I just don't like you being over there. I can feel it in my bones, all this worry, and I don't like it."

"Mom, really, there's nothing wrong. Everything's just taking longer than I expected. That happens a lot with estates." Ilka didn't mention that she was the one who'd messed up a transfer agreement at the last moment. "I have to know what's going on with the business before I can put it up for sale. By the way, I met my half sisters today," she added, hoping the abrupt change of subject would distract her mother. "It doesn't look like we're going to be great friends, but both Leslie and Amber have inherited Dad's height, and the youngest one has the same stringy Jensen hair. But honestly, it doesn't look all that good on her." As if it looked good on anyone! Ilka laughed to lighten the mood.

"Were they nice to you? What did they say?"

"Mom, I have to run—there's someone at the door. I'll call you tomorrow." She hung up, hoping her mother didn't hear her voice starting to thicken. She closed her eyes and sat for a moment, tried to swallow the lump in her throat.

"Are you okay?" Artie asked as she stuffed her phone back into her pocket.

"I'd better get back. Are you coming in tomorrow? McKenna's daughter is coming to view her father."

Ilka didn't know what Sundays were like in the funeral home business. Many people were protective of their days off, but she had the feeling Artie wasn't that way.

"See you tomorrow," he said, sitting expectantly as she stood up and grabbed her sweater off the chair. He had another think coming if he thought she was going to kiss him! She nodded shortly before walking to the car.

The drive home was strange. She felt loose after sleeping with Artie, sad after talking to her mother, and tense after meeting her father's new family. But most of all unsure of how things would turn out.

She drove into the parking lot and noticed a light in one of Sister Eileen's windows, while the rest of the funeral home was dark. She parked and got out. Stood for a moment, enjoying the mild late summer evening, though she still felt bad about being so short with her mother.

Why the hell did you even come here? she thought, scolding herself as she walked up the steps. She decided to spend Sunday going through the last drawers and boxes in her father's room. She would send the whole mess to Denmark by FedEx, so her mother could see what he had left behind.

On the way up, the thought struck Ilka that it might help her mother stifle some of her anger if she knew what had happened back then. Even though she had found Hanne and had gotten on with her life, it was obvious to everyone that being abandoned still plagued her.

She walked in, threw her bag on the floor, and turned the desk lamp on. Suddenly she heard breathing and something moving on the bed, and she whirled around.

Amber sat cross-legged on the bed; she hadn't even bothered to take her boots off. She leaned lazily up against the wall. Nothing about her hinted at how long she'd been waiting for Ilka to come back.

"Hi," Ilka said. She held on to the back of her father's chair, which she had grabbed in shock a moment before. Now she tried to act nonchalant, though her heart was in her throat.

"Don't come by the house again," her half sister said. Slowly she leaned forward and slid her legs off the side of the bed. "It's not good for Mom. It's not good for anything."

"How did you get in?" Ilka tried to calm her heartbeat; her temples were pounding like shutters in a hurricane.

"Dad gave me a key several years ago."

Ilka heard the provocation in her voice; she wanted to show she could come and go as she pleased. Apparently without Artie and Sister Eileen noticing. But why had she sat out on the bench when she could come inside?

Ilka walked over to the bed. She was so frightened, so angry, that she had to fold her arms to keep from hitting her youngest half sister. "What is it I've done to all of you? If it's about this"—she held her arms out—"you can have it; I didn't ask for it, this business. Really, I'd rather go back to Denmark. You're more than welcome to take over, right now. In fact, I think it's totally unfair that I'm the one who has to put things right, to get out of this horrible situation our father put his employees in. And none of you even come by and offer to help. What's wrong with all of you? Don't you know how much money this place owes? What kind of daughters are you?"

Amber was standing now, and for a moment they stood face-to-face. But she shrugged. "I'm sorry it has to be this way."

Ilka listened to her footsteps fade down the stairs; then she threw herself on the bed.

What was it with these people? It was one thing if they didn't care for her, didn't accept their father having had a family before them. That she could handle. But not caring about what had been his daily life—that simply wasn't normal. It was almost as if they were afraid of something.

26

"Wake up! You've got to come downstairs," Artie said as he banged on the door.

Ilka lay still for a moment with her eyes closed. Fragments of his face close-up, the sense of freedom she had felt after their quickie, kept his voice and the sunlight through the curtains at a distance. She thought about Amber, about her father, everything she didn't know about him. She had sat up half the night, going through the storage boxes piled up against the wall. Racetrack results and old programs, with notes written in ornate script in the margins. Winning tickets and receipts from losses that had been added to expenses. There were lots of those.

She had found several pictures in the bottom of one of the boxes. Photos of her father with his parents, her grandparents. She had seen them only sporadically after he left, and finally not at all. Both had died before she was twenty.

In several of the old photos, her father was with boys Ilka didn't recognize. Cousins, maybe? One box held old clippings from newspapers, again mostly having to do with racing. Which driver had switched stables. Who had new sponsors; trainers moving around. Some of them in a plastic folder were about a Danish trotter manager brought in to Maywood Park racetrack, Melrose Park, Illinois, in 1982. In the article, the manager was proclaimed to be one of Scandinavia's most promising, with extensive experience and several Derby victories by drivers he represented under his belt. Ilka wondered about that. Her father had certainly not understated his accomplishments.

Her father. She had recognized him immediately from the grainy photo. Farther down in the article, she read that Paul Jensen was co-owner of the all-star team, that he had chipped in three hundred thousand dollars, the same as the other investors, but he was the only one involved in managing the stable. He looked exactly the way she remembered him: tall, with a tweed cap pulled down over his forehead. He smiled for the camera. A man of the world.

So. Her father had gotten a job over here. But three hundred thousand dollars! She couldn't imagine where he'd gotten hold of that kind of money, with the funeral home in the red when he left Denmark. He did have his winnings, but they didn't even come close to that amount. Her stomach sank.

Artie knocked again. "Shelby's here. It sounds like all hell is about to break loose. You've got to come down and talk to her."

Ilka reached for her watch; it was almost eleven. Quickly she swung her legs over the edge of the bed. "What's breaking loose?" She wrapped her father's striped robe around her and stumbled over to open the door.

"It's best to let her tell about it," he said, his voice serious. "She's just come from the police station."

Not a word about what had happened yesterday. Nothing in his expression, either. That was fine with her. "Give me two minutes."

She shut the door and pulled her clothes on. Before rushing down, she hurriedly gathered up the clippings spread out over the floor and tossed them back in the box. She was getting used to people invading the room whenever they felt like it, but she didn't want anyone to see she'd been delving into her father's life.

Coffee! The smell hit her as she stepped into the arrangement room, and her stomach cramped from hunger. Shelby stood at the window, her back to the door, gazing out at the parking lot. She looked so tense that Ilka hesitated a moment before walking over and putting her arm around the woman's shoulder. "What's the matter?"

She turned to Ilka. She'd been sobbing, and her face was pale, on the edge of collapse. "It was Phyllis Oldham who paid my son," she whispered. "She gave him twenty thousand dollars to leave town, even though she knew he didn't kill Ashley Simpson."

The words came out of her mouth, but it was as if someone else were speaking them. Her expression was frozen.

Ilka held her close before leading her carefully over to an easy chair and pouring her a cup of coffee.

"The police came this morning and asked me to follow them to the station. They felt I had the right to know after everything we went through back then. The young officer asked if I had someone who could take me down there, but I don't. I thought about you and Artie, but it's Sunday, and I didn't want to bother you."

"You can call us, anytime," Ilka said. "But what happened?"

She sat as stiff as a board, her eyes unfocused as she spoke. "Last night Phyllis Oldham came to the police station after most of the policemen had gone home. She admitted she'd pressured Mike to take the blame, but he wouldn't do it. So instead she offered him money to leave town, to make it look like he did. I knew it wasn't him."

Her hands were clenched. "There wasn't any evidence, either. She's a witch, and this is only happening because both her sons have been arrested. If it hadn't been for them, she'd never have confessed."

Ilka poured herself a cup of coffee and grabbed a few small cookies from the bowl before leaning back in her chair. She was determined to let Shelby talk, even though she couldn't make sense of the woman's story.

"It's terrible you can get away with something like that, just because you have money," she wailed, her voice firmer now that she was worked up. "They destroyed my son's life. Our lives. And then when he comes home after so many years because his sister is dying, they kill him!"

Her pale cheeks reddened; tears streaked from her eyes.

Ilka reached across the table and held her arm, her fingers gently stroking the sleeve of her green blouse, buttoned at the wrist. "Who was Mike supposed to take the blame for?" she asked, her voice low. "Why did Phyllis Oldham try to make it look like it was your son?"

After a moment, Shelby looked up. "Because her husband killed Ashley." Her voice was so cold that Ilka pulled her hand back. "Phyllis told the police she saw him walking down from the fisherman's cabin when Ashley was killed."

Ilka pushed the box of Kleenex over to her and waited as she pulled a few out. She blew her nose and dried her eyes; then she cleared her throat. "Phyllis told the police it was a coincidence she saw him on the path from the cabin. She'd wondered about it; it's not a place he normally went to. Later, when she heard about Ashley, she put two and two together. But she didn't say anything."

"And now finally she tells this to the police?"

Shelby nodded and pursed her lips but quickly got hold of herself again. "She's only doing it because she hopes to get her sons out of jail. By sacrificing her dead husband."

"And what do the police say about this coming out now?"

"Phyllis says she kept quiet because of her children, the funeral home business, and the family reputation. She made her choice, to be the silent wife. She did nothing. Except she likely drove him to his death, little by little."

"What do you mean?"

"Douglas Oldham hung himself in the embalming room." She paused for a moment to let her rage and despair die down. "The oldest son found him. I think the whole town knew he'd taken the easy way out. The story was that he suddenly felt sick and lost consciousness because of the dangerous chemicals. But everybody talked about a rope. It was rough on the sons."

"What about the daughter?" Ilka asked.

"Carlotta has always been a mama's girl, but of course it affected her too. After his death, it seemed like the boys sort of dropped out, and it wasn't long before they left to go to school. They didn't come back until they were grown and ready to enter the business."

"So all these years your son was gone, Phyllis Oldham knew her husband killed the young girl?"

"Yes." Shelby stared at the dark mahogany table and nodded, as if she was slowly becoming aware of the extent of the tragedy.

"Do the police say the Oldham sons are responsible for killing Mike?"

After a few moments, the woman shook her head. "But they don't need to. Isn't it obvious?"

Maybe, Ilka thought. *If they thought he had come back to expose the family...*

Her hunger was gone, replaced by an emptiness inside her. She thought about all the years the secret had hung around Racine like a dark cloud, casting its cold shadow, particularly on Mike's mother and sister.

Shelby stood up. A handful of balled-up Kleenex lay on the chair. While buttoning her coat, she turned to Ilka. "Phyllis claims she didn't know anything about Howard falling in love with the girl. Just like she didn't know her brother-in-law broke into your garage and desecrated my son's body."

She looked away. "What kind of people are they?"

She shook her head and left the room.

So. A young girl had turned the heads of two grown men. *Nothing new there*, Ilka thought.

Sister Eileen appeared in the doorway. "She'll be here in twenty minutes," she announced, adding that Ilka might want to change into something more respectable before Ed McKenna's daughter showed up to view her father.

The nun was right. She didn't look like someone who should be meeting a grieving daughter. But first, she needed some clarity about finding her father's clothes in the Dumpster. The whole thing was confusing, and Ilka just couldn't let it go.

"I keep meaning to ask you," Ilka started, turning to Sister Eileen. "Why were my father's things thrown into the Dumpster?"

A look of sheer surprise crossed over the nun's face as she stared, with seeming bewilderment, into Ilka's eyes. "What are you talking about?"

"I know; it was so strange. I saw them in there and couldn't figure out why you would have thrown them away."

"I most certainly didn't," Sister Eileen said assertively. "You must be mistaken. I would never have done that. Never. Oh my goodness, no."

It was all so odd, but Ilka didn't want to cause any more upset or spark an argument. Apologizing for the mistake, she excused herself to change into something more appropriate, and headed upstairs.

Up in the room, still shaking her head, Ilka grabbed her father's black suit. Her uniform, she thought. Once again she felt homesick for her own bathroom and bathtub, her clothes, which might not have been the most fashionable, but at least they hadn't been bought for a man in his seventies.

27

"Please, have a seat." At the doorway, Ilka gestured discreetly toward the oval table in the arrangement room. Lisa McKenna entered without a word, leaving in her wake a strong scent of lavender, which Ilka followed.

"This won't take long," Lisa said, her voice deep, almost masculine. That surprised Ilka; Ed McKenna's daughter was light in complexion and thin, her hair set up loosely in a very feminine look. "We haven't really seen much of each other the past several years."

"Of course," Ilka replied quickly. She wished Artie was there, but she knew he was busy reconstructing Mike Gilbert's face. He had told her what to focus on: coffee, kringle, and Kleenex. Sister Eileen would bring everything in, he'd said. And then just talk to her, or rather, let her talk. Anything she wanted to talk about. "And call me if she wants to know what it takes to prepare her father for transportation by air."

Ilka had asked if they should also show the dog. "Only if she asks," he'd said.

Ed McKenna was prepared for viewing, and he lay in the front part of the chapel, which had been curtained off so the room didn't seem so big. The two large altar candles, one on each side of the coffin, were lit. For a moment, Ilka considered mentioning that the dog had licked her father's cheek off before lying down to die beside him, but Artie had done a fantastic job of reconstruction, and she probably wouldn't even notice that part of his face was wax now. There wasn't any reason to let her in on this macabre detail.

"Coffee?" Ilka kept her voice down, thinking it would help the woman feel at home, cared for.

"No, thanks, but I'd like to use your bathroom before we go in."

The woman's voice surprised her again. "Of course. This way." She pointed and led her out into the front hall.

The daughter's hair was graying, and a fine net of wrinkles softened her face. In her fifties, Ilka guessed.

"I couldn't stand him," Lisa McKenna said when she returned from the bathroom. "If it was up to me, you could pour his ashes in a can and take it to the dump."

Ilka froze; so much for her plan of action. It looked like they wouldn't be needing the Kleenex.

"He was an egotistical, self-centered asshole. But for some strange reason my children want him to be brought home and buried in our cemetery."

Sister Eileen stood in the doorway. She must have heard what the daughter had just said, and Ilka was sure she spotted a glint in the nun's eye after the outburst that left the room silent. The daughter's anger was deep, savage; her attractive face had morphed into a grimace as she spat the words out.

Ilka had no idea what to say, but fortunately Artie stepped into the room and saved her. He wore a black coat with a white shirt attached over his Hawaiian shirt, though part of the turquoise collar stuck out at his neck.

Still unable to speak, Ilka walked over to the section of the chapel being used as a reposing room and opened the door. "If you want to see him, it's this way."

The daughter glanced at her and, seemingly in spite of herself, walked over to the coffin.

"If you need to be alone, you can just come out whenever you're ready. Then we can take care of the practical details about transporting him."

Ilka was about to close the door, but the daughter said, "No, that's fine. I'll come with you now." She turned on her heel and followed Ilka out of the room. "What happened to Toodie?"

"The dog?"

The daughter nodded.

"It's being kept cold," Ilka said. "We didn't want to do anything before you arrived."

"May I see her?" The anger on her face was gone.

Artie stepped forward and said of course. If she could wait just a minute, he would bring the dog in.

"My father didn't care about us. About me or the kids. He was never there when we needed him. The past twenty years, we've only seen him the few times I came from Albany to beg for help. I've been alone with the kids since they were small, since their father . . . well. And Mom died before the kids were born."

She looked as if she'd made up her mind not to cry. "I gave him Toodie, and he loved her. I thought the company might mellow him out. Thought maybe we could have a connection that way. But he just didn't want anything to do with us. Maybe you think he was lonesome, but I can assure you, he chose to be lonesome. Nobody should feel sorry for him."

Artie came in one of the side doors, pushing a small cart in front of him. He looked like a hotel worker delivering room service. A white sheet covered a mound on the cart.

"Just a second." Lisa McKenna took a moment to gather herself. She looked like Ilka had expected she would when she went in to view her father. "Okay, I'm ready."

Artie lifted the sheet, and he and Ilka stepped back. Ilka looked questioningly at him.

"You poor little thing, were you all alone?" She spoke to the dog as if it still were alive. "Did she die of starvation?"

Ilka wasn't expecting that question. She looked at Artie, who was rocking on his heels. "I'm afraid so, yes," she said.

While the daughter continued talking to Toodie, Ilka couldn't help glancing at the coffin where Ed McKenna lay; he should be the one she was grieving over.

"I don't know what it would cost to have the dog embalmed," she said, after they returned to the arrangement room and coffee. "But my father had plenty of money, so I'm bringing her home and burying her in the yard."

After saying good-bye, Ilka stood in the reception area and watched her leave. In a way, she could relate. The difference was that Lisa McKenna had known where her father was. But the rejection must have felt the same.

28

The next morning, coffee, a soft-boiled egg, slices of bread, and a newspaper were lined up on the table in front of Ilka. A large photo of a young Mike Gilbert was plastered on the front page of the paper. The photo bore no resemblance to the ruined face Artie had spent all Sunday afternoon and evening on, shaping it to match the photo his mother had brought. By the time Ilka said good night and went up to her room, the face had been transformed from a bloody mass of broken bones and swelling into a sleeping man with slightly too prominent eyebrows and lips painted on, but it was still far from the big, smiling, happy teenager on the front page.

Ilka guessed it was a school photo. She would have arranged it similarly, but unlike the smiles of many of the students she had photographed over the years, Mike's smile reached all the way up into his eyes. It wasn't just a reaction to the photographer saying, "Smi-i-ile!"

The photo had probably been used often following Ashley's death. In the accompanying article, all the details of Mike's death were described, at least as well as the journalist could with the few facts that were known. Nobody had been found who had seen Mike Gilbert back in town; that was clear. No one had any idea how long he'd been hanging around before being murdered. Judging from the reactions of the people on the street interviewed by the journalist, most were surprised that Mike would dare show his face in town again. The owner of the tobacco shop even believed that Mike Gilbert had tempted fate by returning to Racine. The short statements were accompanied by small head shots to prove the journalist had done some leg work before writing the article.

The long and short of it was that apparently no one saw him before he was killed. Which was why no one knew when he'd returned. The only new information in the article came from a former pathologist, who colorfully described how little it took to crush a skull, with the right weapon.

His guess was that Mike had been murdered with a baseball bat. "Incredible," Ilka muttered to herself. Then she skimmed a description of Ashley Simpson's death. The journalist had found an old school friend and asked her what she remembered from back then. The woman, who obviously hadn't been taking good care of herself, was photographed behind the warehouses where Mike's body had been found. She stood with folded arms and stared grumpily into the camera. In the article, she claimed Mike Gilbert had been cursed.

"Everyone around him dies," she was quoted as saying. Ashley, himself, and now his sister was dying, too.

"Idiot!" In her irritation, Ilka spilled coffee on the newspaper. Beside the article was a small box containing a short statement from the police. Two people detained for questioning that weekend had been released.

Poor Shelby, Ilka thought, sad and tired now as she glanced over the local announcements and sports section.

Soft rain fell from the gray Monday morning sky, streaking the window and blocking the sunlight. But Ilka enjoyed the peace and quiet. For the first time since she'd been in Racine, her morning hadn't been disrupted, no one banging on her door to rouse her out of bed; that alone was enough to loosen her shoulders up, relieve her tension. She'd planned on spending the day going through her father's business papers. Yesterday she had found a cabinet filled with files, but it had seemed far too much to tackle. She'd also called her mother and explained why she had to stay in Racine. Everything was up in the air—finances, creditors. No one knew much about the orders that had come in. Or how many prepaid funerals the funeral home had. She'd realized these things made up the business's actual worth.

"I've got to take care of this. You know yourself how much work it takes to turn around a funeral home in debt."

The moment she said it, she knew how rotten it sounded to bring her mother's struggles into this. But at least it would help her mother understand why everything was taking so long. Ilka had begged her to take care of the photo shoots until she could find a solution. She still hoped Niels from North Sealand Photography could take the jobs. If he'd ever answer her.

Her confrontations with the suppliers who had bailed out

on Jensen Funeral Home had pissed her off. It was okay for people to drop a customer when they got tired of unpaid bills. But she wasn't going to stand for suppliers not giving her a chance to right the ship. And she wouldn't accept that the problems could have been avoided if Sister Eileen had made the calls. They were damn well going to do business with her! She stood up to answer the phone out in the reception area.

"We've booked a business meeting today at twelve thirty," said a man whose name Ilka didn't catch. "Two consultants will be there, and the meeting will last one hour, so please bring along the books for the last two years."

She set her coffee down. The carefree morning mood had evaporated the second she heard his brusque voice. At first, she wasn't sure that Artie had been able to hold the IRS off.

"Excuse me, who are you again?"

"We spoke last week. We informed you of our interest in taking over Jensen Funeral Home. And now I understand there are no longer any other transfer agreements standing in the way. We're prepared to reach an agreement quickly to take control of your family's business."

Ilka had pulled Sister Eileen's chair out and was sitting on its arm. She remembered the call, but back then the voice had been ingratiating and as smooth as melted chocolate. Now he sounded ice-cold and arrogant. "There is no 'your family.' It's 'my' business, and I've decided to run it myself, so I'm not interested in your proposal. Jensen Funeral Home is not for sale. Thank you anyway."

She was shaken when she hung up. Not so much because the call had sounded more like a demand than a polite business inquiry, but because something in the man's tone made her skin crawl.

Sitting briefly in thought, she shook her head. If she'd had any doubts about the wisdom of taking up the challenge and righting the ship, they were gone now. The decision had been made.

Something else stirred underneath her anger about the call. Sitting there at Sister Eileen's desk, she realized she'd just made the first clear decision of her career. It may have been spur of the moment; it was definitely a rash decision. And it was stubbornness, not ambition, that had motivated her to become a funeral home director. But she didn't give a damn, because she was going to show them.

The phone on the nun's desk rang again. Ilka stood up to return to her breakfast; if it was that man again, he would have to wait until the sister was back. But then she changed her mind and picked up. "This funeral home is not for sale, and it will not in the future be for sale either. And any business meeting has to be approved by me."

"Excuse me," a woman said warily. "Is this Ilka Jensen? I was referred to this number when I called her cell phone."

"Yes, this is Ilka."

The woman began speaking in Danish. "I'm calling from Linde School in Virum. We're very dissatisfied with the photographer you sent. It's disgraceful that the photographs are taking so long."

Ilka was startled. She'd never worked for that school before, and she had the feeling the school secretary was just warming up.

"The woman you sent only managed to get through two classes today. I've never seen anything like it. You can't expect students to have the patience to be steered around so much. This isn't about details and shadows; you should know that. We're talking about school photos here. And they missed far too many classes!"

Ilka tried to get a word in, but the woman ignored her. "This is about giving students a memory of their time in school, of their schoolmates throughout the years. We're not paying for all the extra time being used. Choosing you was obviously a mistake. And it's going to be difficult to give you a good review on Trustpilot."

Ilka finally broke in. "Yes, I would say it was a mistake that I sent our prize-winning portrait photographer out to you. But I've heard that for years, parents with children attending your school have been complaining that the individual photos were taken like the students were on an assembly line. If your school administration doesn't appreciate higher-quality work, you shouldn't be using us. You should go back to the standard you're used to. I'm afraid we can't offer that." She could almost hear Erik cackling up on his cloud. "I think we should stop here. We don't serve clients who prefer discount work."

"But, you're not...you're not finished."

"No. It seems you weren't well enough prepared. I suggest you contact another school photographer. I will send out photo orders only to those students we photographed. Have a good day." She hung up.

Okay. One less client to hand over to North Sealand Photography. Her mother of course would want to take good pictures of every single child. She should have realized that.

She could see it now: her conscientious mother using far too much time in placing the students properly, getting the light just right, adjusting the height of the chair so everything would be perfect.

She smiled. What a mess.

29

"Shall I order the zinc coffin for Ed McKenna, or will you?" Sister Eileen asked. She looked disapprovingly at Ilka, who was sitting in her chair.

The white band of her veil sat tight around her forehead, hiding the short dark hair Ilka had noticed the night she roused the nun out of bed to help with Mike. She stood erect, with a closed, dismissive look of professionalism—*Get out*, it seemed to be saying to Ilka.

"We also need to make reservations on the plane for the coffin. The dog will need its own zinc coffin. It will be embalmed this morning. I can imagine it would fit in a child's coffin."

Ilka nodded. If this was how it was going to be between the two of them, then okay. She'd given up on trying to follow the shifts between the warmhearted sister who brought tea and cookies and the person in front of her now, the one trying to freeze Ilka out. But if Sister Eileen wasn't going to cooperate and accept she had a new boss, she'd have to go. Ilka didn't have the same devotion to nuns as her father.

"What about putting the dog into the coffin along with him? That way we'd save one coffin."

Stone-faced, the sister said, "You'll have to talk to Artie about that." She laid a pile of envelopes on the desk. "Bills."

Ilka looked them over; she should start handling the mail, if she was ever going to have a clear understanding of their situation.

Artie stepped into the reception area. "Let Sister Eileen order the zinc coffin so we don't risk having him stranded here."

Ilka had the feeling he'd been standing out in the hall, eavesdropping on them. And that the sister knew he was listening.

His long hair was now gathered in a bun on his neck, and the gaudy red shirt with the palms and surfers hung outside his pants. He walked over and set his glass of Red Bull and coffee on the desk; suddenly Ilka felt trapped between the two people who knew the daily routines of the funeral home and her own ignorance. Again, she sensed they had a secret agenda, while pretending to be going down with the ship.

She went into the arrangement room, where her breakfast lay untouched. Her coffee was cold. Artie appeared in the doorway after she sat down.

"What about the dog?" she asked. Without looking at him, she started in on her egg. "Can't we put it in his coffin?"

"Ed McKenna wasn't very tall; let's see if there's room for it at the foot end." He asked if she'd like fresh coffee, but he'd already picked up her cup and walked out to fill it. When he returned, he set a bag from the bakery in front of her.

Ilka surrendered and pushed her cold egg aside. She stuck her hand down in the sugary, oily brown paper, brought out a warm glazed doughnut, and laid it on her plate as she told him about the call from the funeral home chain.

"Damn!" Artie said. "Guess they didn't get the message. I thought I'd made myself clear yesterday."

"Yesterday?"

"Yeah, they called me and wanted to set up a meeting. I told them we weren't interested."

"And then they call again after that? Why didn't you say something? So I could have been ready for them."

"I didn't think they'd be so stubborn. American Funeral Group is always on the lookout for acquisitions. What did you tell them?"

"They definitely heard about the deal with Golden Slumbers failing, but I told them Jensen Funeral Home wasn't for sale, so there was no reason for a meeting. I think we three should sit down sometime today so I can tell you about my plans for the funeral home. When is a good time for you?"

Artie had been leaning up against the doorframe, his coffee in one hand and a doughnut in the other. Now he laid everything down and fished out a cigarette, which he lit on the way out the back door. "I'm going to start embalming Mike Gilbert now," he said over his shoulder. "Then I'm driving Mrs. Norton to the crematorium. But I'll have time when I get back."

Clearly he wasn't happy about it being *her* plans, not *their* plans. She walked back into the reception area and asked Sister Eileen if they could all meet that afternoon.

The sister nodded, friendly now, as if the little episode they'd just gone through had never happened. "I have an errand to do in town around noon. I should be back around two."

Ilka thanked her, but before she could leave, the nun added, "Would you please consider how much we can give to the fall church bazaar next month? Your father was known to be very generous with donations."

Ilka squelched her anger and studied Sister Eileen for a moment, wondering if she even realized that the business was almost completely underwater, gasping for air, that she should count herself lucky if she ended up keeping her job and room. Then Ilka reminded herself that even factoring in the generous donations, the sister probably was the least drain on the budget, given that she wasn't paid for her work. And besides, tongues in the community would start wagging if they were less generous to the church. Not a good signal to send if they wanted to give the impression that the business was stable and under control.

"We'll give the same as last year," Ilka decided, even though there wasn't much left in her private accounts. She asked how the sister wanted the money to be donated.

"Cash would be best. Two thousand dollars. It will be greatly appreciated. Shall I order the zinc coffin?"

Ilka was sitting at her father's desk with the mail when Artie knocked on the doorframe. "You want to come by for a beer tonight?"

Beer was the last thing he was interested in; she could

hear that. She shook her head as she sorted out the advertisements and threw them in the wastebasket. He stared at her for a moment, then nodded and walked out.

It didn't take her long to go through the letters. She opened a yellow envelope from the local racetrack and pulled out a bill. It was time to renew her father's weekly racetrack ticket. Occasionally back home she bought a ticket herself; once she had even had a subscription. She could handle that if she stayed away from the racetrack and the smell of horses, the excitement as they neared the finish line. Ilka was about to wad the renewal up, but instead she stuck it in her pocket. She was almost finished going through the bills when Artie showed up in the doorway again. "You have a visitor," he said, his voice muffled by his mask. He was wearing his white coat, and he smelled of formaldehyde.

"If it's that man who wants to hold the business meeting, tell him no, he'll just have to leave."

"It's not him. It's some guy who wants to talk to you. You want me to send him in?"

She eyed him for a moment, unused to him playing the secretary and unsure who wanted to see her. But she nodded, and a moment later the guy from the bar appeared at the door. She ignored Artie's look. "Thanks," she said, and she gestured for him to leave.

"Hi," Larry said, a bit hesitantly. He glanced over his shoulder when Artie left. "You have a moment?"

"Not really," Ilka said, quickly covering up how flustered she was by his suddenly stopping by. Before she could find a way to get rid of him, he was standing by the desk.

"I was just thinking that maybe you'd like to go out to eat some evening? Or for a drink?"

Ilka was standing behind her chair now, as if that would stop Larry from reaching her. The rain had plastered his dark hair to his skull, and his blue Windbreaker clung to his chest, but there was a sparkle in his eye, something she couldn't totally resist. She had to stop herself. Immediately. That was the whole idea with casual relationships.

"I'm sorry." She started for the door to follow him out. "I'm just way too busy."

She could hear how lame that sounded, and she was being mean, too. But damn it, it was a one-night stand, with no obligations, nothing that committed her to having seconds.

He followed her reluctantly. "Can I call you?"

She shook her head. Out in the hallway she noticed Artie ducking back into the preparation room. Presumably he had been at the door, listening.

"How did you find me?" she asked as she opened the door to the parking lot.

"People are talking about you." She was relieved he didn't say anything about her rejection. "There aren't that many supertall foreign Viking women in town right now. And not so many of them who came to take over a funeral home."

She smiled at him. So, people in town knew who she was and what she was doing here.

The door to the preparation room was closed, and Ilka assumed Artie was at work inside. Out in the foyer, Sister Eileen was stuffing brochures in the holders beside the glass case displaying charms. The brochures contained information about the funeral home's services and gave the dates for the next senior citizen fair, where Jensen Funeral Home would be explaining about their offers and the advantages of making payments on a preordered funeral. Ilka would have to learn about all this, too, if she was going to try to lure more customers in.

Though she'd never done anything remotely like selling funeral home services, she already knew she was going to hate it. That and going around holding home parties, like Golden Slumbers did. The question was if she could afford not doing these things; the only way to turn the business around was to increase revenues.

Her mother and Hanne would be perfect for something like this. They would come off as trustworthy, and they were both good at talking to people. And her mother would throw herself into it body and soul, like when she started her online yarn business and the knitting courses she taught.

Unsure of what to do now, Ilka felt a bit useless. Artie was working, and the nun was taking care of her duties; she felt she should be the motivating force, the engine in her father's business, but the others had the fuel to make everything run. They knew the routines; they had the experience—they should be the ones trying to get the business back on track so it could be sold. So Artie could take over the house and start his own business.

Determined now, she walked over and knocked on the preparation room door. She had to knock again a few times before he unlocked it.

"Is there anything I can do to help?" She walked inside and looked around for a white coat. "It would be good for me to know how this is done, and I promise I won't get in the way—"

She looked down at the steel table. The exhaust fan hood loomed over Mike's body, which was covered by a white sheet from the waist down. It was so very different from seeing the bodies they had picked up. There was something clinically dead about this, yet it seemed almost intimate, vulnerable.

"Are you okay?" Artie joined her. She stood motionless, her eyes stuck on the exposed upper body like thin skin to a frozen iron pipe.

She knew bodies were pumped full of formaldehyde during the embalming; Artie had explained that. But she hadn't imagined a person could seem so lifeless.

He'd made an incision on each side of the throat. On one side the embalming fluid entered through a tube, while on the other side the body fluids drained out. A pump whirred, and at short intervals it emitted air. It sounded like sighing.

In her head, she heard Erik's calm voice, and she tried to imagine him explaining how to photograph the body in bright light: Use a filter and change the aperture. But she was still unable to move. She struggled to find a suitable expression, one that would look professional.

Artie was back at the table, but occasionally he glanced over his shoulder, as if making sure she was still standing.

"During the embalming, you remove the eyes," he explained, after she'd gotten a grip on herself and put on the white coat he'd handed her. She fumbled to put on the mask. "Eyes are too fragile to handle the process."

He turned and pointed at some small plastic boxes on the

shelf beside the door. "We have fake eyes over there, but I don't put them in until I'm done. And it's only for cosmetic effect, the facial expression. The eye cavities have to be filled, because I close the eyes."

His deep voice was calm, something like her mother's in schoolteacher mode when she forgot that Ilka wasn't one of her students, not to mention an adult.

She nodded and watched. The skin over Mike's stomach was bumpy—the fluid had gathered in pockets—and Artie concentrated on smoothing the skin by stroking it carefully with the flat of his hand.

The odor in the room stung her sinuses when Ilka breathed through her nose. She opened her mouth and sucked in air through the mask, which hopefully filtered the poisonous particles. But the rough paper didn't stop the sensation of breathing in fumes from a putrefying body. She pressed her tongue up on the roof of her mouth to hold back her nausea.

Though slightly dizzy, Ilka stood beside Artie while he finished up. She was determined to file away every single detail of his work so she would understand the process.

He turned off the pump and pulled out the thin tube. "You thinking about coming along to the crematorium to watch Mrs. Norton burn up?" He took the tube over to the sink, but he didn't shut off the exhaust fan. "Everything has to be rinsed and washed; otherwise, it's too dangerous to be in here."

"I'd like to go along to the crematorium, yes." He mumbled something behind his mask. "If you don't mind?"

She had the feeling her presence made him uncomfortable, prevented him from getting into his work as he normally did. He nodded and said she was welcome to come along; they could leave as soon as Mike had been laid in the coffin and wheeled into the cold room.

"It's too hot in here for him; he needs to be cool. I got a coffin ready out in the garage. You want to give me a hand with it?"

Ilka nodded and asked if she should keep the white coat and mask on.

"The mask doesn't matter; it's only for not breathing in too much poison. But keep the white coat on so you don't get your clothes dirty."

He went outside and opened the garage door. He'd already covered the bottom of the coffin with a white sheet. There was no embroidery or decoration, just a common white sheet and a small flat pillow up at the head. He tossed her a thin blanket in a plastic sack and asked her to unwrap it. Then he rolled the casket carriage over to the door. "You want to help me with the step here?"

She leaned over and grabbed a small handle on the front of the carriage. The coffin looked like the coffins common in Denmark, not like the ones she had seen since she'd arrived. Apparently, this was the discount model.

He parked the coffin in the hallway. "Normally I'd wheel the body out and lift it over, but since there's two of us, we can carry him out."

She nodded and tried to conceal her discomfort. Though it wasn't the first time she'd lifted a corpse, she wasn't really used to it. Though Mike Gilbert now looked more like a wax dummy than a real person. But she followed him, and when Artie told her to grab under his knees and lift while he lifted his upper body, she did so without batting an eye. A moment later the body was in the coffin, and she covered it with the blanket and swept the wrinkles out until it looked as smooth as a tablecloth.

"Do they want anything in the coffin with him?" Artie asked.

She shook her head. "Not that I know of, but maybe they'll bring something along at the viewing."

"When are they coming, do you know?"

"Five o'clock. His father is coming too; he's driving up here, so they couldn't make it earlier."

Artie nodded. "Do they need anything for the funeral service, or maybe that's been arranged already with the sister?"

"There won't be a service. They just want to sit with him and say good-bye."

"Okay. Make sure the stereo system is ready so there's music in the background. Otherwise it can be really hard for the relatives to take the silence."

Ilka nodded.

They rolled Mike's coffin in and parked him beside McKenna and his dog, who were to be flown out Wednesday or Thursday; the details weren't taken care of yet—they were waiting on the final papers.

"Ready?" Artie grabbed the casket carriage with Mrs. Norton's coffin. "I'll clean up when we get back."

Ilka wanted to take a quick shower, but Artie was already on his way to the hearse. He asked her to find Mrs. Norton's death certificate in the office while he loaded the coffin.

"And bring the urn with you," he said.

"Is there a specific urn, or should I just pick one out?"

Artie let go of the carriage, obviously annoyed. No, she couldn't just pick one out. "Which urn did they pay for? It's on the order sheet. That's not ready?"

She looked at him in confusion and asked if this was something she should have taken care of.

"It's something Paul always did, anyway."

Ilka was about to defend herself, but instead she straightened up. "Starting today, that will change. From now on, the person driving the body to the crematorium will also take care of the urn." She stared at him until he gave her a nod.

Ilka turned and left the room. She almost slammed the door, but she thought better of it. After a moment, she walked into the garage. Artie was over on the other side, opening the rear door of the hearse.

"I'm sorry," she said. "I'll go in and find the papers."

Artie turned to her. They stood for a moment, letting their anger seep away. Then he offered to help find the urn if she would look to see which model Mrs. Norton had ordered.

Now that they'd cleared the air, Ilka scolded herself. She was going to have to make this work.

In the office, she brought out the folder on Mrs. Norton's funeral. A clay urn had been ordered and paid for, nothing fancy. Just a common model to be put in the grave where her husband already lay.

Before going over to the storage room to find the urn, she noticed two men in dark suits about to get out of an expensive car. They walked across the parking lot toward the front entrance. She stepped back just inside the door, out of sight. There was something purposeful about them, the way they walked silently, straight to the door.

Curious now, also a bit nervous, she moved closer to the reception area. The doorbell rang, and Sister Eileen said something Ilka didn't pick up. A dark, masculine voice replied. She stayed in the foyer and listened. It seemed that the American Funeral Group hadn't accepted her refusal to meet with them. Or else they were extremely hard of hearing. Which she doubted. Either way, she was annoyed.

She walked up to them and introduced herself. "Like I already said earlier today, this business is not for sale." She didn't want to sound directly rude. Just almost.

Instead of backing off, however, one of the men simply walked farther inside and looked around, as if he'd been invited to take a tour of the house. It was a conscious provocation, obviously, and insolent, which worried Ilka. The sister sat behind her desk, her eyes lowered, while the other dark-suited man stood to the side like a silent threat.

"I want you to leave, now," Ilka said. She walked over and opened the door. As she held it open, she caught Sister Eileen's eye; she looked guarded, uncertain, sitting there slumped in her chair. Ilka briefly thought about getting Artie, but instead she again told them to leave.

"I don't think you know who you're dealing with," said the smaller of the two men, the stocky one standing beside the desk. His hands were stuck deep into his pockets, as they had been since the two men had walked in.

"Dealing with? I don't plan on dealing with anyone. I'm just telling you my father's funeral home business is not for sale. Not now, anyway. Which I told you on the phone this morning."

"But it'll be up for sale later?" he said.

Ilka immediately regretted her choice of words, but she

was losing patience. "There's no reason for you to think that. Right now it's not for sale."

There was something in his eye that stopped her from being more forceful. *Don't burn your bridges*, a small voice in the back of her head was telling her; *these people could prove to be useful*. But they couldn't just barge in this way, and besides, it was none of their business whether or not the funeral home would be for sale in the future.

"We knew your father," the taller man said, walking over to her. "We also know about his problems. What I think is, you're making a big mistake, not listening to our organization's offer."

He was in her face now, inches away; they were the same height, and it felt as if his eyes were burning straight through her, which enraged her. She stared straight back at him. "Leave, now."

They stood there without moving; then he broke the tension by glancing over at his partner. They turned and walked out without closing the door.

After they drove off, Ilka slammed the door and glared at it. When she turned around, she saw the nun was pale and frightened. "Have they been here before?"

"They've never showed up in person. But American Funeral Group contacted Paul; they've been trying to monopolize the market here in Racine for some time. Several years ago, they took over a funeral home on the outskirts of town, an old family business. He should never have sold."

"Are they trying to control prices?" Ilka still felt uneasy. She would never claim they had threatened her, and perhaps she was just sensitive. But what that tall man had said about her father was about as close as he could come to a threat without being direct about it.

"Paul said they had a reputation for ruining undertakers who didn't go along with them. But he always managed to avoid them."

"But they contacted him?"

Sister Eileen nodded. She still looked pale. "They did, a few times. But Paul wasn't interested in being part of their chain, even though they offered to let him run the business. Changes would of course have been made; we would have had to follow their way of doing business. All their funeral homes are run the same way. But he would have kept his position as funeral director. Your father called it a monopoly, and he kept them at a distance."

Artie stood in the doorway now. He spoke quietly. "This is exactly what I wanted to keep you away from."

She turned to him. "What do you mean?"

"If we'd gone through with the deal I set up with Phyllis Oldham, they wouldn't have targeted us. Now we won't be able to shake them. American Funeral Group wants to take over everywhere. They undermine businesses, pressure people to sell. I've seen it before, and it's not pretty. They're brutal. They'll stop at nothing. If they can't scare us into selling, they'll make sure no one dares do business with us. They'll ruin us, take everything we have so we can't fight them. And they won't give up until we surrender or close down."

"They can't do that," Ilka said. "It's not like this is the Wild West."

"Oh no?" the sister muttered.

"Matter of fact, they can. They're financially powerful,

and they've got connections in places that make us vulnerable. They can see to it that we can't renew our license. Or they can get the IRS to come in and check every last detail in our books. That would be trouble for anybody. They can invent problems for us we never even heard of."

Ilka listened without speaking as she tried to ignore the knot growing inside her, the one that made her bend over a few inches and fold her arms.

"Just look at Gregg, like Sister Eileen says. He was forced to sell his funeral home to them a few days before declaring personal bankruptcy. You've seen him around town; he usually hangs out on the square or in Oh Dennis!, when they let him in. He's a shadow of himself. The rest of him disappeared the day he turned over the keys to his funeral home. Drive by and you'll see how they've let the place go. Like, the flag outside the door is ripped; they've boarded the windows. The best thing they can do for the place is level it. American Funeral Group closed it right after they took over. They weren't one bit interested in running the business. All they wanted was one less funeral home. No one knows how they managed to ruin him, but it was a lesson for all of us."

Artie fished a cigarette out of his pocket. His voice was thin now. *He's under pressure*, Ilka thought. *And he feels bad. Maybe he's even scared.*

She watched him walk out of the foyer; then she turned to Sister Eileen. "I'm going along to the crematorium to see how everything is done. If we're not back before you leave, just lock up."

The nun forced a faint smile and nodded.

30

Artie had already driven the hearse out of the garage. He asked if Ilka had remembered the urn and papers.

"I've got it all right here." Carefully she laid the urn in the hearse. Mrs. Norton's death certificate was in her bag. She hoped Artie had calmed down.

"Ready?" He pointed to the coffin. "We're putting her in feet first."

Ilka looked up in surprise, and he smiled. "That way, if she wakes up and sits up in the coffin, she'll be able to see out the front windshield. Paul taught me that on our first trip together."

They grabbed the handles on each side of the coffin, lifted it over onto the small rollers in the back of the hearse, and carefully pushed it in.

Ilka noticed several rusty spots around the rear door as she closed it. In fact, a few places looked almost rusted away.

Iron peeped through the uneven rusty brown splotches, which looked like scabs. She inspected the back; the rust was worst at the bottom of the door. But as long as it drove okay, she thought, it would do. At a distance, it looked decent enough. It wasn't something she had to take care of right now, and anyway, if the funeral home business was sold, it would probably end up at an auto salvage yard.

She got in. "Is it a long drive?"

Artie shook his head. "The crematorium is on the edge of town. Douglas Oldham was going to build onto Golden Slumbers, but Phyllis didn't want the soot from burning dead bodies bothering her when she was out on her terrace. Douglas promised there would be a particle filter and machinery installed to remove the mercury in the smoke, and he got permission from the city, but not his wife. So they built it at the end of a residential street where the Oldhams owned a big lot. Now the neighbors out there get to enjoy the crematorium's chimney."

"Why didn't they just build it outside of town?" Ilka fastened her seat belt as the hearse slowly swayed out of the parking lot. Their mood lightened as they chatted.

"Probably for practical reasons. So they wouldn't have to drive so far. And I think Douglas wanted to show everyone who's boss, after the county gave him permission to build within city limits. The people living there raised hell, of course, but that didn't change anything. You got the bucks, you can get it done. It was a great status symbol for his funeral home."

Ilka looked over at him; she didn't understand.

"A lot of people think funerals are cheaper if the funeral home has its own crematorium. That's not true, of course, but the Oldhams hoped it would bring in more customers."

Gray two-story buildings slid by. Failed businesses, abandoned industry, empty back lots with graffiti smeared on walls visible through mesh fences and open gates. Construction waste and trash had been bulldozed into large piles. It looked like no one had taken responsibility for cleaning up after everything had closed. So much of Racine was like a ghost town that Ilka could hardly imagine the lively trade center where many Danish immigrants had settled. And her father had been one of them, though he must have arrived at the end of Racine's glory days. *What the hell were you doing here?* she thought. She leaned her head against the window and watched it all pass by.

They crossed a four-lane bypass that led to the freeway, and after a church and a gas station, Artie signaled and turned off into a residential district with tall trees on both sides of the street. The hearse swayed.

They had ridden silently most of the way, but suddenly he asked, "So we're not going to see each other? Privately, I mean?"

That took Ilka by surprise. She glanced over at him and smiled. "Like you said, it's probably not so smart." She looked out at the front lawns with their low hedges and neat lawns.

"You didn't think it was so wrong the other day," Artie reminded her quickly.

"It's not at all that I think it's wrong. We're adults; we don't owe each other anything. I'm just not so good at planning. Anyway, not at this sort of thing."

"We don't have to plan anything," he said. "It was nice that you just showed up. But it might be even better if I was a little bit prepared."

"You mean so I don't walk in on you and your other women." She expected that would embarrass him, but he didn't react. Maybe he'd already forgotten the woman who had driven off the first evening Ilka came to get him. Then she thought about the guy at the bar who had showed up at the funeral home. She dropped it.

Artie hummed something she couldn't hear. At the end of the street, a low, square brick building with an enormous chimney came into sight. A small paved driveway to the left led around the building. CREMATORIUM was written in the same gold cursive script as on the sign at the Oldhams' funeral home. But there was nothing pretentious about anything else. The chimney rose above the treetops, pointing to the sky like a symbol of death.

Artie drove around the building and backed the hearse up to a green door. He'd just gotten out when an older man wearing a black shirt tucked into a pair of heavy canvas pants stepped outside. His Irish cap pulled down over his forehead shaded his eyes. Ilka sensed a problem, and sure enough, the man folded his arms and shook his head when Artie approached. For a moment, the two men stood talking, but before she could loosen her seat belt, Artie was back in the hearse. He slammed the door angrily and turned the key.

"This is fucking blackmail; I'll be damned if I'm going to stand for this."

They roared out of the driveway, as much as the hearse could be said to roar, and the chimney disappeared behind them as he floored it.

"Blackmail?" Ilka didn't understand.

They drove for a while in silence while he calmed down.

"He demanded cash before he would accept the body! And they're charging us thirty percent extra for being late on our payments." He was furious again. "If they think they can run us out of business because we backed out of the deal, they've got another think coming."

"Can they do this? I mean, I'm sure they can demand cash if we owe them. But can they add thirty percent? Isn't that a lot? Isn't it usually just a few percent for a late payment?"

Artie shrugged and stared straight ahead, though he kept his eye on the cars crossing the highway ahead. "In principle they can do whatever they want; they own the place. But we're not taking this lying down. I don't know if Paul had a special arrangement with them. It wouldn't surprise me if he'd been paying extra to keep the peace, since the Oldhams didn't try to cut prices and run him out of business. But if I know Golden Slumbers, they profited from it."

"Do we have to take Mrs. Norton back? Or are there other crematoriums we can just show up at?"

Artie nodded. "There's a private crematorium just outside of town; it's open twenty-four hours a day. We can drive up there, but it's expensive. And there's one down in Kenosha. They also burn pets; not all crematoriums do. Right now, they're closed, though. They're renovating the place."

Ilka thought of the crematorium at Bispebjerg Hospital back in Copenhagen. It was hard for her to understand that Americans could charge whatever they wanted, though she didn't know anything about it. It just seemed so improbable that there weren't regulations. But then, she didn't know if pets could be cremated in Denmark, or if cremations were done twenty-four hours a day. She'd never needed to know.

Artie had turned off, and now they were headed west, away from Lake Michigan, according to Ilka's sense of direction. Which wasn't particularly reliable. "We're not going north?"

Artie didn't answer, but soon, when the trees seemed to close in on the narrow road, he turned off again. They drove through hills with large, open fields, sectioned off into enormous squares. "First let's see if Dorothy has her oven up and running," he said.

He slowed down and turned off onto a winding gravel road leading to a farm nestled in the hills. Ilka couldn't spot a sign, which made her wonder, but she waited for Artie to say something.

"Here we are," was all he said.

Two long ells of a farmhouse lay at angles to each other. Potted plants stood in the windows of the one Ilka guessed was the living quarters. A building with an oddly shaped tall roof lay farther back. *The crematorium*, she thought, when she noticed the tall chimney at one end. A thin, almost invisible wisp of smoke rose out of it. There were no other cars in the parking lot, no signs indicating this was a crematorium. In contrast to the wooden and masonry houses in town, the buildings were made of red stone.

Artie punched the hearse's horn several times, and soon a middle-aged woman in coveralls, her medium-length gray hair held in a scarf, came out and stood on the front steps. When she saw the hearse, her face lit up in a big smile. She waved.

Artie jumped out of the car and walked over to her. She didn't look at all like someone who ran a crematorium, nor did the place even look like a crematorium to Ilka. Beside the building with the chimney, though, the ends of two coffins stuck out from under a tarp, with firewood stacked beside them. An ax stuck up out of a chopping block.

She looked back at the woman. Obviously, she and Artie knew each other well. Something in the way they faced each other told her they might have been lovers. Curious now, Ilka leaned forward for a better look. Suddenly the woman stared over at the hearse; her smile disappeared as she concentrated on what Artie was saying. They seemed to be negotiating.

Being ignored this way annoyed her. She got out of the car, walked over right past Artie, and introduced herself.

"She's from Denmark," Artie said. She waited for the woman to measure her up. Reluctantly she held a surprisingly big, strong, dry hand out to Ilka.

"Dorothy Cane."

When she stepped down to face her, Ilka was surprised to see they were the same height. They eyed each other for a moment before Artie broke in. "We can carry the coffin ourselves." He pointed out at the hearse.

"What is it?" Dorothy asked. "The cold room is shut off; I can't have anything sitting around here. And I'm busy."

"This is one of the quick ones," Artie said. "A small older lady."

She nodded. "Okay, then."

Artie smiled at her; then he got back into the hearse and slowly backed up toward the red building. He waved Ilka over to help him with the coffin.

"What about the money?" Dorothy said.

"We'll pay you right here and now," Ilka said. Not that she had any idea how much it would cost to burn Mrs. Norton, but the two thousand dollars she'd promised to Sister Eileen was in her pocket, and she wanted so badly to shut Dorothy Cane up. For some reason, the woman irritated her.

Ilka felt the woman's eyes on her as they lifted the coffin out. She straightened up and concentrated on gripping the two handles. It wasn't pretty, but they managed to keep the heavy coffin level so Mrs. Norton wasn't shaken too much on the way across the farm's parking lot.

Dorothy held a small gray gate open for them. "There's a catafalque over there by the wall. Go ahead and set the coffin on top of it."

She pointed at a long box the length of the coffin, equipped with two tracks to slide coffins in. With her foot, she unlocked the catafalque's wheels, and they pushed it into a room across the tiled hallway with two empty coffins, lids open. As if two people had just gotten up and walked away.

Ilka looked around. Whitewashed walls, clean reddish brown floor tiles. The place was nice, not musty at all, and a bit cool, though there was a faint odor of an extinguished fire out in the hall. In here, though, where they left Mrs. Norton, she couldn't smell anything. Cool and dark; that was it.

"Cash would be fine," Dorothy said. "You want a look at the oven?"

She started down the hall before Ilka could answer. At the end, she opened a heavy double door. The noise was more pronounced than the heat when they walked into the room, which was open all the way up to the roof. An iron monster with glass doors stood in the middle in front of the brick chimney. Flames leapt up on one side. Underneath the

265

glass doors was a broad trapdoor. The box the ashes fell into, Ilka guessed.

Artie and Dorothy stood behind her, their voices drowned out by the noise from the oven. She resisted the temptation to walk over and peek inside the glass doors, not knowing what she would see. An iron cupboard with doors and drawers stood against the far wall, with a few iron boxes on the floor in front of it, filled with something. Bolts, it looked like, only bigger than the ones in Ilka's toolbox back in Copenhagen. She walked over to check it out.

From behind, Dorothy said, "Hip operations and artificial knees, complicated broken bones. All the reserve parts from the dead end up here. I sell them; I get a good price for titanium. The former owner donated the money to the local athletic club. Nowadays it takes a long time to fill the box up."

"How long does a cremation take?" she asked, now that Dorothy had warmed a bit to her.

"Three, four hours. If it's a kid, it doesn't take quite so long. It's all a matter of size."

Interesting, Ilka thought. There was something in Dorothy's eye, now that she was talking about her work. As if fire was a craft she could control. A passion she wanted to share. "How hot does it get in there?"

A long iron rod with a short, wide scraper on one end stood up against the wall. Dorothy walked over, opened the glass doors, and stuck the poker inside. She pushed around whatever was in there, and the flames leapt up again. "It can get hotter, but you cremate at between a thousand and twelve hundred degrees. It takes a while for the bodies to start burning, but when they start the heat is stable. It helps if the body is in a wooden coffin so the flames have something to work with."

Ilka nodded. Not that this interested her, but suddenly it felt important to break the ice, even though she had no plans to see this woman in coveralls again.

While they stood talking, she remembered the urn. She went out to the hearse to get it, and on the way, she heard Artie ask if it was okay to come by after supper. The woman nodded and suggested he bring along a bottle of wine.

It was quiet outside. A slight breeze whispered in the trees surrounding the farm buildings; on the steps stood several large, elegant glazed pots, blue, green, and yellow, that didn't at all match the tall woman in working clothes. Despite the circumstances, Ilka wasn't uncomfortable. The relationship between Artie and the woman did bug her a bit, which surprised her. She picked up the box containing the urn, walked back, laid it beside the coffin, then waited for Artie to say good-bye. On the way to the hearse, she noticed an old metal sign leaning against the end of the house by the covered coffins. CREMATORIUM.

She looked around for a moment, but other than the old sign, nothing pointed to this being an authorized crematorium.

"What *is* that place?" she said as they drove up the hill. She was still upset about being rejected at the Oldhams' crematorium, and she was tired of it all. All the enthusiasm she'd felt that morning, the determination to turn things around, had gradually slipped away without her realizing it. And now this. It felt like they'd been let in through the back door to get a body burned. A body they otherwise couldn't get rid of. "It can't be a legal crematorium, can it?"

Suddenly she felt old, older than these hills, and she shivered even though the sun was blazing. She couldn't take any more. Maybe it was the men from the American Funeral Group that morning, acting as if they already owned the business. That had seriously shaken her, surprisingly so, and as the hearse rattled down the gravel road, she couldn't see any use in staying to fight for the funeral home.

Artie forced the hearse up the last stretch of hill. "It is; it's actually legal. It's a closed crematorium, or not really all the way closed, of course; it's just that Dorothy doesn't run it as a crematorium anymore."

"Who is she?" She stared in the side mirror. At the bottom of the hill, the farmhouse, the red stone building, the tall chimney with wisps of smoke curling up out of it as if it were about to vanish from sight.

"Dorothy is a potter and artist. She bought the place five or six years ago to use the big ovens for her work."

"She burns clay in those ovens! *And* bodies?"

Artie sighed and ignored her outburst. "She fishes down at the lake occasionally. That's where I met her. She went to an art institute in Ohio where an old friend of mine in Key West went. Though they didn't know each other. When she told me where she'd moved to, we talked some about that, and she's helped us a few times with interments where there weren't any relatives."

"The homeless, you mean, who also deserve a decent burial," she said, repeating what she'd heard one of the first days she was in Racine.

"Your dad made a big deal about everyone being treated

with dignity after their death, including people without much money. Not all funeral directors in town see it that way, but Paul did. So, Dorothy let us use her oven."

"But is she allowed to do this?"

"She's not allowed to do the burning herself; you're supposed to be a certified undertaker. But I am. All she has to do is renew her license every year; then it's a hundred percent legal."

"But Mrs. Norton has paid for her cremation."

He nodded. "And she will be cremated. We're paying Dorothy for helping us, of course. Just not as much as the Oldhams charge."

"And we get the same out of it?"

He nodded again. "We'll get her ashes in an urn. Any pieces of bone, silver fillings, and any screws she might have from operations are filtered out. And we'll get her teeth in a bag to give to the family. We put them in small boxes stamped with our logo and deliver them with the photos from the funeral service and our final bill."

"Did we take photos?"

He looked at her as if he didn't know what she meant, but then he nodded. "The sister always takes pictures of the coffin during the services. And then some mood photos. Pictures of the buffet and the flowers. And then she gathers up all the condolence cards. We take care of everything so the family doesn't have to worry about remembering. And when it's over, we give it all to the relatives."

Ilka wasn't aware of all that. "But surely someone knows about Dorothy Cane's little moonlighting business?"

"She doesn't do it that often. If someone brought it to the government's attention, she might have some problems. The

IRS would probably be who's most interested; they might check to see if she's not reporting some income. I doubt she'd actually be in trouble. The crematorium meets the environmental standards, but of course the Oldhams might be pissed off if they found out about it. They'd make as much trouble for her as they could. But Dorothy isn't interested in competing with all the others. She's just making a few extra bucks so she can do her pottery thing."

"Does the government keep an eye on crematoriums?" Ilka said.

"Sure, of course. But every state has their own cremation laws, and like I said, Wisconsin requires a valid license, and cremations must be done by a certified undertaker. It's possible the oversight is stricter after what happened down in Georgia, but I doubt it."

"What was that about?"

"There was this guy who inherited a crematorium from his father in the mid-nineties, and five or six years later, bodies began showing up at the place. It was a major scandal. If I remember right, the first person to notice something was a driver delivering gas or oil to the crematorium. He said he saw body parts lying around, but nothing was done because the local sheriff thought it had to do with regulations, nothing criminal. The driver complained again, and the deputy sheriff went out there, but he didn't find anything."

"All they did was go out there and look? They didn't talk to the owner?"

Artie shook his head. "Guess not. Then the next year someone reported seeing body parts in the forest near the crematorium. This time the sheriff went out, but he didn't find anything either. Then finally two years after the first report, someone walking their dog stumbled onto some human bones in the forest, and the authorities moved in. They found fifty body parts spread around."

"That sounds insane."

"Yeah, it was unbelievable. They brought in a federal disaster team, and things really heated up. It was hard to identify the bodies; they were so decomposed. They found— I think it was three hundred thirty-four bodies on the property. Some of them were in the forest behind, some in sheds; there were bodies in coffins out in the yard. I think one body was even stuck halfway inside the oven. There were bodies everywhere. Some of them had been lying around for five years."

Artie shook his head. "The entire funeral home industry was in shock, of course, not to mention the relatives. Some of the deceased were in their Sunday clothes wearing jewelry, others in hospital clothes. The police found out that over twenty years, several thousand bodies had been sent there, the Tri-State Crematory. It was the only crematorium in the whole region. But all this happened after the son took over."

"How in the world could something like that happen?" Ilka realized she was sitting with her mouth open and fists clenched.

"I haven't followed the case since he was sentenced to twelve years in prison. But back then they called him the Mad Hatter; somehow he got poisoned and went crazy. Mercury poisoning can do that, make people insane and lazy, and mercury just so happens to be one of the dangers with cremation. The regulations are strict about filters, to avoid just that, mercury poisoning. Some people claim something went wrong when he left school to help his dad.

They say he'd always been popular, a nice kid, but he didn't want to take over the crematorium, and something in his head just went 'click.' What do I know, though? He's the only one who does, but I don't think he ever spoke out."

"How did the relatives take it? It must have been horrible for them."

"Yeah, no shit. It really stirred people up. And it turned out he'd been filling urns with cement dust and giving them to the families. They had no idea about all this until the story hit."

"*Hold da kæft,*" Ilka muttered. Incredible. She couldn't imagine anything like that happening in Denmark.

"It didn't exactly promote trust in the funeral home industry. Other things have happened, just not as big a tragedy. The authorities found eight bodies in the house of another licensed undertaker; the guy apparently was in trouble financially. Over three hundred bodies, though, that's a whole different level."

They were almost back in Racine. Neither of them spoke the rest of the way; Ilka couldn't shake the terrible feeling inside her, and she badly needed a cup of coffee and a sandwich.

31

The back door out to the parking lot was unlocked when they returned. Ilka ignored it; even before they'd left Dorothy Cane's crematorium, she'd been holding back the call of nature, and now she rushed through the foyer to the guest bathroom while Artie parked the hearse in the garage. She heard him call out for Sister Eileen; then he walked by the bathroom toward the reception area and called her name again.

Ilka came out of the bathroom and said, "Do you need help with something?"

"I asked Sister Eileen to clean up after the embalming, and she didn't put the key back."

"Where do you usually put it?"

"I told her to lay it on the desk in the office, but it's not there. Usually I keep it on me."

"I'll look on her desk," Ilka said, turning to go.

"I already checked; it's not there."

She walked back to the reception area anyway to see if she'd stuck the preparation room key in one of her drawers. "Is it on a key ring?" she yelled back.

"There's two keys, on a leather string with a ceramic amulet on the end of it. You can't miss it."

Ilka tugged on the drawers. Two of them were locked; the top one was open. Paper, stapler, tape, envelopes, but no keys. When she closed the drawer, she noticed the nun's bag beside the desk chair.

A small, dark gray woman's bag.

"I don't think she's left," Ilka said after she returned empty-handed. "Her bag is still here. And I told her to lock up if she left before we came back, and she didn't. She must be in her apartment."

Ilka walked up the stairs to her father's room to pack up all the folders containing the business's accounts. She'd planned on going through everything, but now she didn't feel like starting on anything that might help save the funeral home. It simply wasn't worth it any longer. What did she think she was proving? Other than that she wouldn't be scared off.

"She's not in her apartment," Artie yelled from the hallway. His voice was higher than usual, and she stopped on the stairs. He sounded worried. She turned and took the last steps down in one jump.

He grabbed the doorknob to the preparation room and shook it as he called the nun's name. He knocked, then slammed the palms of his hands against the door, as if he hoped it would cave in.

"Why do you think she's in there?" Ilka asked. What had gotten into him?

"I don't necessarily, but she might be; maybe she started feeling bad while she was cleaning up."

She heard the worry in his every word; she hadn't thought much about the relationship between her father's two employees, but clearly, Artie cared about her.

"Maybe she lost track of time and suddenly realized she had to go," Ilka said, wanting to reassure him. "And forgot about returning the key because she was in such a hurry."

"And forgot to lock the back door?" He didn't believe it. "Her apartment door wasn't locked, either, and her lunch was on the kitchen counter, half-eaten, and her tea was cold."

He knocked again.

"You're afraid she's locked herself in," Ilka said.

"It's dangerous in there when the exhaust fan isn't running. The fumes are poisonous."

"But surely she didn't stop in the middle of her lunch to come over and clean up. Don't you think she finished cleaning first?"

He banged on the door again and called her name. "You said her bag was in the reception area. Was her wallet there?"

"I didn't look for it," Ilka admitted. Artie said he would run home for his extra key.

The house was oddly quiet after he left. As if no sound could get in or out. She felt jittery, agitated, and the feeling spread throughout her body. Suddenly it was as if she were in a house of farewell, a house filled with loss and sorrow. Not a chilling feeling, but empty.

She went over to the preparation room and slumped to

275

the floor beside the door. The stillness was intense; it spread under her skin like a gust of wind.

When Ilka heard Artie drive in, she opened the back door. Infected by his worry, she followed him to the preparation room and stood behind him as he unlocked the door and opened it.

The room had been cleaned. Every surface had been washed; water still stood on the floor here and there after the hosing down. But the sister wasn't there. The only thing that caught Ilka's eye was the thin gold chain Mike had worn around his neck, lying flat under the architect lamp on Artie's small worktable.

"If we're giving the chain to Shelby, I can put it in an envelope for her so it doesn't get lost."

Artie shook his head; then he walked over and picked it up. "I forgot to put it on him. I'll do it right now."

He looked around the room as if making sure the nun wasn't in one of the corners; then he turned off the light.

Ilka stayed while he walked over and punched in the code to unlock the cold room door. She was hungry. She could pick up some tacos over at the Mexican place. Or she could start packing the old accounts, like she'd planned on doing before, and lay aside everything she wanted to take home to Denmark. She was halfway up the stairs when she heard the scream.

Sister Eileen lay on the floor just inside the cold room. The temperature was in the thirties, to hinder the decomposition of bodies without freezing them.

The nun's body was limp; her head covering lay beside

her. Artie quickly kneeled; then he told Ilka to hold the door so he could carry her out.

They took her into the office, which had a thick carpet. Artie spoke quietly to her, shaking her lightly. Finally, she opened her eyes, but she was so confused that Ilka couldn't understand a word she said. She was alive, though, and Ilka let out a sigh she'd been suppressing for several minutes, as if she'd been holding her breath.

Artie checked her pulse, and Ilka grabbed a thick blanket from a chair in the arrangement room. As she wrapped it around Sister Eileen, her hand grazed the nun's ice-cold skin. She closed her eyes again, but her eyelids were quivering in fright. "I'm calling an ambulance," Ilka said after she'd tucked the blanket around the sister's feet.

"Let's see if she comes out of it first," Artie said. Carefully he lifted her head and stuck a pillow underneath. Her short dark hair, damp from the cold, clung to her forehead. He rubbed her arms.

"She's not really conscious. It's like she's in and out. I'm calling." Her hand was on the phone to call 911.

"Wait!" Artie ordered. "She'll make it. It's not life threatening until the body is under seventy-nine degrees; that's when you need special treatment to survive. The important thing is to warm the body carefully."

"I'm not taking responsibility here; we're calling an ambulance. If you're afraid we don't have insurance to cover this, I'll pay for the hospital. She's not conscious. This is irresponsible."

She lifted the receiver, but before she could call, he shocked her by wrenching the phone out of her hand. "We're going to wait."

Sister Eileen stirred, and Ilka hesitated. "Okay. But being cooled down this way can kill you."

He nodded. "Go up and see if there's a hot water bottle or an electric blanket in your father's room, and fill the bathtub with hot water."

Artie kept rubbing the sister's arms, as Ilka remembered her mother doing when she'd been out sledding and came in freezing, her cheeks red and fingers tingling from the cold.

"Right now the important thing is to get her own heat regulation going," he explained when Ilka came down with a heavy electric blanket. "But we have to be careful. Her skin can be numb from being cooled down. Make sure the blanket isn't too hot."

She went out to fill the bathtub. When she came back the sister had lifted her arms, and she was moving her fingers one by one, as if she were making sure they were still there. She stared at a spot behind Artie's shoulder, her eyes fluttering as if she'd just woken up.

"How in the world did this happen?" Ilka asked. She squatted down and massaged the sister's feet. "It's way too unsafe if the door locks automatically when it shuts."

"It doesn't," Artie murmured. "The door only locks when you push the red symbol in on the doorknob outside."

"So what does that mean?"

He stared at her, his eyes doing the talking: The nun hadn't locked herself in the cold room.

"We need to call the police." She got up to call, but the sister spoke, asking her to come back.

Ilka sat down again beside her. "What happened?"

Sister Eileen tried to sit up using her elbows. Her body wasn't cooperating fully; her movements lagged behind. She

278

groaned and lay back down, and Artie tucked the electric blanket around her.

"Did you see who it was?"

The sister shut her eyes again, but this time her voice was clear. "Forget about it. It was an accident, and everything's okay now."

"What are you talking about?" Ilka said. "You could have frozen to death in there if we hadn't found you."

"Let's just drop it." Artie stood up. "If Sister Eileen doesn't feel like being questioned by the police, she shouldn't have to. Right now, the most important thing is to warm her up."

He slid both arms under the nun and helped her sit up. "I'll walk her out to the bathtub; you can get everything ready for Shelby and her daughter. They're coming at five."

Ilka wasn't sure whether what had just happened was the last straw, or if she'd already made her decision after leaving the old crematorium. But instead of preparing for the two women's farewell to Mike Gilbert, she went into her father's office and plucked out of the wastebasket the transfer agreement Phyllis Oldham had brought.

She smoothed it out and dabbed at the oily spots that came from its lying in the trash. Luckily there were none on the back side where Phyllis Oldham's signature was written in steep, loopy handwriting. Ilka thought it almost looked like it had been written with a fountain pen. She reached for a cheap plastic pen with their logo on it and signed her name on the dotted line. The document now had both of their signatures.

"Are you sure?" Artie said from the doorway.

Ilka hadn't heard him. "Yes. I'll have to sell sooner or later anyway, and now I guess it's going to be sooner. I've had enough of the funeral home business."

The thought of driving around to schools in Copenhagen and photographing students was more attractive than ever to her.

"She's going to be all right," he assured her. "It will help when she gets into the warm water."

For a few moments, they looked at each other. Then she walked over to the desk for the keys to her father's car. She stuffed the transfer agreement in her bag and left the office.

32

Ilka drove into the enormous parking lot behind Golden Slumbers Funeral Home. The spaces closest to the building were taken, so she parked facing Lake Michigan. Across the street, a flag hung at half-mast over the door of a building, and she hesitated at the prospect of going in during a funeral service. But she got out anyway and headed for the employee entrance Artie had used on their previous visit.

She walked down the long hall decorated with family portraits. The soft, deep blue carpet engulfed her sneakers with each step, and the pungent odor of the embalming fluids was every bit as nasty as it had been the first time she'd been there.

She took the few steps up to the desk, where the nun wearing the same garment as Sister Eileen had greeted them the other day. Now the desk was cleared and the chair empty. She looked around, then walked on to the office. Just before reaching the door, she noticed someone with his back to her, looking out over the river. Ilka recognized the youngest son, Jesse. He didn't seem to remember her, because when he turned he simply smiled politely and said it was going to be a beautiful evening on Lake Michigan.

Ilka asked if he knew where she could find Phyllis. Jesse pointed to his mother's office and walked up the steps.

The door was open, and she knocked on the doorframe. Phyllis was sitting behind an old mahogany desk. She gave a start when she saw Ilka. She must have been lost in thought.

"May I come in?" Ilka asked.

After a moment of silence, Ilka walked to the chair across the desk from Phyllis and laid her bag on the floor. "I'm sorry I behaved so badly earlier. Now that I've thought about it, I can see the right thing to do is sell the business to you."

She smiled apologetically and tried to show that she knew she had behaved childishly. But Phyllis Oldham sat staring straight ahead, stiff and unresponsive. Petrified. Had she heard Ilka?

Ilka fumbled around and finally brought out the transfer agreement she'd signed. She laid it on the desk; then she saw the woman was shaking her head.

Phyllis Oldham was dressed in an elegant blue suit with a blouse underneath buttoned up to her neck; a heavy gold cross rested on her breasts, and her slightly wavy hair was perfectly brushed. In short, she resembled herself. But when Ilka looked closely, she realized that in reality, nothing was the same. The pale woman seemed older than the last time she'd seen her, only a few days earlier. What really struck her, though, was Phyllis's stare—was she even aware Ilka was in the room?

"Phyllis," she said, but the woman didn't answer. It was almost as if she wasn't there. Had she gone into shock? Maybe that made sense, given that she'd just admitted to paying Mike Gilbert to leave town.

Ilka said her name again, and suddenly Phyllis looked at her. She reached for the transfer agreement and tore it in half, and without a word she swiveled her chair and turned on the shredder under the window. Before Ilka could react, she'd stuffed the two halves of the agreement in the machine. A second later they were reduced to confetti.

Ilka watched silently as the agreement she'd just gathered the courage to sign disappeared into a wastebasket.

"My offer no longer stands," Phyllis said, her voice flat and a bit rough edged. "I've decided to sell the family business. From now on Golden Slumbers Funeral Home will be a part of American Funeral Group. It's best you go now."

Ilka opened her mouth, then closed it as what Phyllis Oldham had just said sank in. "But I don't understand—"

Phyllis waved her hand. "No questions. I'm not at liberty to speak about the deal, but you're welcome to contact the new owners."

Ilka simply stared at her, unable to move, while thoughts of her own situation and the future of her father's funeral home ran through her head, now that selling to the Oldhams was no longer possible.

"This is my last day at the office," Phyllis said. "I've been told that I mustn't remove anything, not even personal belongings. Not even the family portraits. No one coming in should suspect new ownership."

283

Ilka backed up toward the door. Suddenly the room felt claustrophobic, airless. Golden Slumbers had been the biggest funeral home in town, but it was nothing compared to the bulldozer forcing everyone else out of business.

"And saying you could take over my father's business at the end of the month won't change your mind?"

For a moment, Phyllis didn't seem to understand what she meant, but then she shook her head. "It's too late."

Ilka nodded.

"Fuck, fuck, fuck!" she yelled, on her way to the car. She kicked an empty cola can at a black Dodge parked in front of the building. Then she turned and took one last look at the funeral home. Things hadn't exactly become easier for her.

33

Back at her own funeral home, Ilka parked the car, shut off the engine, closed her eyes, and rested her head against the steering wheel. What she wanted most of all was to call her mother and ask her to come and help her out of the mess she'd gotten herself into.

She pressed her temples and tried to control her breathing. They were going to be crushed; she had no doubt about that. The smartest thing to do was to look for a new buyer before word got out that American Funeral Group had bought Golden Slumbers. Otherwise no one would dare take over a small operation like hers. And now that the funeral home chain owned a big funeral home in town, they probably weren't interested in hers. She just didn't understand why Phyllis Oldham had decided to sell when she so recently had planned on expanding.

As Ilka saw it, she had only one option left. Determined

now, she jumped out of the car and trotted across the parking lot to find Artie. His car was still there; he couldn't have gone home, she thought. But the hearse was gone, and she found a note on the desk: "We've got a pickup. I'll try to be back before Shelby and the family arrive."

Ilka had forgotten all about them. It was almost four thirty, and she hadn't opened up the chapel or prepared the music.

She rushed in and switched on the light. The room was cool; the curtains had been left closed. Ilka wasn't familiar with the stereo system, but she pressed the CD button. Soft Muzak streamed out of the hidden speakers. She found a box of matches and walked over to the candles to be placed around Mike Gilbert's open coffin. Even though the rear section was closed off, the room seemed much too big and impersonal. They should have a room even smaller, Ilka thought. Then she shook that idea off; it wasn't her problem, or at least it wouldn't be.

A car drove in. She went outside to give Artie a hand.

"That was quick," she said, as he got out of the hearse to open the garage door.

"It was just down at the nursing home. She died yesterday; it was expected. The family was there today to say their good-byes."

"When do we meet with them? Are they coming here, or do we go to them?"

"No meeting necessary. They've said their good-byes; they just want to know when to pick up the urn."

Ilka stared. "So we won't be involved? Except for the pickup?"

"And the cremation."

Here we go again, she thought. She started to walk over for the casket carriage, but Artie stopped her. "She's there on the stretcher; there's no coffin."

Ilka gave up and simply waited. "Is something wrong?" she asked. "Isn't this just something to get over with?"

Artie looked in the back of the hearse at the body covered by a white sheet. "Irene was only thirty-four years old. She was born with a mental handicap, and it's been years since she recognized her parents. She's been in the nursing home the last fourteen years. She was too much for the family to take care of at home."

"That's so terribly sad." She walked over to the hearse. "Shouldn't we put her in a coffin? We can't have her lying there like that."

Artie looked at her. "Incredible how much you remind me of your dad."

Ilka pointed over toward one of the coffins by the wall. "Can't we use one of those?"

"Yeah, why not? Irene might as well get some use out of it before the Oldhams take over and clean everything out."

Ilka stopped. It took a moment for him to realize something was wrong. "What?" asked Artie.

"The deal is off. Phyllis tore the transfer agreement up and shredded it."

Artie started laughing. "She'll come around; she's just trying to show you who's boss."

"No, she won't. She just sold Golden Slumbers to the American Funeral Group."

Though he was thirty feet away, she saw his face fall. "She didn't!"

Ilka nodded. "They're taking over immediately. We won't be selling. Unless we sell to them."

He swiped at his forehead, as if he needed to clear his mind. He shook a cigarette out of his pack and lit it, even though they were in the garage.

"Shelby's coming in ten minutes," he said. "You better go in and get ready for her. I'll get Mike's coffin. We'll take care of Irene later."

Ilka nodded and went back into the house. She unlocked the front door so the family didn't have to use the back entrance, as Shelby had been doing. A door slammed and something rolled across the floor; then she watched Artie maneuver the catafalque through the doorway. She went out to start the coffee, fill a bowl with chocolates, and find a new box of Kleenex.

The doorbell rang, and Ilka walked out to let them in. Shelby entered with her arm around her daughter, who was using a cane. She'd been allowed to leave All Saints Hospital to say good-bye to her brother. Emma was frail, almost translucent. She wore a black cape over her much-too-loose clothing and a scarf over her bald head. A gust of wind could almost scoop her up and carry her away. Ilka knew she was on her second round of chemotherapy; the tumor in her brain was still too big for an operation that Shelby wasn't even sure she could pay for. It seemed unbearable to Ilka, so different than in Denmark, where it wasn't a question of money, but of whether a treatment was good enough.

Shelby was also dressed in black. She seemed more poised than before. "The only one missing is Tommy," she said, with a long-suffering annoyance in her voice she surely wasn't aware of. "He's always late."

"Let's sit down while we wait," Ilka said. She picked up a small stack of laminated photos of Mike, on which the date of his birth and death were printed. Sister Eileen had been a bit unsure of whether or not it was appropriate, since this wasn't a real funeral service, but Ilka had thought it was a good idea, that the family would appreciate something to remember him by.

She had already given up trying to figure out whether or not something was appropriate; American burials were so different from the ones back in Denmark. Her main impression was that nothing could be too much over here when it came to commemorating deceased loved ones.

Inside the arrangement room, Shelby helped her daughter sit down in the armchair while Ilka brought in the coffee and chocolates, which she set on the table.

Ilka noticed something different about her. Something lighter, even though in a few moments she would be going in to say good bye to her oldest child. Ilka smiled and looked away when Shelby met her eyes.

"Emma is a bit nervous about seeing her brother in there," she said, glancing affectionately at her daughter. "But I told her not to worry, because Artie Sorvino has taken good care of him."

"He does look very good," Ilka said. She asked Emma how she remembered her brother.

At first Mike's sister stared down at her hands. Should she not have been so direct? Ilka wondered. But then Emma looked up with a big smile on her face. "He always needed a haircut. And he wouldn't put on a shirt, even though Mom told him to. Isn't that right, Mom?"

She turned to Shelby, who nodded. "I'm sure it's true,

even though I can't remember about the shirts." She smiled. "But I do remember he always got holes in the toes of his tennis shoes. They'd start fraying, and you knew it was just a matter of time before they'd fall apart." She shook her head at the memory.

"I always did like Ashley," Emma said after a few moments of silence. "She was always nice, and she asked me several times if I wanted to go down to the harbor when they went to look at the ships. Back when Mike hung out with Jesse and the other guys, I never got to go along."

Her mother tilted her head, as if she were surprised that her daughter had suddenly spoken about something that had happened years ago. "But you and your brother spent a lot of time together," she said.

Emma nodded. "Maybe it was mostly Jesse who didn't want me along."

"Were they together a lot back then?" Ilka asked. "I mean, Mike and Jesse Oldham?"

Shelby said the two boys had been in the same class, but it wasn't until they were fifteen or sixteen that the younger Oldham boy started acting friendly toward Mike.

"And it was only because Mike was the starting quarterback," Emma said. "Jesse wasn't any good at football, but he hung around, a real wannabe."

She snorted. "But when Mike started going out with Ashley, he stopped hanging around with Jesse."

"Yes," Shelby said. "And look where that got him."

Emma slumped in her chair. The film of old memories had stopped abruptly; reality had returned.

Shelby looked at her daughter, then turned to Ilka. "Phyllis Oldham came up to us at the hospital today." Her expression changed, and again it looked as if her sorrow had lightened, but there was anger, too, in the furrows around her mouth.

"She offered to pay for the rest of Emma's treatments. No matter how long it took, how many treatments were necessary. And if the doctors at some point think it's no longer too risky to operate, she'll pay for that too. She's even offered to have Emma moved to another hospital, if we can find one with better specialists."

Again, her daughter stared down at her hands, intertwined in her lap.

"I accepted her offer. Maybe I shouldn't have; she shouldn't be allowed to buy her way out of responsibility for what she did to Mike. Of course she shouldn't. But I said yes and thank you."

Mostly Ilka sensed some sort of embarrassment. As if she was ashamed of having to accept the offer, though she surely wanted nothing to do with the Oldhams after what they had done to her son. "Of course you should let her pay. It's so wonderful for the both of you."

Shelby simply nodded, as if she was relieved to have said it. "We'll give him ten more minutes. This is so like him. He could just have said he didn't want to drive all the way over."

"You can't know; he might be parking outside right now," Emma said, looking at her mother.

The doorbell rang, and Ilka smiled.

"You stay right here; I'll go out and bring him in."

Ilka put on a professional smile as she walked through the foyer to greet Mike Gilbert's father, but she stopped at the sight of a woman with short blond hair holding the hands of two small children. She'd been sobbing, and she seemed utterly crushed and exhausted.

"Hello," Ilka said, feeling a bit awkward as she approached her. How was she going to deal with this right now, when Shelby and her daughter were about to enter the chapel?

She might want to talk to Artie about the woman he'd brought in, Ilka thought. She could be a relative who had changed her mind and wanted to view her anyway.

"May I help you?" It annoyed her that Sister Eileen wasn't there, even though it was totally unfair.

"We're here to see Mike Gilbert," the woman said. The two children looked as if they had just woken up. Shy and a bit frightened, they glanced around in confusion. The haggard woman's lips trembled. "We first heard what happened this morning, and we've been driving all day. Tommy called and told us you're holding a funeral service for him."

"Tommy?" Ilka tried to gather her thoughts.

"My father-in-law. I'm Mike's wife."

"Of course," Ilka said hurriedly, though she didn't know what was going on. "Come inside. Do you need anything?"

She looked down at the boy and girl. Two or three years old, she guessed. "The bathroom is right over there." She pointed it out. "Mike's mother and sister are here. Actually, we thought you were Tommy arriving." Ilka hoped that explained some of her confusion.

"It would be nice to use the bathroom." She began herding the children over.

"I'm hungry," the girl said, her voice thin and tired.

"So you didn't come with your father-in-law?" Ilka said. The boy whined about wanting to sleep.

"He's not coming," the woman said.

After the door closed behind them, Ilka thought about what to do. Shelby hadn't mentioned anything about grandchildren; Ilka doubted very much that she knew about her son's family.

She returned to the arrangement room, where the two women were whispering. They stopped and looked up when she walked in.

"It wasn't Tommy. It's three people who were very close to Mike. They only heard what happened to him this morning, and they're very shaken up. They've been driving all day, and I think you should all have a little time together before we go into the chapel."

A child yelled out in the foyer, "Thirsty, too!" It sounded as if she was about to cry.

Shelby sat up. Emma looked uneasy as she lifted her hand to her scarf. The woman appeared in the doorway carrying one child and holding the hand of the other.

No one spoke for a moment as the three mourners looked at each other. Then the woman stepped inside uncertainly, set the girl down, and ignored the small whimpers, which quieted when Ilka offered the children crackers in a bowl.

"I'm Kathy. I lived with Mike." She held her hand out to Shelby. "This is Ellen and Don. They're three years old."

Mike's mother shook her hand mechanically, but otherwise she looked completely paralyzed at the sight of the twins. Finally, she tore her eyes off them and turned to the woman, but Emma was already standing with tears running down her cheeks and arms spread, reaching toward Kathy.

Shelby stood up uncertainly, as if everything was going too fast, but then she hugged her daughter-in-law and squatted down in front of her grandchildren.

"There's soda and juice in the refrigerator," Ilka said. "And there's bread and stuff for sandwiches. And more crackers. You're welcome to it all, and please take your time. Just say when you're ready."

Ilka caught her breath for a moment before going in to Artie and telling him who'd just walked in instead of the father. "It's not okay at all that she drove this far with two small kids, right after hearing about her husband's death," she said. "The father-in-law surely could have driven them. Or she could have called. We could have waited until tomorrow."

Artie shrugged. "I'm guessing she wouldn't have waited until tomorrow anyway. It's normal for people to not believe a relative has suddenly died. They have to see with their own eyes."

"Of course. But his father apparently didn't need to see his son. Or his daughter, for that matter. That's so damn tragic," she muttered. She nodded when Artie asked if she would give him a hand with Mike's coffin.

The candles were still flickering slightly when they opened the chapel door. Music streamed out from speakers on the wall.

Artie had covered the catafalque bearing the coffin with a black sheet. "You want it all the way up to the podium, or should we just roll it over to the wall so the room doesn't look so big? Seeing as there's only a few people here."

"Let's put it over against the wall. It'll be a bit cozier. And I'll move the candles over there. Leave some space between the coffin and the wall so they can stand around it."

Ilka had just moved the last floor candelabra when Shelby appeared and said they were ready.

"Lift the lid of the coffin," Artie said. "There's an arm that holds it in place when it's up." While Shelby and the family walked over to the coffin, he told her he was driving out to Dorothy's to cremate Mrs. Norton. "Just close it again when you're finished. I'll roll it back into the cold room when I get back."

"Can't I do that?" Then she remembered what had happened to Sister Eileen, and she gestured that she would leave it there until he returned. "Okay, we can do it then."

Shelby's arm was around Emma when they walked in. Kathy followed. The children must be right outside, Ilka noted. Shelby hesitated at her son's coffin; then she turned and reached for her daughter-in-law's hand. They waited while Ilka walked around to lift the coffin lid.

She moved a few feet to the side, the family stepped forward, and all four of them looked down—at an empty coffin.

For a moment, they all stared, as if they expected Mike to appear. Then the three women looked at Ilka.

"Oh my God!" Ilka apologized profusely, said it had to be a mistake. She rushed out of the room in a rage and found Artie outside walking toward the hearse, his back to her.

"What the hell were you thinking?" she yelled at him, striding over as if she were about to grab him by the collar and drag him back. "You put an empty coffin in there! How could you? How hard could it be? There were only three coffins, and he was the only one in a wooden coffin!"

Suddenly she realized what she'd just said. Mike Gilbert lay in the only wooden coffin they had. Artie hadn't made a mistake after all.

She stopped. "Shit," she muttered. Her legs were about to give out from under her. Quickly she explained what had happened, and they went back inside. Artie's hand rested on her back, as if he were nudging her along.

Ilka felt herself walking like a mechanical doll as she followed him into the cold room. Irene's blue coffin was just inside the door. Her hands were folded over a blanket, and a small flower stuck up from between her fingers. Artie must have plucked it out from among the bouquets in the foyer.

At the far wall stood the zinc coffin with Ed McKenna and his dog, to be flown to Albany. Ilka waited just inside the room while Artie unscrewed the coffin lid, which took some time. Even from a distance, she could make out the elderly man.

Without a word, Artie screwed the lid back on. Ilka pulled herself together, returned to the chapel, and asked Shelby to follow her into her father's office. They sat down across from each other.

"Something absolutely terrible has happened, and I can't explain it." Ilka told her about finding the sister in the cold room earlier that day. "But I didn't think it could have anything to do with Mike."

296

Shelby listened silently; she looked as if she expected Ilka to make some sense out of all this, to help her understand why it had happened to her. She leaned forward. "Is Sister Eileen all right? Is she hurt?"

"She's okay. We found her in time. She was lying on the floor, with a weak pulse. She wasn't breathing well. Her voice was…blurry, and she wasn't making much sense. But at least she was conscious."

Artie appeared in the doorway. "The police are coming, but the dispatcher couldn't say exactly when they'll be here. There's a big accident outside town. They're still cleaning up."

Shelby asked if they could go home. "The children need to go to bed, and Kathy looks like she's about to collapse, the poor girl. I don't know what she knows about Mike's background, either, and what happened back then. She deserves to hear about that."

"Of course," Ilka said at once. "I'll call you as soon as we find something out."

She nodded, but before she stood up, she said, "Did you see how much they look like him? Both of them. It's like looking at Mike when he was three. And Kathy seems very nice, don't you think?"

Ilka nodded.

"They've known each other five years, but they weren't married. Her parents live in Oregon. I'll never forgive Tommy for not telling me about them. He knew, but he never visited them, even though he had their address. And he didn't come here to say good-bye, either. He's always been an asshole."

Ilka followed them outside. Shelby and Kathy each carried a child, while Emma opened the car doors for them. Her head felt frozen as she watched them drive away. Frozen, or emptied out and stuffed with cotton. Artie came over and stood behind her.

The red taillights disappeared in the dark, and she turned and accepted the cigarette he held out to her.

34

"No," Ilka repeated, "we have no idea who broke in and locked Sister Eileen in our cold room. No sane person would do such a thing. She could have died if we hadn't found her."

"Can she describe the assailant?"

Artie shook his head. "Sister Eileen didn't see anything. Someone pulled a shroud over her head."

Ilka stopped listening. She sank into a funk; she'd given up trying to make sense of it all.

"But we know that Sister Eileen was locked in the room," Artie persisted. "And we know we didn't shut and lock the door from the outside, because we weren't here."

"Where were you?" Officer Thomas said. He pulled a notepad out of his pocket.

"At the crematorium."

"Which crematorium?"

The policeman looked up when Artie hesitated a beat. "Oldhams'," Artie said. "And then we drove to Kenosha to see if they could do it quicker, but it was closed. I'd forgotten about that. And then we came back."

"So you delivered a body to the Oldhams to be cremated?"

"Look, do you really think we locked Sister Eileen in? Shouldn't we be focusing a little bit on Mike Gilbert disappearing from his coffin? Christ, don't you think he and his family have suffered enough? If nothing else, take it seriously for Shelby's sake."

Officer Thomas grunted; then he straightened up, still holding his notepad. "What about the surveillance cameras? They must cover the back too; you should be able to see who comes in."

Ilka glanced over at Artie. He looked tired. "They still haven't been activated. But Sister Eileen was here. It was the middle of the day."

The officer leaned over the table, his stomach rolling over the edge. He also looked tired—exhausted, in fact. And sad. "I understand if you're thinking Howard Oldham might be on the warpath again. But it's not him. Right now, he's being operated on; the doctors are trying to save his life. He was involved in a serious traffic accident earlier today. For some reason, he lost control of his car out on the highway. He hit a truck head on. He'd been in Chicago, meeting with the family's lawyers. I don't know if you've heard, but he and Phyllis recently decided to sell their funeral home to the American Funeral Group, the big chain."

"We don't suspect Howard Oldham," Artie said, none too politely. "We're just asking you to help us find Mike Gilbert's body. It's been stolen, and we're just trying to file a report about it."

Officer Thomas looked away and nodded. "Agreed. Let's keep our focus here." He wiped his forehead and straightened up again. "When was the last time you saw him in the coffin?"

"Right before we drove to the crematorium. Just before noon. And we were back around two."

"So it's within that time frame?"

"Yes. At the same time that Sister Eileen was locked in the cold room."

"But that's where the coffin was, too. Is that correct?"

Artie and Ilka both nodded. Ilka knew it was going to be a long evening if everything had to be spelled out. Artie seemed to realize that, too, along with the policeman, who stuck the notepad back in his pocket and stared blankly for a moment before wiping his forehead again.

"Two people died in that accident." He sounded distant. "They'd been at the swimming pool. They rammed into the back of the truck that collided with Oldham."

Ilka shifted in her chair. She wasn't sure he'd even been listening closely to them; he might have been too much in his own world. She slumped when he started in again.

"Howard drove into the opposite lane on purpose. I'm sure of that. It was a straight stretch of road, no dangerous curves. Nothing blocking his sight. Witnesses said he'd been driving at a steady speed, and nobody noticed him swerving, or anything that might have meant he was feeling bad. Suddenly he just pulled into the other lane, and that was that."

No one said anything for a moment. Then Officer Thomas pushed his chair back. "It was my neighbor in the car behind the truck. A father and his five-year-old son. I'm sorry. It's just that some days on this job are better than others. How's Shelby taking it? Was her daughter there when you discovered Mike's body was missing?"

Suddenly the mood was personal, close. As if it had helped him to get that off his chest.

Ilka nodded. "And the daughter-in-law and Mike's two children. The only person not there was his father."

The policeman looked puzzled. "What? Mike had a family?"

"Yes, and I think it will help Shelby get through this. And, of course, knowing that Phyllis Oldham is going to pay all the bills for Emma's treatments."

Now it was Artie's turn to be startled. There simply hadn't been time to tell him before now.

"I'll get some men together and we'll get a search started immediately," he said, adding that he would keep them informed.

35

Artie left for Dorothy's old crematorium. Ilka hadn't noticed if he had brought a bottle of wine, but she didn't really care. She was up to her neck in shit, as she had put it earlier that evening, when she called home for moral support.

"Come home, then," her mother had said. She brushed aside what Ilka had told her about having to sell off the business first. "Why do you feel it's your responsibility? You'd be better off coming back and focusing on your own business before it goes down the drain. Honestly, these school secretaries aren't all that easy to please." Several times she had emphasized that Ilka didn't owe anything to anyone. Not to Artie or Sister Eileen or, especially, her father.

"If this Artie Sorvino guy is interested in the house, sell it to him. Let the business go. It sounds like that town has plenty of funeral homes. Surely people will find another place to go to."

She was right, of course. They would; no doubt about that.

"And then it's Sorvino who decides if the nun will stay or not. You don't have to get involved in that. And under no circumstances should you let anyone threaten you into doing anything."

This was Karin Jensen in a nutshell. Black or white. Ilka didn't care to explain that her staying to fight for her father's business had nothing to do with the American Funeral Group. Or with the business, not really. It was him, her father. She still had almost no idea of why he had abandoned them. Walking around the funeral home, she sometimes imagined she could feel his presence, but no more than that. She hadn't found out more about the life he'd led in Racine. Occasionally small fragments of his working life came out, but there was so very much she didn't know. All the things still in darkness, things that appeared only in short, unpleasant glimpses. The unpaid bills, what people talked about indirectly. They knew things about her father that Ilka didn't. Things he had done or messes he had gotten himself into. As if he had a shady side to him. Things they hinted at but never elaborated on.

She's right, Ilka told herself after she shut the door and started down the steps. Through the dormer window she had noticed Sister Eileen's light was out. Which wasn't so strange. She'd just gone through a terrible experience. Ilka had bought sandwiches for herself and Artie, and she'd taken one over, but the sister didn't want it. She lay in bed under a thick blanket, pale, still unable to remember what had happened, even right before the attack.

She hadn't seen anything; she hadn't heard anything; she hadn't noticed any smells, sounds, voices. Nothing. She didn't remember if there had been someone in the cold room with her, either. Suddenly the door had slammed behind her. She didn't answer when they asked if she had gone in there under her own power.

Something had scared Sister Eileen out of her wits, Ilka sensed, and she either couldn't or wouldn't remember what.

She stuck her hands in her pockets and strode down toward Oh Dennis!. The next day, she decided, she would hand everything over to Artie. Except the things from her father's room she was taking home with her. And he could do anything he wanted with it. He could get rid of the business and move into the house. He could set up a studio or get together with Dorothy and spin pottery with her and fire it in the crematory oven. Or he could doll up corpses to his heart's content. Ilka didn't give a damn.

She didn't even notice if there was anyone in the restaurant when she went up to the counter and asked for a hundred dollars' worth of coins. When the young guy asked if she wanted something to drink, she just shook her head, grabbed the coins, and walked to the one-armed bandit in back. She began stuffing the coins in the machine and soon disappeared into a world where nothing existed except the rush when she won.

Coin after coin fell in. Ilka didn't move her left hand from the buttons on the bottom controlling which wheel should spin and which should be held back. She kept the wheels going, following the Native Americans, tents, horses, fruit, and stars when they showed up on the line in the middle of the glass. Most of the time the combinations didn't pay out, but she was in a frenzy, caught up in surges of adrenaline.

A dark voice spoke next to her ear. "Would you like a beer?" Someone rubbed against her right arm resting on the machine just beside the coin slot. She smelled fresh air, light aftershave.

Without looking, Ilka shook her head.

"Wine, maybe?"

She shook her head again and noted that he didn't move. Coins rattled into the cup when she won. He yelled out; then he said something—Ilka didn't know what. She concentrated on sticking the coins back into the machine, and she shut out every sound, every person, the sense of even being there, and focused on the line behind the glass. Finally, he gave up and walked away.

Maybe an hour or two went by, maybe only half an hour; Ilka had no idea. She walked up to the counter and laid another hundred-dollar bill in front of the bartender. This time he didn't ask if she wanted a drink; he brought the coins out to her and shoved them across the counter. They weighed a ton, but she hardly even noticed. Just returned to her machine.

The restaurant was almost empty now. An elderly couple sat by the window, and at the table in the rear next to the bathrooms sat a small man in a light blue windbreaker much too big for him. There were spareribs on his oval plate, French fries in a dish. Leftovers served by a cook who had taken pity on one of the town's losers.

Ilka didn't pay attention to these things either. She stared straight ahead and disappeared into her own world.

36

The next morning, Ilka had just made toast and a cup of coffee when her phone started ringing. Her head felt leaden, her soul numb; she'd given in to the thing that clouded her judgment and left her vulnerable, and she'd spent half the night cursing herself for it. What the hell had she been thinking? Now that she'd decided to throw in the towel and go home after her failed mission.

She'd put a sign in the front-door window. CLOSED. She hadn't talked to Artie since he'd driven out to Dorothy Cane's place the evening before. Maybe he was still out there, for all she knew. She didn't even know when she'd gotten home herself. The guy behind the bar had followed her, but all she remembered was that it had been a long night. For him. She'd paid him to let her sit glued to the one-armed bandit, and she'd spent her last cent. Had tried to talk him into letting her use her credit card, but he'd refused.

She recognized the number. Artie. "Yes?"

"We have to go out and get Mike Gilbert. I'll take a quick shower and I'll be there." He told her to find a roll of plastic and get the stretcher ready. The one they'd used to pick up Ed McKenna. "And we'll need a body bag."

"What happened? Where did they find him?"

"Up in the fishing cabin where Ashley died."

Ilka dropped her phone while pulling a sweater over her head. "Hello!" she yelled, to make sure he was still there. "Does Shelby know?"

"I don't know. All the police would say was that we should come get him."

Ilka rushed down the stairs and into the garage to look for the roll of plastic they'd taken when they picked Mike Gilbert up in the morgue. It was on a shelf beside boxes of masks and plastic gloves. She grabbed a handful of both, along with two disposable white coats.

It was almost ten thirty when they drove out of the parking lot. Artie's hair smelled clean and lay plastered to his head. Ilka had never understood older men with long hair, but she was getting used to it. He hadn't said much since picking her up. He asked what she'd done last evening but didn't seem particularly interested when she told him she'd lain around reading. And she didn't ask about his night.

She had in fact planned to tell him right off about her decision to hand everything over to him. He could decide whether to continue her father's funeral home or close it and pursue his dream. The alternative was that she simply lock up and call it quits. She wanted to get it over with, but that moment, in the car, didn't seem like the right time.

From a distance, they could see all the police cars parked at the foot of the path leading up to the fishing cabin. The path where Phyllis Oldham had seen her husband when he shouldn't have been there.

An ambulance was parked a bit farther on. Artie slowed and stopped when a uniformed officer approached them. "Pull behind the ambulance," she said. "We're waiting for the techs to give the okay to remove the bodies."

"What's going on?" Artie asked. He undid his seat belt and leaned farther out the window. The tips of Ilka's fingers were cold. She wasn't sure she wanted to hear the answer to his question. She shouldn't even have come along, she thought. She wasn't trained to handle dead people, and to-day, feeling completely defenseless, she just wasn't up to it.

"Who's up there with him?" Artie yelled out when the female officer walked away. Ilka's stomach lurched.

The officer didn't answer, but she unfastened the barrier tape so they could drive the hearse in.

"Sorry, I can't tell you anything," she said as they drove by.

Artie followed orders and parked behind the ambu-lance. Officers Thomas and Doonan were coming down the path when they got out of the hearse. The two po-licemen spotted them and waved them over. "Bring the stretcher," Thomas said, his voice unusually deep. "You get to carry him down."

Closer now, Ilka saw that Doonan's eyes were red, and there were deep lines around his mouth, as if he had pulled a mask over his face to shield himself.

Thomas's emotions were more open; his round cheeks quivered when he shook his head. "This is about as tragic as it gets," he said, his voice almost a whisper. He looked so miserable that Ilka involuntarily reached out and squeezed his arm. "This is just so sad, so, so sad, and it makes no sense at all. You'd better go on up."

"Does Shelby know?" Artie asked again.

Thomas raised a hand to his forehead, and a few seconds later he began massaging his temple, as if he hoped everything would go away if he rubbed hard enough. "Not yet. This changes everything about what's happened. I guess I'll have to show her the letter; otherwise, she'll never understand."

He turned and walked back up. They followed, though Ilka lagged behind. The two men carried the stretcher, while she bore the body bag under her arm.

Lyme grass grew on both sides of the path; tangled wild roses stood out in windblown bushes. They followed the winding path, and finally Ilka caught sight of the cabin, a wooden shack with small windows. Fish traps and nets hung from the end of the structure; the wind and foam from the lake had weathered the unvarnished boards. The cabin looked like it had been built from driftwood.

She counted eight police officers before they reached the cabin. A technician squatted, packing up a camera.

"We've been waiting on that tech, but now it looks like he's finished," Thomas said, gesturing at the man. "The dogs found them a little past eight this morning. And nothing has been moved; they're lying just like they were when we came."

Again Artie asked what had happened as they walked to the door, which hung crookedly on two hinges. The police stood off to the side now, speaking quietly among themselves. None of them looked at the cabin when Thomas led them in.

Ilka couldn't stop from crying out when she saw the two men on the floor. Mike Gilbert had on the same clothes as when he'd been in the coffin. He looked like a wax figure as he lay with his head in Jesse Oldham's lap, his hands folded across his chest. The undertaker's son sat slumped in a corner, his hair hanging over his closed eyes, hands resting on Mike's shoulders.

"The letter was on the floor beside them," Thomas said, his voice breaking. He cleared his throat.

The policeman must have known the two men on the floor since they were in school, Ilka thought. His face was gray, and it was obviously difficult for him to look over there.

The cabin was otherwise completely empty; no furniture, nothing indicating it was used by some of the many sport fishermen along Lake Michigan. Jesse Oldham had placed himself and Mike so they faced the crooked door that opened to a magnificent view of the lake.

"The door was open when the dogs found them," the policeman said. "Must have been hard for Jesse to drag Mike up here, though he was a strong guy."

"But why?" Ilka asked, after they'd all stepped out of the cabin. The wind whipped her hair around in front of her face; all she could see was the image of the two men on the floor.

The stocky officer crossed his arms as if he were freezing, even though the sun bore down on them. He cleared his throat again and said that in the letter, Jesse Oldham admitted killing Ashley.

"But the way he tells it, it was a mistake; he didn't mean to kill her. He was jealous, and he snuck along behind when

311

Mike came up here to meet her. He waited outside and saw them together. Then when Mike left to go to work, Jesse knocked and went in. They argued, he got mad, got upset, and he yelled at her, told her to stay away from Mike. He wrote that Ashley made fun of him, taunted him about falling in love with Mike. She told him, 'Do you really think he wants anything to do with a fag like you?' And he pushed her. And she fell."

"Oh God," Artie said.

"He wrote that he had been in love with Mike already back in school. At first he thought Mike was interested, too, but then Mike met Ashley. Jesse was the odd man out."

Before continuing, Thomas gestured for two broad-shouldered men with MEDICAL EXAMINER printed on the back of their coats to go on in.

"Forensics is finished. They're taking Jesse to the morgue. They'll do an autopsy today or tomorrow. Though I'm sure the cause of death is the pills he says he took from his mother's medicine cabinet. When they bring him out, you can go in and pick up Mike."

Suddenly Ilka was so dizzy that she wavered a bit before plopping down on the ground. Artie pulled out his cigarettes and looked at the officer, who simply nodded and held out his hand. They lit the cigarettes and sat down beside her.

"Jesse also wrote that he hadn't heard from Mike for almost eight years; then all of a sudden he shows up and wants to meet him. Jesse thought he'd come back to see him, but it turned out he was only interested in money. He wanted help to pay for his sister's treatment. That hurt Jesse."

Thomas snubbed out his cigarette. Then he explained that Jesse had also felt threatened. Not that Mike would reveal what happened back then, because he didn't know. But he did know the Oldhams had something to hide. And he was putting Jesse under pressure to help get the money. It wasn't until Mike told him about Kathy and the twins, though, that Jesse lost control and started beating him.

"The letter is pretty mushy," Thomas said. He didn't try to hide that he couldn't care less how a decent, sensible young guy could end up so bizarrely deranged.

Artie had been quiet, but now he said, "It's not really so strange for young kids to experiment with their sexuality. But in a little place like Racine, you don't do it in public."

Ilka could imagine that two schoolboys in love was something people whispered about here. Twelve years ago, people had probably not even talked about it.

"Jack drove over to inform Phyllis and the rest of the family. We finally managed to contact them right before we called you. They were at the hospital all morning. Howard Oldham died, about the time our dogs found these two."

Thomas shook his head and began rubbing his temples again. Artie was smoking another cigarette, sitting and staring out over the lake. The wind blew hard enough to flatten the small, stiff bushes, but they ignored it.

Ilka had seen Jesse Oldham only twice. During their first meeting with Golden Slumbers and then yesterday afternoon, when he was gazing at the river. She shivered when she remembered what he'd said about the lake. He had been handsome, not very tall, but muscular and friendly-looking. From now on, though, when she thought about him, no matter how hard she tried not to, she would see him sitting on the floor in the fishing cabin with Mike Gilbert's head resting on his lap.

"So it wasn't Douglas Oldham who killed the young girl," Artie said, stubbing out his cigarette. "Wonder if he'd still be alive if Phyllis had known he didn't have anything to do with it."

Officer Thomas struggled to stand up. "Yeah, like I said," he muttered. "This job, some days are just better than others."

37

Leaning against the back wall during Mike Gilbert's funeral service, Ilka realized why her father had stayed with the funeral home business all his life. And why working with the dead was more meaningful to Artie than what he had been doing in Key West.

She barely remembered carrying Mike's body down from the fishing cabin. She had been in shock from the sight of the two young men. When they got back, Artie immediately began reconstructing the parts of Mike's face damaged on the way up to the cabin. At one point, she opened the preparation room door and watched him leaning over Mike's face, fully focused. When she closed the door carefully, not wanting to disturb him, she heard what was missing—noise, specifically music. Not so much as one note of the Beach Boys was going to distract him.

The Racine Police Department had permitted the Gilbert family to hold the services already planned for the day after the tragedy. Ilka had the feeling that the quick release of the body was connected with Officer Thomas wanting to see the whole agonizing case put to rest; everyone, including local TV news journalists who were on the love tragedy like dogs on a bone, pointed out that the Racine Police Department hadn't investigated Ashley's death thoroughly enough back then.

Candles were lit in the tall candelabras up by the coffin. She didn't notice the music in the background, but it filled the room with an air of serenity. She'd asked Artie to lay Mike in the showy coffin taking up space in the garage. The coffin with the large golden handles and the shiny white satin liner looked like something for a head of state. It had been delivered by mistake, and someone might come to pick it up, but that wasn't her problem now. After all Mike Gilbert had been put through, he wasn't going to be sent out of her house in some shabby wooden coffin.

Artie had dressed him in a suit Kathy brought in. He threw the old clothes away.

Officer Thomas had stopped by Ilka's office earlier that day to tell her and Artie that the police considered the case closed. They had ransacked Jesse Oldham's apartment and found several letters Mike had written him after he left town. Jesse had placed the letters on his desk in his small office. They had also confiscated his laptop and cell phone.

"What about his mother?" Ilka had asked. She was surprised to hear that Phyllis had known about everything. The morning before he committed suicide, Jesse had told her he was the one who pushed Ashley and killed her. He had panicked and called his father, who then came to the fishing cabin. Douglas sent Jesse home and got rid of every trace of Jesse's presence. And Phyllis had seen him after he'd finished, when he was on the way down. By keeping silent all those years, she'd thought she was protecting her unfaithful husband, when in truth, he'd saved their son.

"I think she realized she'd been living a lie all these years," Thomas had said. "After Jesse confessed, she called in her son David and told him. Then they contacted the American Funeral Group and initiated the sale. It's like she's given up. She's home. Staring off into space."

Ilka thought about Douglas's suicide and the accusations Phyllis had made against him. But in a way, Howard Oldham's story was even more heartbreaking to her, his suicide on the highway after discussing with his lawyer the sale of the funeral home that had been in the family for several generations. An era was definitively over.

"Why didn't Jesse just keep quiet?" Artie sat with his head in his hands. "He didn't need to admit he'd pushed the girl; he could have gotten away with it, easy."

Thomas thought that over for a while. "He wasn't a murderer," he finally said. "Being rejected was what broke him. It wasn't about getting away with it. I don't think he thought that way. He wrote at the end of the letter that they were leaving together. Neither one of them would be left alone again."

Artie had looked sullen. "Yeah. Two little kids and a woman get left behind instead."

Ilka closed her eyes and took in the deep sense of peace in the room. That morning, when she and Sister Eileen were preparing for the service, they had closed the back part of the chapel off and pushed the plush sofas closer to the coffin, to create a more intimate atmosphere.

Kathy had asked to say a few words up by the coffin, and without thinking Ilka had asked if she needed a microphone. Shelby had said a few of Emma's friends might show up too, also some of Mike's old school buddies who had stopped by the evening before. The news about Jesse Oldham had spread through town like wildfire, and most people now knew that Mike had been innocent.

Ilka was unaware of when those attending the services had begun streaming in. At first she thought it must be Emma's friends and Mike's classmates she was hearing. But suddenly someone came up and introduced herself as his grade school teacher. Then some of the people he'd worked with at the Italian restaurant on the harbor walked in, then some from the shop where he'd worked afternoons. Finally, Sister Eileen suggested they open the back part of the chapel so there would be room enough for everyone.

It also took a while before Shelby discovered what was happening behind her. She was sitting on the plush sofa, a grandchild on each side of her. When the twins came in the room and saw their father, they called out his name. And they cried when he didn't answer. Kathy hugged them for a long time, and finally they calmed down. Now they sat on the sofa, staring up at the glittering black coffin.

Finally, when Emma tapped her mother's shoulder and pointed, Shelby turned and saw the chapel was full. Ilka had already sent the sister out to call the town's Danish bakers, to hear if they had enough kringles for an emergency delivery. Artie was making coffee and setting out more cups.

A bewildered Shelby stood up and gazed at all the people.

She began walking around, greeting everyone who had showed up to pay their respects to her son.

Ilka smiled at her. *How could the entire town so quickly find out the time of the funeral service?* she wondered. Apart from the family, only the police had known. Maybe this was Officer Thomas's way of apologizing to Mike. She was a bit upset that they weren't better prepared; there were no hors d'oeuvres or bouquets of flowers on the round table in the foyer. The fireplace in the chapel wasn't even lit.

Fortunately, the people attending didn't notice much other than the elegant coffin. After they greeted the family, they filed past the coffin and took their seats.

From the snatches of conversation Ilka overheard, it seemed Artie had done well. She shut out all thoughts and enjoyed the peace in the room as the voices died down. It was like sitting in a church just before a pastor began the sermon. And it occurred to Ilka that she hadn't thought much about her father the past few days. Suddenly, though, he was here again, like an almost physical presence.

Quietly she stepped out into the hallway and closed the door behind her. Then she walked upstairs and lay down on the bed.

The mood of the funeral service had moved her deeply, and now she felt closer to her father than she had ever before. She tried to imagine the version of him she'd never known. And she realized it was too early for her to go home, with so many facts that didn't add up, so much left unsaid, so many things still a mystery to her.

Another letter had arrived, at the bottom of the pile of advertisements, bills, and an offer for washing windows. A white envelope with the same feminine handwriting as some of the letters her father had hidden in the desk drawer. Ilka hadn't read the older letters yet, but she had opened the new one after recognizing the handwriting.

"You have a week to pay, otherwise the truth will come out."

To be continued...

ACKNOWLEDGMENTS

The Undertaker's Daughter is a work of fiction. Some of the places in this book are real, and certain people have been sources of inspiration. But the story comes from my imagination.

The idea for the book came to me in 2013. My parents died within three days of each other, and six weeks later, my beloved Aunt Kirsten followed them. Throughout my entire life, these three people have been my closest family.

All three funerals were handled by the same undertaker. I'd known nothing about her or her funeral home before then, and it surprised me when a young, smiling, and very sweet woman stood at my door.

In the chaos of all my sorrow, I felt that she picked me up. She took care of everything in the most caring and professional manner. Even when I called three days after meeting her and asked her to delay my mother's funeral, because my father had also died. And after I hung up, after we had planned all the practical details for the funeral of both my parents, it was clear to me that my next main character would be an undertaker.

ACKNOWLEDGMENTS

Therefore, a special thank-you goes out to Christina Gauguin from Elholm Funeral Home. First and foremost, because of the perfect farewells arranged for my parents and Aunt Kirsten. But also, because you, Lone, Marianne, and Victor kept your doors open to me, answered all my questions, and allowed me to take an apprenticeship in undertaking. You are the greatest inspiration for *The Undertaker's Daughter*.

I would also like to thank the Wilson Funeral Home and Ann Meredith from the Meredith Funeral Home, both in Racine, for allowing me to come in and ask my many questions. Thank you for showing me around and teaching me about an undertaking tradition very much unlike that in Denmark.

Thanks go out to Steen Holger Hansen, a forensic pathologist who throughout my writing career has taken time to explain how my fictional ideas would take place in the real world.

Thank you, Trine Busch. You were the first person I shared my new idea with, and you believed in it right from the start. Thanks for accompanying me to Racine and helping me find my bearings in this area so new to me.

My publisher, People's Press, also deserves my heartfelt thanks. You were immediately receptive to the idea of a new series. It's so enjoyable working with all of you. And thanks to Rasmus Funder, who once again succeeded in designing the perfect book cover.

Thank you, Ditte Degner, for continuing as my social media manager, even though as a law student you have more than enough on your plate. I simply would have hated to see you go. I appreciate you staying on the team.

ACKNOWLEDGMENTS

My editor, Lisbeth Møller-Madsen, is my better half when it comes to my books. We constantly remind each other that it must be fun, and I thank my lucky stars that it was this time, too. Dear Lisbeth, thank you so much for so quickly agreeing to take care of Ilka and my new world. Working with you has truly been a gift to me.

It's also been fun working with Malene Kirkegaard Nielsen from the Plot Workshop, who helped form the framework for my undertaker universe. You're the best sparring partner I could have asked for, Malene. Thank you.

Also, thanks to my fantastic PR agent, Elisa Lykke. You know me very well, and you have an incredibly sharp eye for knowing what's in my best interest. Thank you for your wholehearted support.

There are four people who mean so very, very much to me, not only because they ensure that my books are published throughout the world but also because they are always there for me, backing me up in every way. Thank you, Victoria Sanders, my wonderful agent, Bernadette Baker-Baughman, Chris Kepner, and Jessica Spivey from Victoria Sanders & Associates, for such a tremendous team effort.

Benee Knauer helped me greatly with research for this book. She answered tons of questions and dug things up every time there was something I couldn't find myself. Thank you for making Racine and my American world familiar to me.

A special thanks goes out to Karin Slaughter, for sharing a story with me when I told her about my new venture. I would never have come up with the story myself. Thank you for your ability to shake me up with bizarre stories from the real world. But most of all, thank you for being my friend.

My greatest thank-you goes out to my son, Adam. You were the first one to read the initial draft of *The Undertaker's Daughter*, and you told me at once to keep on working because you wanted to read more. You're the best.

And finally, to my fantastic readers and my followers on Facebook—thank you so very much! You are my greatest incentive. Thank you for always trusting me to come up with what you want to read. It means all the world to me.

—Sara Blaedel

ABOUT THE AUTHOR

Sara Blaedel's suspense novels have enjoyed incredible success around the world: fantastic acclaim, multiple awards, and runaway #1 bestselling success internationally. In her native Denmark, Sara was voted most popular novelist for the fourth time in 2014. She is also a recipient of the Golden Laurel, Denmark's most prestigious literary award. Her books are published in thirty-seven countries. Her series featuring police detective Louise Rick is adored the world over, and Sara is excited for the launch of her new Undertaker's Daughter suspense series in the United States.

Sara Blaedel's interest in story, writing, and especially crime fiction was nurtured from a young age. The daughter of a renowned Danish journalist and an actress whose career included roles in theater, radio, TV, and movies, Sara grew up surrounded by a constant flow of professional writers and performers visiting the Blaedel home. Despite a struggle with dyslexia, books gave Sara a world in which to escape when her introverted nature demanded an exit from the hustle and bustle of life.

Sara tried a number of careers, from a restaurant apprenticeship to graphic design, before she started a publishing company called Sara B, where she published Danish translations of American crime fiction.

Publishing ultimately led Sara to journalism, and she covered a wide range of stories, from criminal trials to the premiere of *Star Wars: Episode I*. It was during this time—and while skiing in Norway—that Sara started brewing the ideas for her first novel. In 2004 Louise and Camilla were introduced in *Grønt Støv* ("Green Dust"), and Sara won the Danish Academy for Crime Fiction's debut prize.

Today Sara lives in New York City, and when she isn't busy committing brutal murders on the page, she is an ambassador with Save the Children and serves on the jury of a documentary film competition.